CW00572028

Games

Andy Slade

Published by Bennie Rosa, 2024.

GAMES

First edition. April 21, 2024.

Copyright © 2024 Andy Slade.

ISBN: 979-8224666454

Written by Andy Slade.

Also by Andy Slade

Betrayal Is Beautiful
Our Shadows Never Die
The Magic Parachute
Games

Table of Contents

Chapter 1

A solitary motionless figure stood silently in the steady rain, peering through a rusted chain link fence. It was Sunday, late afternoon. The rain came down gently, dripping down the brim of his black baseball cap, his large hands sticking through the chain links, pushing through as far as they would go. His name was Vic Mason, a New York City Detective, but not that Sunday. He was just a man alone, waiting for a miracle. He didn't move at all, except for his eyes.

His ex-wife Melanie usually took his two daughters to the park around that time. He knew they wouldn't be there; Melanie wouldn't bring them there while it was raining, but he had to go anyway, just to be there. Just being near the park was enough because he knew that's where they went to play. The rain stopped and Mase remained, hoping to catch a glimpse of his family. Their last name was now Stanton, from the successful lawyer Melanie had married, Gregory Stanton. He hated Vic because he knew Melanie still loved Vic but couldn't deal with his drinking anymore.

As the sun fought its way through the clouds and Vic was about to leave, he caught a glimpse of Melanie and the girls walking to the park. The girls, Gina and Mia on either side of their mother, were holding Melanie's hands and skipping and jumping their way to their favorite spot. Melanie saw Vic and immediately stopped. He looked as sad as anyone she'd ever seen. She stood there staring at the man she'd always loved, ever since High School where they'd met. They were locked into each other's faces, unable to move, drawn to each other, when she suddenly turned around with the girls and headed back.

He thought about calling out to the girls, but he stopped himself. He'd already caused them enough grief. When Melanie turned around for one last glimpse, Vic was gone.

***

Vic always ended up hanging out in Washington Square Park in the Village on Sunday's. After seeing his kids and his ex, the idea of watching and waiting for the old hippies still clinging to their wasted pasts gave him that warped justification he needed for his own visits to his own wasteland. This wasn't Eliot's Wasteland or Leary's Get High and Die for Peace not War wasteland, it was Vic Mason's feel better about your wasted life wasteland.

He spotted the boy known as Miguelito hawking his knockoff watches to the old Deadheads roaming their only good memories. When Miguelito saw Mase, short for Mason, he smiled and walked over to the forlorn Detective. Mase put his pint in his jacket pocket as the little boy covered his arm that had all the watches. He sat down next to Vic.

"Thought I told you to knock it off with the knockoffs, last week. Didn't I? And where are your parents for chrissake? How old are you, twelve?" Mase put him arm gently around the boy's shoulders and smiled weakly.

"Twenty-Eight. That's what I am. I'm twenty-eight," Replied the youngster. "Thought I told you to stop drinking Mase, it's gonna get you in trouble one day."

"Been in trouble."

"Exactamente! Oh, excuse me Mase, my customers are waiting..."

Miguelito jumped up and ran over to an older couple from Indiana who declared their home pride with their Pacer's T-shirts. Mase took a swig from his pint and walked over to Miguelito.

"Here, shake my hand you little Madoff you." Vic extended his large hand to Miguelito, shook his hand and gave the boy a hug. Miguelito looked into his hand and found a twenty."

Vic took another swig from his paper bag pint and walked away, waving off Miguelito who wanted to hug Mase. The young boy looked sad as he watched Mase weave and stumble his way through the tourists.

***

From his hospital bed, Detective Vic Mason was trying to remember what exactly happened that Sunday night at the gaming bar in The Village, the one on Eighth Street called The Bottle Royale. He vaguely recalled Corso, the bartender, solver of all problems, asking him something, or telling him something, something like:

"Go home Mase. You've had enough."

"The only thing I've had enough of is you."

"See, that's what I mean. That's not you Mase. I mean, come on."

Mase looked down at his drink and turned the glass around slowly.

"I like video games. I play better when I drink. And ... I..."

"I like you Mase, but not when you get like this."

"I don't need a fucking shrink, I need a drink... See, I'm a fucking poet and I don't even know it." Mase laughed at himself and tried to lift his glass, but it tipped over. "I'm likable, ain't I?"

"You're not my type, besides, you've got bad breath," Said Corso.

"Well, I love you, Curso, or Corso, or whatever the fu your name is."

Corso reached over the bar and gently put his hand on Mase's hand and patted it softly.

"Look, it's like this Mase. Either go home, or we'll send you home. Get it?"

He remembered Corso putting his fat Italian hand on his hand, the one with the spinning drink, and him patting it like a big sister. Then he tried to push Mase's hand down on the bar and...

"You wanna be a one-armed bartender?" Said the wasted Detective.

He found out later that the small crowd in the bar was getting fed up with Mase the drunk, leaving the bar almost empty.

"Look man...I'm sick of you and your fagg... way. You just shu the fu up or I..."

The black dude at the bar seemed to have unlimited patience. He tapped Mase on his shoulder, as Mase held on to the edge of the long mahogany bar, and then turned around...

"1v1?"

"Wha...."

There were display monitors above the bar to show its patrons what was happening as other patrons played their video games. No one was playing because everyone had left. The screens were blank. The bar was empty.

Corso was wiping down the bar. It was clean, but he continued to wipe it down as he glared at Mase.

"1v1?"

"Wha...?"

"For twenty bucks, one game. You pick it."

"Wha the fu..."

He told Mase his gamer-tag was blackToast and Mase told him his was 'who gives a fuck'. The game lasted five minutes and Mase's last twenty, was about to transfer itself into blackToast's pocket.

Sometimes, especially when you're wasted, it's hard to tell the hustlers from the rest of humanity or games from life. Bruh put his hand out for the twenty and Mase just stared at him like he didn't know a goddamn thing about what he was talking about.

Bruh grabbed him by his belt, pulled him into the street and into a small alley furnished with dented trash cans, cats in heat, and a god damned raccoon. Bruh was thick and wide and tall and very strong and Mase had no chance. He helped himself to the detective's twenty, smashed his head into the brick wall behind the trash cans and kicked a field goal with Mase's head.

Now, he was in and out, mostly out, and when he tried later to recall what had happened, it was like he was in a half-dream, swimming in a cosmic washing machine and the harder he tried to stop it the faster the spin cycle took over and that was that.

But, he remembered the raccoon and how he lifted the top of the garbage can and he was replaying a podcast in his mind where he'd heard about how a rabid raccoon had sunk its teeth in this female jogger and wouldn't let go for five and a half hours, gave her rabies, or, was he the one with rabies?

He sort of remembered hearing the siren and the conversation of the two uni's that showed up, which he found out later was Troy Levin and Kyle Mansfield, two incompetent weasels if ever there were two. They never saw a problem they couldn't ignore. They couldn't tell if he was dead or just sleeping it off.

Levin pushed him with the tip of his shoe. Nothing. He toed him again. Nothing again. "Hey. Hey. Wake up."

"Roll him over bro," Said Mansfield.

"You roll him over. I just polished my shoes this morning and this guy's a fucking mess."

Mansfield squatted down and rolled him over, looking disgusted. Then he looked up at his partner. "It's Mase."

"Again?"

"Yup."

"Is he breathing?"

"I can't tell for sure. He kinda looks dead to me, but you know ..."

"How many times is it this month?"

"At least a half dozen...maybe more," Said Mansfield.

The green and white ambulance from Lenox Health Greenwich Village had just arrived and as they shut off the siren and stopped, Mansfield looked up, tilted his cap up on the back of his head and stepped back to allow the EMTs to bring in their stretcher and life-saving gear. He was still out of it but heard one of the EMTs laugh when they bent over him.

"Guess you didn't need us after all. Look like he's gone."

"Really?" Said Levin.

"Wait a minute, wait a minute, hold on. Nope, nope. He's still with us. He's breathing. Son of a bitch!" Said the chubby EMT with the gold nose ring. "He's in pretty bad shape. Tony, get me a cervical collar and head immobilizer."

Levin tried hard to look like he cared as they carefully lifted Mase onto the stretcher.

"He gonna make it?"

The half shrug and doubtful look on the EMT's face told Levin everything he needed to know.

Corso was still hanging around where the alley met the sidewalk. As Levin and Mansfield walked back to their patrol car, Corso asked if Mase was going to make it. Both cops looked at each other and smirked at the bartender but didn't answer the question, as it screeched away into the blackness.

"Corso, just tell us what happened." said Mansfield.

"Well, it was like this. Mase had a few too many and I tried to cut him off but he wouldn't have any of it. I mean nothing. In fact, he was getting pretty mouthy, you know how he gets. Then, we argue a little bit and this big black dude walks up to him and challenges him to a game of War Zone. I'd seen that guy before and I'm pretty sure he hustles gamers for a living. Anyway, they bet twenty and Mase loses, of course."

"You pressing charges?"

"Charges?"

"Yes, charges. Yes or no?"

"No, hell no."

"Works for me," Said Levin.

The cops left and sat in their unit as they looked at each other like life was a waste of time and doing anything right was an exercise is stupidity.

"Cap's gonna be pissed!" Said Levin.

"He's always pissed."

"Yeah, but we'd better call him right now. I know for sure he's going to want to know anything about his golden boy."

Mansfield used his personal cell phone to call Captain Vrain's personal phone number. This needed a light touch to see what Vrain wanted to do.

All Vrain said was for the two cops to keep their mouths shut and go about their business and that he would take care of it from that point.

Sucking up and keeping their mouths shut were Levin and Mansfield's specialty, their finest qualities, probably their only qualities.

Chapter 2

Melanie Stanton peered through the ICU window, deep worry creasing her brow. At first, she couldn't even recognize her ex. He had tubes going everywhere and a huge gash over his left eye and a head bandage over his entire skull. She couldn't believe it.

Mase saw her for a split second when he opened his right bloodshot eye and lifted his right hand, the one with the IV.

The middle-aged nurse with the sleeve tattoo of a dragon with a rose in its mouth held his hand and took his pulse. Mase shifted in his bed slightly and she told him to be still while she checked him out.

"Am I in a hospital?" asked Mase.

"It ain't the Waldorf, honey."

He was asleep before she answered him as she shrugged a 'that was a waste of time' at the door as she left. Mase opened his eye again for a second. He had just enough strength to point at Melanie with his trembling index finger. That was all he could do before he closed his eye and floated back to unconsciousness.

Melany forced her upper lip into curl into a faint smile as Mase recognized her. The smile left instantly as Mase fell back into unconsciousness. She shook her head and looked disconsolately down at the ivory colored linoleum. She was in deep thought while distant memories ripped through her mind. Most of them were fond memories but were veiled behind the Mase that tore their family apart with his drinking. Despite that, the good memories were still there. She felt someone tapping her shoulder. It caught her by surprise, and she whipped around while dabbing her wet eye. It was Captain Richard Vrain.

"Still love him, don't you?" asked Vrain.

"Love doesn't really end, does it?"

"I know."

He hugged her gently. He could see the awful fear in her eyes that Mase might not make it. It's an awful thing, fear.

"Sorry to call you so late this evening, but you're the only one any of us knew was important enough to come here. He doesn't really have anyone else."

"I'm glad you called me. I should be here. What happened?"

"The usual, drank too much, mouthed off too much, got his ass kicked big time. You know."

Melanie nodded.

"You know, Mel, Mase is important to me like no one else in the department. He's the young brother I never had but wished I had. So, I've kind of adopted him. Kind of like a stray dog that sleeps at your front door hoping you'll open the door."

"You and Mase were always fighting for the underdog no matter how hopeless."

She put a gentle hand on his shoulder and forced another weak smile out of an exhausted face.

"I hope this is a wake-up call, because he needs one."

There was a brief but definite look of doubt on Melany's face. Vrain changed the subject.

"So, how's married life? Everything working out OK?"

"Oh, sure. Greg's a great guy, and a perfect dad for the girls. Told him Vic was in the hospital, which didn't go down well, but..."

"How long have you been married now?"

The small talk wasn't working very well because Melany kept looking over her shoulder at her ex., even as Vrain kept prattling on.

"What are the doctors saying, Dick. I mean what are they seeing right now? He looks pretty bad."

"Actually, it's what they're not saying that worries me the most."

"And what does that mean?"

They both turned to Mase in his bed and the more they looked at him the more concern took over their faces.

"Well, that's just it. I don't know because every time I ask them about his condition they keep saying it's too early to tell."

"Too early to tell?"

"Exactly."

It seemed like hours had passed as they both looked through the window at Mase. Nothing more was said until Vrain took a deep breath.

"I've got to leave now. I've told the doctors to call me if there are any changes, good or bad, and I'd come right over. I'll let you know if anything happens."

"Thanks Dick. I appreciate that more than you know."

Vrain walked quietly away through the silent door. She could hear his footsteps start out loud and fade to silence. Once again, it was just her and Mase. She tried not to think that it might be the last time.

It was a few minutes past midnight and it looked like the entire ICU staff had left for the evening. Melanie wanted to talk to Mase. Maybe she should leave. She stared at her ex-husband and then the heart monitor went flat. It had nothing, no beats, no beeps, nothing. She raced to the nursing station and the one lone nurse was playing a video game on her phone and she wore earphones. The monitor on her desk was blaring at her and she ignored it like it wasn't there. Melanie ran over to her and shook her.

"Hey, look at that, look!" She pointed to the monitor on the desk. "Don't you see that? Look!"

Melanie pulled the earbuds out of her head and pulled her hair towards the screen. "He's dying in there. Can't you see, you stupid bitch? He's dying in there."

"Take your hands off of me. He's fine. It's that stupid machine. It does that all the time. Look, I'll show you, honey. Come with me."

They both walked into Mase's room and the nurse smacked the machine a couple of times and it came back to life. Mase's heart was still beating.

"Look, honey, I can understand your worry. Really, I can. But next time, go a little easier on us nurses. We're just tryin' to make a living like anyone else. OK?"

"Can I kiss him? He looks so tired."

"Sorry, not allowed. But..." She pretended to look around if someone was looking. "But go ahead anyway. It won't matter."

"Thanks."

She walked down the lonely corridor. And the nurse said, "He's tough. He'll make it. That kind always does."

Melanie's feet had a mind of their own. She told herself that she had to leave, but her feet stopped as if they were stuck in cement. She stood at the door to the elevator until it opened and she walked in as slowly as she could. The two metal doors closed silently behind her and whatever was left of Mase and Melanie became fused with the forces of fate and destiny. There was absolutely nothing she could do now.

The security guard had to open the locked entry doors because it was past operating hours.

He was an old man, but he read her face like he'd known her all his life.

"Have a good evening Ma'am and don't worry. The doctors here will take good care of your man. They will. I promise you."

Chapter 3

"I've got to get the fuck out of this place." Thought Mase as a burly nurse removed his bedpan.

"You're the girl of my dreams. Do you know that?"

"Oh, absolutely. It's true love." Said the nurse as she left, holding the bed pan.

There was light, bright sunlight streaming through the window. It was like a sun room. The ICU equipment was in the spotlight. He could see fluid in the tube that fed him. He thought everything was like some kind of science experiment gone wrong.

Nurse Frankenstein returned and glanced at the monitors in emotionless review. It was her job, and Mase could see she did it well.

"You need to get some rest Mr. Mason. So, what else can I do for you before I let you rest? Doctor's orders."

"You can run away with me, have my children, and live in a fantasy world with me, just you and me; how about it?"

Nurse Frankenstein shook her head and gave him the grimace he knew was coming. She shut the blinds in the room and as she left she smiled.

"You're not my type."

"Such a pity..."

She waved him off and disappeared.

There was a tube in him somewhere that gave him the needed sedative. He didn't know which one it was, but it was about as good as Scotch, only different. Scotch was his Dad's best friend and never let him down and now it was his. It was always there for him and made him feel confident and wise and calm. Now he was just tired.

***

"Pop? When's Mom comin' home? I'm hungry."

"Soon boy, soon. Saturdays are always busy at the market. She's always late on Saturdays."

Just then, a loud knocking at the apartment door broke the conversation between Victor Arthur Mason and his father McKinley Mason. The two looked at each other. When Mac opened the door, a patrol officer asked him if Moira Mason lived there. Mac answered yes.

"What's going on, officer?"

"She passed out at work and they took her to the hospital."

Both Mack and Victor left immediately to the hospital to see the woman who ran everything in the house and ruled her palace with dignity and grace, the woman they both adored and couldn't live without.

Moira had instructed the doctors not to divulge what was wrong with her to her family. She told them she would handle it her own way and that she had to leave because they didn't have the money to afford any health treatment. They told her she needed to stay for a least a couple of days until all the tests were completed and she told them it was unnecessary and that they should all have a wonderful day, a day of blessings for themselves and their families.

Mac and Mase took her home, but they could see she was not feeling well. Mac made her lay down in bed as he fixed their dinner and cleaned up the kitchen. Victor helped him but kept staring at his father. He wanted to know, even though he knew.

***

Then Mase woke up momentarily to find his best friend Chuckie Carlo sitting in a chair next to his hospital bed. He closed his eyes and Chuckie responded.

"Oh, no you don't. You're not going to sleep now. I've been sitting here on my ass for forty-five minutes. Oh no. No way."

"You're always sitting on your ass, so what's the problem." Responded Mase with a small wry smile.

"Well, at least I'm not lying down pretending I'm all hurt and wounded."

"Funny, you little shit."

"Alright, so enough of this. When you gettin' out of here and back to work? Aren't you sick of it already?"

"Believe me. I'm sick of it. But..."

There was a small lull in the banter as both of the two childhood friends stared at each other. Chuckie had been the first to join the force and then Mase. It was just pure luck that they wound up in the same precinct. But, they were good for each other, Chuckie always trying to center the daredevil golden boy and Mase always being a protector for his smaller and weaker friend. Mase had the detective chops and Chuckie had the tech smarts. They kept smiling at each other until Chuckie broke the ice again.

"Remember when you got busted for jumping from roof to roof on Rivington Street and the cops brought you to Principal Cohen's office. You were stupid then and you're stupid now."

"How pissed is Vrain?" Asked the now somber Mase.

"Oh, he's pissed!"

"Yeah, but how pissed?"

"Well, somehow you've singlehandedly created a new level for him. It's beyond, way beyond anger now. He said he's ashamed and angry, plus he's under enormous pressure."

"From the brass?"

"From the brass."

Mase waved Chuckie away and moved slightly on his right side to look out the window at the cloud filled sky. No sun today, not a ray.

***

It was the same sky that buried Moira in her final resting place in a pauper's grave on Staten Island. All she ever did was love her husband and her son, and it never stopped for one solitary second of their lives. After she was buried, one lone dirty seagull decided her grave marker was a fine place to rest. Moira would have been OK with that.

The silent ride back on the ferry and the subway was solemn and final. Mac was lost and Vic was furious about life. *This was life? What was the point of it? Why bother with everything in life when the end is yours whether you like it or not.* He didn't like any of it.

Mac drank more than he ever had and since they didn't live too far from the Bowery, he soon found a permanent place to stay and Mase was out on my own. The Carlo's took Vic in; they said temporarily, but it was permanent, and they treated him like their son.

***

"Mr. Mason, open your eyes. It's time for your sponge bath. Come on, Mr. Mason, wake up. I know you can hear me."

"You're right, you're always right nurse. I was just enjoying the beautiful sound of your beautiful mellifluous voice. It's so beautiful and, inspiring."

She grimaced as she took the steps to sponge down the snappy detective.

Chapter 4

Mase had the feeling that it was time to go, at least it felt that way. He caught bits and pieces of medical talk between the now familiar voices. They talked in murmurs about his vital signs, his respiration, his concussion until it raveled and unraveled so many times that he couldn't understand any of it. It was a floating mass of words and meaningless chatter that came and went and disintegrated into mish mashed murmurs. And that's where he was, lying on his back and listening as the endless inane bullshit that meant nothing to him except that he would get discharged soon.

Was that Melany that just left. I can't see her, but it felt like her. She held my hand and whispered words I couldn't hear, but I know it was her. It had to be her.

She was wearing a pink jogging suit and her hair was in a ponytail like she always wore when she ran errands. He remembered that. He pressed the call button for the nurse, and she arrived quickly.

"Yes, Mr. Mason. Is everything OK?"

"Was that my ex-wife that just came by?"

"Yes, that was her. She came to check on you but didn't want to wake you. She's been here quite a few times."

"She has?"

"Oh yes. You've had many visitors, but you were too ill to see them. Apparently, you have many friends who care about you."

"Thanks."

Mase dosed off with a slight smile on his face.

***

Mac had recited poetry to Vic many times before. He never knew when Mac would read poetry, but when we did, Vic remembered almost every one. It was the way he spoke, with that slight Scottish accent in his voice, and the way his eyes lit up as he read them. Mac had wanted, with all his might, to be a university professor. Too much drinking and not enough intention. His field was the History of English Literature and he loved it about as much as a man can love anything other than the woman of his dreams, which he already had, his wife Moira.

He could always tell when Mac was about to begin the poetry recital. He would take a shot of Scotch, put a little in a spoon for Vic and toast the spoon with his shot glass and always say:

"To the juices flowing my boy, to the juices."

He decided on Keats's "Oh Solitude! if I must with thee dwell" when they came home from Moira's funeral. They sat in the small living room with the small chair and the table that had a photo of Moira when they were first married. He read to a small old lamp that flickered from time to time, as he did, any time he thought about Moira. He could hardly contain his grief as he read the words, tears flowing, and lips quivering with the saddest, most sorrowful look on his face that Vic had ever seen:

O Solitude! if I must with thee dwell,
Let it not be among the jumbled heap
Of murky buildings; climb with me the steep,
—Nature's observatory—whence the dell,
Its flowery slopes, its river's crystal swell,
May seem a span; let me thy vigils keep
'Mongst boughs pavillion'd, where the deer's swift leap
Startles the wild bee from the fox-glove bell.
But though I'll gladly trace these scenes with thee,
Yet the sweet converse of an innocent mind,
Whose words are images of thoughts refin'd,
Is my soul's pleasure; and it sure must be
Almost the highest bliss of human-kind,
When to thy haunts two kindred spirits flee.

It took everything he had to finish it. Vic hugged him with everything he had until his father finally pushed him gently away.

***

The doctors all agreed that Mase had made enough progress to finally go home. Chuckie Carlo got the day off to take Mase home. Mase could do most physical activity again and as he packed his stuff in the large plastic bag they give to patients, he heard a light knock on the door frame of his room.

"Vacation finally over?" Asked Chuckie.

"Not really."

"All the docs say you're ready to get the hell out of here. So, are you?"

"Define ready."

"To face the world again?" There was a slight doubt in Chuckie's voice and tone.

"It's not the world I need to face."

"I'm here as your obedient servant and chauffeur." He did a bow that was as fake as his British accent.

Mase threw the bag with his things at Chuckie who caught it like a professional second baseman getting a toss from the shortstop to finish a double play. Nothing that Mase did ever surprised him. Mase put his arm around Chuckie's shoulder to wordlessly show his appreciation, not to mention the physical support he still needed to get around.

***

Almost a week had passed and Mase was in full lock-down cabin fever. There was another week to go before he was scheduled to return to work to who knew what. The Mets were playing a day/ night doubleheader and he had his feet up on the coffee table watching but not watching his TV. He always hated the Mets and always considered them a fake New York team. *Sure, the Giants and Dodgers had abandoned the city decades before, but please, come on, the Mets. You've got to be kidding.*

The third beer commercial had finally gotten to him. He had the most uncontrollable craving for beer he could ever remember, even on his worse days as a raging alcoholic. He got up, felt strong enough and walked down to the GO MART convenience store two blocks down. He bought two Michelob Ultra six-packs and could easily have consumed all twelve before he reached his apartment. He waved meekly at Mrs. Kaplan and her psychotic poodle as he gained speed up the stairs to his second-floor residence.

The rest of the evening became another predictable a nosedive into bad places. All those days in the ICU and all that medication to get him back to world, all for what? He was back in the same situation as he was in before. Only now, he suffered head-splitting headaches that wouldn't go away. He'd never had headaches like those. Maybe, he thought, it was the concussion. Maybe it was payment for what he was doing to himself, or maybe, it was...

The excruciating pain was only slightly relieved by screaming into his sweat stained pillow. He couldn't sleep, couldn't eat and couldn't do a damn thing for himself. He bought six more six-packs and stacked them up in his bedroom. *Fuck the headaches! Who gives a fuck?*

Chapter 5

Mase couldn't figure out why the bright sunlight made him sick to his stomach. He looked at people walking on the street to their useless jobs and their petty lives. They looked determined to get wherever they were going. Did they really want to go where they were going? They made him sick as well.

He wasn't ready for his first day back. He'd been drinking steadily since he'd returned home from the hospital. The usual thoughts came and went, along with any remaining self-respect, with the same results. But, he had no choice. It was drink or go completely insane. It was that simple. Go completely off the deep end or get himself nice and relaxed and pleasantly aware of the world around him. It was easy once he had his drink. Who doesn't want everything to make sense?

***

The next day unfolded in front of him he found himself driving into the employee parking lot. That familiar thought occurred to him that he didn't give a shit about any of the people in there and that the feeling was mutual. He knew he was a good detective, and everyone else knew it. Those who just played at their jobs hated him, those that should have been kicked off the force years ago, hated him. If you're good or even great at your job, you'd better watch your ass. So why waste your time?

The bump he felt as he parked was probably nothing. He parked crooked in his space and didn't lock his car, the old gray Camry he bought in 2001, just days before 9/11. He ignored all of it as he shambled into the building, taking his sweet time delaying the inevitable.

Eyes glanced his way as he found his desk in the center of the large room. Whenever he came into the office, he avoided the white linoleum squares because they were bad luck, just like ballplayers who won't step on the baselines when they entered or left the dugout. He passed Chuckie Carlo who shook his head ever so slightly. This wasn't going to be pretty, and everyone knew it.

"Where is he?"

"Brass." Chuckie's thumb pointed upstairs.

"Wonderful."

His old wooden desk was too neat for Mase. He liked messy everything, especially his desk, papers sticking out from the drawers or scattered everywhere on his desk, maybe on the floor. Suddenly, he felt a hard tap on his left shoulder. It was Vrain. As he continued into his office, the large stocky Captain held up his right index finger and curled it at Mase a few times. No words were exchanged. None were necessary.

Chuckie Carlo's face tightened when he noticed Mase didn't follow the Captain immediately. *What was he waiting for?* He knew the Captain hated smart-asses.

After what seemed like back-to-back eternities, Mase walked slowly into Captain Richard C. Vrain's office. The bright rays of sunlight caught Mase right in his eyes, but he didn't react. His pupils didn't react. He was granite, but cracks were showing.

Vrain was pacing back and forth in front of the window, occasionally looking out at the street below, occasionally looking at the ceiling. He didn't look directly at his best detective.

"Sit down Vic."

Mase stayed still until the Captain stared at him using his death ray look, and only then did the detective sit down in the chair in front of the desk.

"I can smell the booze from here."

Mase refused to answer because he'd already decided to quit, or leave the station and go home. Besides, it wasn't a question, so why bother.

"On Sunday, June 23, you spend your day off, first scaring Melanie and your kids, then at Carlo's apartment playing stupid video games. Then, after drinking your ass drunk there, you hang out with low life at Washington Square Pare and then you decide to have a night cap at The Bottle Royale. You were already drunk enough not think straight so you try to strong arm the bartender for more, more, more, and more." Vrain pounded his desk each time he said 'more'. " Then you get hustled for twenty bucks and get your ass destroyed and handed to you in a dark alley next to the bar. You're within minutes of the end of your life when two EMT's save your worthless ass and you spend the next two and a half weeks, at taxpayer's expense, in the ICU where God knows how they pulled you through."

Mase squirmed a little in his chair and looked at his filthy fingernails.

"Your point?" Although the words wanted to sound strong, they came out as a whisper.

"My point is, grow the fuck up and quick. That's my point. And stop playing the role of the tough guy because you lost that privilege in the ICU. God took it away from you, right then and right there."

Mase tried to stand but had trouble. It didn't matter because Vrain wasn't finished.

"To tie a big fucking bow around this entire pile of shit, I had to sit in front of Chief Rodriguez for an hour, an hour, while he practiced pathological proctology on my pathetic ass for supporting you from day one in your career and how you've managed to single-handedly destroy the stellar reputation of the entire 7th Precinct."

Mase nodded and a slight smile curled around the edges of his mouth.

"You think it's funny. Well, it's not funny. And it certainly won't make you laugh when you hear what you have to do to stay employed here, if you want to stay employed here, because you're certainly not acting like someone who wants to keep his job. Do you?"

Mase's eye opened a little wider and his attention was now properly focused.

"I suppose."

"You suppose?" Screamed the Captain.

"Alright...I do."

"Well," Vrain was staring straight into Mase's eyes. "If you really want to keep your job, you're going to have to take a two month medical leave to attend behavioral therapy sessions with a therapist approved by the Department. You must cooperate fully with the therapist and work with her to help you get over this, this, this...issue. You'll be able to come back to work, with your issue resolved, only, and I mean only when she reports to us that you've worked hard to resolve this, this, this thing you've got. Otherwise, you can't come back, the brass won't let you come back, and you can drive a garbage truck for the rest of your life if that's what you want."

Mase shook his head and stared back at Vrain.

"You in, or not?" Asked the Captain.

"What choice do I have?"

"None. Well? You in?"

"I suppose..." The Captain stared him down. "Yes. Alright."

Mase stood up strongly and left.

"Wait a minute. Here..." Vrain handed him a slip of paper with the name, address and telephone number of the Therapist. "Here's the information you'll need to get your shit together and only you can do it. You hear me, son?"

Mase took the paper and walked out mumbling.

"Yes, I hear you, sir."

"Before you go, leave your badge and your gun with me. It's policy."

Mase turned around quickly and tossed his stuff on Vrain's desk and walked out. Nobody looked up at him as he stormed out.

Chapter 6

A long week later, Mase walked into the Manhattan Center for Cognitive-Behavioral Therapy. Even in his current state, Mase made mental notes of the stark white office made softer by LED lights throughout the suite. In the waiting room were three ergonomic chairs with one small and one large ficus plant that couldn't grow in the place if they were real. On the coffee table were three magazines: one architectural digest, one healthy living and one Mediterranean Diet magazine. The bleached wood floor was made to look real, but you could tell that it was a laminate miracle with fake cracks and mold around the edges. *Enough already,* he thought to himself. *"Do what you have to do to get through this. Stop the detective bullshit already. Look worried but interested."*

Lara Deming, LMHC, Licensed Mental Health Counselor, had her name on the closed door of her office. Lara's Assistant, Paolo Manteo, a tall thin young man with curly black hair, busily scurried around looking for things to do to make himself look engaged in his work. To his credit, he had a good routine. It was very convincing. He dutifully greeted Mase with a limp hand and gracious look that made Mase look apprehensive. He was certain it was the expression they expected to see on his face. So that's what he offered them as he entered.

He tucked in his shirt as sat down, ergonomically. He worked unenthusiastically on his patient profile form: **Height**, 6' 4 1/2", **Weight** 205, **Color of** eyes Light blue. And then Lara's door opened and she walked into the waiting area. His head lifted and he couldn't believe how strikingly beautiful she was.

She was tall, thin and had the exact curves of a perfect Scandinavian goddess. He was mesmerized and frozen in space and time. It was all he could do to catch his breath, which he tried to hide by looking down at his profile form. She wore a beautifully tailored light gray business suit that must have been custom made because it fit her like skin. She somehow walked silently as she approached Mase with her thin long hand held out for a business hand shake.

Mase did something he never did. He stood up in the presence of a lady and offered his hand. She looked a little surprised at how tall he was. The rest of his appearance was less than impressive, but she hid it well under the tight facial control that all therapists probably have, the good ones anyway.

"Mr. Mason, I'm Lara Deming."

"Nice to meet you, Lara." All of his training at being composed at all times went away as soon as he shook her soft and pliant hand. "You can call me Mase. Everyone does..."

"OK, well, as soon as you've completed your patient's profile, just give it to Paolo. Then we can start. Is that acceptable?"

"Completely."

"Great. Take your time. It's important that you put in all the information."

Mase took longer than he should of because he couldn't get her out of his mind. Each question was interrupted by her long narrow hips, her full mouth and thin lips, the slightly square jaw and high cheek bones, her light hazel eyes with just the right amount of intensity, and her natural blond hair...

"Are you almost finished Mr. Mason?" Asked Paolo who appeared in front of him without a sound. It caught Mase by surprise.

"Oh, yes. Here."

"Follow me, please." Paolo walked with a hip swing that made no sense to Mase.

Mase had been beauty shocked but was back in the real world as Paolo led him into the office of Lara Deming. He smelled flowers as he walked through the door or was that her. The room was acoustically silent. Mase's power of observation couldn't abate even when he was being consumed. The room was obviously intended to be affirming and calming. The pastel colored walls had the usual diplomas, the long thin sculptures on the tables and two well-padded light green tweed chairs that faced each other in front of the desk. Lara got up, sat in one chair and motioned gracefully to Mase to have a seat in the other. He bumped into it as he moved because he kept staring at her face. Paolo closed the door behind him as he left.

As she reviewed his profile, she noticed a few of the questions were left unanswered. Mase kept staring at her as she prefaced.

"Mase, let's fill in the blanks together so we can develop the best treatment plan for you. So, Mase, what brings you here today?"

"An undeniable urge to kill myself by drinking too much, and too often."

She seemed to take copious notes as he kept his tongue safely in his cheek.

"Have you ever seen a counselor, therapist, or psychologist before?"

"You mean other than my mother?"

A very slight smile was quickly extinguished on Lara's face.

"What do you see as being the biggest problem?"

"My O.C. addiction to play video games, my very poor attitude about wasting my life away by drinking too much, and my unwavering sense of justice."

"That's three Mase. Give me the one that's the biggest."

"I'm an officer of the law. I seek justice when a crime is committed. I feel useless when justice doesn't happen."

"How does this problem make you feel?"

"Like a complete failure."

"What makes the problem better?"

"When, no matter what, justice is served."

Lara paused for a second as she made sure she recorded her notes accurately. She took the time and attempted to complete her initial thoughts. She crossed her long and shapely legs in front of him as she finished.

"You're a detective I see. What do you think of your job?"

"Would it be OK if I call you Lara?"

"Certainly."

"Well Lara, it's like this. My job is to find and bring to justice people who commit crimes, usually murders. That's what I do and if I don't say so myself, I'm pretty good at it. You know how some people have a knack for certain things, take you, for instance. I'm sure you always had a knack for finding out what makes people tick. Now you do it for a living. Me, I found out I had that knack only after I became a cop. I had no intention ever of becoming a detective."

"We'll get into all of that later Mase. But for right now, I just want to make sure I've got your entire profile finished, and I think we have. And then I'll work with you on the best strategy to help you work on the things that bother you the most. Does that sound like a good way to begin?"

He glanced at her legs as she stood up. At over six feet tall herself, she wasn't used to looking up at people, but when she stood next to Mase, he was taller. Her eyes seemed to widen. They stood fairly close to each other as they ended the session with a handshake.

"Paolo will set you up for our next session in a few days."

He held her hand a little too long as she gently pulled it back with a smile.

"Thank you Lara. I look forward to it."

Chapter 7

After a five day wait, Mase took the elevator to the third floor and entered Lara's office. He had taken the time to make sure he was more presentable to Lara. His straight black hair was combed neatly in place, his hands and fingernails were clean, and most of all he had made sure he didn't drink anything the day before so he wouldn't reek. He thought about Lara for the entire five days and knew that his previous appearance that he'd been an embarrassment.

As he entered the carefully lit waiting room, he noticed Paolo was there and that he heard muffled conversations coming from one of the therapy rooms. He closed the entry door softly and heard the muted bell that told Paolo he was there for his session. Still, no one came to greet him. He figured they must have been dealing with a challenging patient. He waited for a few minutes and still no one arrived, so he lifted a magazine off the coffee table and riffled through its pages until he came to a picture of a log cabin in the Adirondacks that looked as though it had been constructed somewhere else and somehow put there in the boonies. The architecture magazine was as shiny as the perfect homes it highlighted. He wondered how much that prefab cabin was worth and whether enjoying nature in the mountains had become a playground for the rich and perfect. He closed the magazine and put it exactly where it had been on the table.

As he was about to sit back in his chair, under an Ingmar Bergman poster, Paolo came scurrying through the waiting area and looked surprised when he saw Mase. He stopped in his tracks and held up his right index finger to Mase and continued his scurrying into the closed therapy room where Lara's muffled voice could be heard through the door that Paolo closed carefully but forcefully.

Mase picked up a tone from the muffled conversation that sounded frantic. He knew it was Lara's voice because it had stayed with him since their first meeting. The conversation inside the room elevated and dropped and elevated again. Mase looked at the ceiling with its modern version of a chandelier. He looked down at his hands, which he now clasped together, and reopened. The conversation in the room seemed to pause, or even stop, because not a sound was heard for a few minutes.

Mase was getting a bad feeling now. It really wasn't any of his business. *Why should it bother me? People have problems they need to solve. People like Lara help them. They deal with difficult people,* he thought, *just like himself and they have to navigate their way through the complex personalities that are always figuring out ways to out think the people who are trying to help them. Seems like a tough way to earn a living. Oh well, it was her choice.*

The door opened once again. Paolo edged his way out, backwards, and closed the door with the softest of touches. The conversation, now a little quieter, continued inside. He did a slight pirouette after he closed the door and walked slowly and quietly over to Mase.

"I am so sorry Mr. Mason. Miss Deming has been dealing with a difficult patient and she and I both apologize for the delay. Can I get you something to drink while you wait, some coffee or tea, perhaps?"

"Nothing thanks."

"Very well, sir, and once again, sir, we apologize for the delay, Miss Deming will be just a few more minutes."

Paolo pirouetted again and disappeared into his world of the professional office assistant. It must be nice to come and go into your own world and leave everything behind. But, the more he saw of Paolo, the more he liked him. He liked people who took their damn jobs seriously and did their best, whatever it was. He definitely looked like a guy you could count on, no matter what. He was glad that Lara had a person like that to help her. *Why did he care about all of that?* The question had a definite answer, and the answer was becoming more and more complicated.

When the hidden talk seemed over, Lara came out and apologized personally to Mase. She told him that his session would begin shortly and to give her a few minutes to get ready. She wasn't as composed as she was in the first session. She had tension and concern etched all over her flawless face. A little 'v' formed between her two eyebrows just above the bridge of her beautiful aquiline nose. Whatever was going on with the 'difficult' patient, she wasn't handling it very well, but the warning flags were flying everywhere.

Mase paced the waiting area. He had the feeling that Lara was trying hard to compose herself but wasn't getting very far. So, he waited some more, and then a little longer until he was about ready to knock on the door as he approached to knock, the door opened and hit him on his knuckles, causing a bruise.

Lara saw it and for a second she almost lost it. But, she recovered quickly using every bit of her professional training to put forth the solid granite front of the consummate pro. Mase liked her now even more, although it was supposed to be none of his business.

"I am so sorry. If I'd have known you were there, I would have been..."

"No worries Miss Deming. I get these all the time, you know, saving the world and all that..."

Lara cracked a smile at Mase's attempt at calming down the situation. She looked him directly in his eyes and lost her cover, but just for two or three seconds. She put her hand gently on his back and guided him into the office.

"Please, have a seat." She brought a manila folder with her as she sat opposite Mase.

Just as she was about to sit down, Paolo rushed in and excused himself to both and gently whispered something into Lara's left ear.

Lara was about to say something when Mase interrupted.

"Look Miss Deming, I can see this has been a challenging day for you and Paolo. I can also see you have to attend to your challenge right now. There's no need to explain anything. I can reschedule our session and we can begin again like all of this never happened. If you're OK with that, I'll leave now to allow you to attend to your business."

"Thank you Mase."

As Mase left and looked into the other therapy room, the door was slightly ajar and he noticed a VR headset sitting on Lara's desk inside with different color lights blinking. He filed it in his tickler file, otherwise known as detective intuition.

Chapter 8

He rarely visited bars on the Upper East Side, but just the idea of being in the same area as Lara Deming was enough to push him. He wound up at the corner of 73rd St. and 2nd Avenue at a gaming bar called Head Shots. He looked through the large plate-glass windows and although it wasn't his kind of place; he thought it looked OK and went in. He was in a Fortnite mood and noticed a couple of good-looking women playing the game in the far right corner of the bar. He ordered the one drink, and only one drink, that he would buy for the evening.

The room was buzzing with people playing and drinking. If you closed your eyes, you'd swear you were in Vegas. But, he was in the mood so he drifted over to the area. One woman, a curvy one with heavy makeup and large breasts, was doing well at her game. When she jumped up and down, all the surrounding men jumped up with her. The more she jumped the more they encouraged her. She knew exactly what she was doing and her game was winning as much at her Fortnite game. Mase wondered to himself if all there was left in the world were games.

A few people gathered around him to watch him play. He played as well as he'd ever played and he kept winning. The crowd was pumped and as he looked back at his groupies; he spotted Lara on the other side of the room. When his Victory Royale screen appeared and he did his victory dance, he walked slowly away from the screen so he could catch another glimpse of Lara.

He stayed hidden in the crowd as Lara continued to party with four young players who were enjoying being with her. She looked slightly drunk and unsteady, but she continued to party. All four men had her circled and she kept putting on and taking off a VR headset. When she offered it to one dude, he took it, put it on and made a stupid joke because everyone started laughing, including Lara. The guys started getting extra friendly and so did Lara.

When Lara tried to retrieve her headset, one guy kissed her and put his hands all over her and as far a Mase could tell, she enjoyed every second. Mase was thinking about playing the hero and coming to her rescue. But, it wouldn't work because she appeared to be having as good a time as the four dudes who were all over her. She finally left with her arms around the shoulders of two of them and the other two following behind. She was laughing too hard to be in trouble.

***

The trouble with subways is that they're a bad influence. Yes, Mase was bummed by the sight of his beautiful Goddess enjoying herself with a stable of studs who looked like nerds on dope. They looked hungry and she looked unconcerned. He waited at the edge of the platform on the 72nd St. Subway.

He soon felt the push of the metallic smelling breeze coming out of the tunnel. It felt warm and soft. It came harder and harder until he felt it move his hair like someone blew their bad breath all over him. One wino was huddled on the last seat near the door that led to the next car. There was no one else on the train. He looked at the wino enough that the wino finally looked up at him with bleary red eyes and a sagging mouth drooling the days' best vintage. It scared the shit out of Mase, because for a split second the wino was him, Victor Mason.

Then Lara entered his mind and took over. Everything about her was captivating and she had a way about her that put her firmly on that Grecian pedestal that Mase created deep inside his painful consciousness. *Was she a nymphomaniac clothed in Psychiatric clothing? Was she a misunderstood party girl who needed to be in the company of as many men as she could handle? Was she something completely different from what she put forth to the world? What was she? Who are you Lara Deming?*

***

The day finally arrived. His second therapy session was scheduled for 9:30 am and he had arrived in the neighborhood almost an hour and a half early. He tried to milk a coffee and donut at a local diner for almost an hour and a half until the wait staff gave him the goodbye look necessary for the rush of breakfast eaters that were coming in.

He straightened himself out for the slow walk to her office. He walked that fine line of love and hate, desire and pain, the past and the future all in total and uncontrolled warfare with each other. He must have appeared to be a complete wack job to the people walking towards him on 2nd Avenue. He knew he was talking to himself and if you had a problem with that, too bad. It was hard work coming to terms with your own problems. But, wait, wasn't Lara supposed to be solving his problems, not creating them?

When he opened the door and the bell sounded, he felt like Pavlov's dog. Only he was Pavlov and the dog combined. This time Paolo was ready as he usually was and greeted Mase heartily as he entered and assured him that Lara would be with him shortly to start his session.

Lara appeared at the door to the office. Bright sunlight was streaming through the window behind her. Her form, with its perfect shape and curve, her hair glowing, almost golden white made her appear as though she belonged to an eternity from somewhere else in the universe.

"Come in Mase, please." Lara used her softest voice and open palm pointing toward the office. "How are you this morning?"

She closed the door as gently as possible behind him as he made his way to the chair he had sat in before. Mase gently nodded his head but did not answer the question with words. Lara knew immediately that something was wrong.

"Well, we finally made it to our second session. Once again, I apologize for the delay."

Mase still wouldn't answer, so Lara tried the direct approach.

"Mase, forgive me for asking, but you seem distant and quiet. It's a different person who I've seen before. Is there something bothering you, something that you and I can work on helping you get past it and move on with your program of progress?"

"Life is too big a topic for our conversation."

"Your life?"

"Life," he stared out the window of her office, "life."

"I'm not sure..."

"Look, maybe today isn't the best day for this. Would you mind if we rescheduled this for another day?"

"Not at all. If that's what you want?"

"Yes, it's what I want."

Chapter 9

It was approximately two weeks earlier that Lara Deming had her first encounter with Creighton LaVelle. She had received a phone call from him requesting her assistance in helping him overcome certain issues. His phone call raised red flags all over the place and she initially declined citing an overly full schedule and the fact that he said he could only do online sessions.

But, LaVelle was persistent. He kept calling until Lara finally agreed to an initial assessment of his so-called 'issues'.

"How did you get my name Mr. LaVelle?"

"I was referred to you by a colleague of mine. Dr. Earnest Raveneaux."

"I'm not familiar with him. What is his line of work?"

"Same as mine. We're both neuroscientists that work independently."

As Lara looked at the computer screen in front of her, she was taken by the handsome good looks of LaVelle. He seemed almost perfect in his speech, in his mannerisms and in his vocabulary that seemed without limits. He dropped names, places, and high-end intellectual references that were intended to impress. He even threw in clever jokes that were sprinkled into the assessment that Lara was doing. She smiled at the attempts at humor, but she knew he was covering something.

"Based on what you've told me so far Mr. LaVelle, I won't be able to help you. In fact, I'm not even sure what your so-called issues are. You haven't really told me what you want."

"You don't understand Miss Deming. Ever since COVID, I haven't been outside of my residence, I order all my food and have it delivered, I'm afraid of interacting with other human beings and..."

"You and about 50 million other people, Mr. LaVelle. COVID isn't a problem anymore. Just take it one step at a time and reach out to the world just like you're reaching out to me, and you'll be just fine."

"I wish I could share your optimistic outlook, but I need help. Can't you see that? I need help."

"Mr. LaVelle, I suggest you seek the help of a Psychiatrist who can work with you to get to the core of what's going on with you. Often, when people become shut-ins they..."

"Look Miss Deming, this is more than just being a shut in, believe me. I can't sleep at night; I hear noises and see dark images everywhere. It's becoming too much for me to handle. I've even had thoughts of suicide. Believe me, I need help. Can't you see that?"

"I understand, Mr. LaVelle, but I won't be able to take you as my patient. If you are having suicidal thoughts and you think you need immediate help, call 911 and they'll send someone over immediately to help you."

A long silence in the video transmission showed the handsome face of Creighton LaVelle morphing slightly, and then returns to its original face. She was taken aback by the quick morphing. For a split second, she thought it looked exactly like her deceased husband, Carl Deming. It couldn't have been. Her mind must've been playing tricks on her.

Chapter 10

Jerry Barlow was always playing the ponies or the sports betting plays or the online video gaming parlors that hid in plain sight because they were too high stakes. During the day, he was a stock broker for Archive Investments on Wall Street. That gambling was for chumps, he always thought, but because he was so good at it, they came to him like flies to shit. It was a shame how much money he took off the flies.

He lived the good life on the Upper East Side until he started betting on himself, which was the worst bet of all. When the blind luck he'd always had ended, he sank into his own misery that some of his friends told him would be the death of him. Most people liked Jerry Barlow because he bought their friendships with booze and compliments and big bear hugs that caused people to cough as he squeezed them like a papa bear.

He knew how to tap into guys or gals who had the money. He knew the right words in the right tone of voice, in the right settings. Recently, he had lost a bundle to an online ghost named 'Call me Death'! It was multiple six figures and the bit coin he'd used to pay the debt had bounced back like a digital Sword of Damocles.

Jerry knew that consequences would come, he just didn't know when or how or how bad. The Champion's Sports Palace had two back rooms and the usual bank of regular video gamer monitors out front. The two back rooms had recently started their VR Gaming high stakes parlays, mid game betting, fast and expensive.

He'd been on a bad losing streak when he tore off the headset and walked out of Champions like an automaton, when a very large human stepped on the set like he was putting out a cigarette. Jerry stood on the east side curb of Third Avenue and waited and waited. Other pedestrians pushed him aside because he wouldn't move. All he could do was stare at the oncoming traffic for what some witnesses said was close to ten minutes.

Around nine o'clock, Jerry Barlow walked in front of a speeding delivery van and cashed in his chips. It made no sense to anyone. He wasn't drunk, as the detectives found out, and he wasn't suicidal, as most of his 'friends' stated.

"No, no, no... Jerry wouldn't hurt a fly. He was a party boy. We all loved Jerry," A patron at Champion's stated.

Standing deep in the shadows of the milling crowd stood a tall and burly, dark-skinned man smoking a cigarette. His face could have been made of stone. All you could see was the red tip of the cigarette drawing down and out. He left after the grim-looking paramedics took the half-dead body of Jerry Barlow and slid him into the chariot of death.

As Mr. Stone face walked away, he glanced over his shoulder at the ambulance, and a huge explosion blew it apart and showered it over the traffic and pedestrians who were stupid enough to watch and wait for death so they could tell someone anyone that they were there. The dark-skinned man took one last drag on his cigarette and tossed it into the street. It rolled back to the curbside puddle that flowed slowly down the street and fizzled into nothing, just like Jerry Barlow.

When the 19th Precinct found out that Jerry Barlow's Savings and Checking accounts had mysteriously been emptied, the wheels started turning. They started reaching out to the other Precincts for any assistance and information on Mr. Barlow. Chuckie Carlo saw the request for information and he filed it away with all the other unsolved crimes and their associated problems. They found out one thing. Mr. Party Animal had an ex-wife who was struggling to make ends meet for her and her daughter. Jerry stopping paying alimony to her for the past year so his lack of usable funds did not surprise her one bit.

She ended her diatribe by telling the detectives at the 19th Precinct to call his damn shrink. She would probably know more about him. She forgot the shrink's name, so the entire conversation, if you could call it that, ended right there. They reached their dead end, which as far as they were concerned was fine with them. They tried one last shot at talking to his employer, Archive Investments.

A buddy of Jerry's told the detective that Jerry didn't enjoy paying his debts and always tried to weasel out of them whenever he could. He knew because Jerry had tapped him for a cool couple of grand a few of months back and gave up asking for his money back. Jerry was too good at sliding and smiling and rubbing people's backs.

Nobody cried for Jerry.

Chapter 11

Jonah Christian lounged in front of his immense fireplace. It was actually a large flat screen monitor. The sound of the crackling flames were programmed, by Jonah of course, to create music. Each lick of a flame was a chord, and the rising and falling of the flame indicated tone and volume. There was nothing he couldn't do with a computer. And every part of his world was driven by and created to enhance his very sad and sick life. He was a tortured man, not by the world, but by himself.

He walked around his mansion in a long smoking jacket. When he walked, he moved with grace and dignity. He had no mirrors in his rooms because that particular piece of reality simply wasn't welcome. He only allowed his two man servants access to him as needed. Anyone else would see what he wanted them to see. He was an avatar to most, a fantasy fiction character to others, and a horror show to himself when he would sneak a look at himself as a reflection in a metal lamp or spoon. He hated looking at himself like that, but just like someone looking at a bad accident, he couldn't help himself. Why? Because he used to be an extremely handsome man. He lived a gentleman's existence, living on his massive inheritance, and gambling. He loved gambling as long as he didn't lose, which he never did. When COVID almost finished him and he caught a flesh-eating bacteria that removed his lips, part of his nose and cheeks he submerged himself deep into a world of computer programming, AI and online gambling via video games. He could live any life he wanted to live and make it seem as real as reality.

This is where we start with Jonah Christian.

Jonah was an autodidact of the first degree. He learned faster than was humanly possible because he had developed a speed/reading/learning program that worked directly in his brain as he learned. He could imprint and form his own engrams that created memory and knowledge. He was so good at this that he soon developed a way of imprinting others to create memories he wanted them to form in their minds. No one else in the world could do this and by doing it this way, when you worked with Jonah, you never had a chance of being your own person.

What Jonah also found out was that the human brain was infinitely more powerful than the most powerful supercomputer. Once a person's brain was mastered, the person was mastered and completely under his control. It all started out as a game one winter evening in 2021. In his research labs on level 2 under his mansion, he had programmed common field mice to act like cats. They were cats, and when he put these mice and a cat in the same cage; the cat acted as if the mice were cats and did nothing.

This was just one of the major discoveries of Jonah Christian. Of course, he was burning through his inheritance at a rapid rate and knew he would have to create a more substantial income to allow him to continue his work. He devised a way of stealing ten cents from anyone with a bank account. He did this so successfully and so easily that he was never suspected.

Everything he had was hidden. His identity was hidden. His name wasn't really Jonah Christian. He wealth, at the fifty billion dollar level, hid in his own bitcoin servers which were hidden below his mansion and water cooled by the underground stream he discovered on his property.

It wasn't actually possible to meet Jonah Christian; however, if you did and happened to look into his eyes, death was available for observation. Who was Jonah Christian His levels were so many and so deep that even he wasn't sure. But, because of his extraordinary abilities, he could easily click an icon and find out almost immediately who you were.

He was a computer programmer, neuroscientist, linguist, research scientist, and far too many more labels; that's who he was.

His actual personal wealth is still a matter of debate but I can tell you that his personal residence on seven hundred acres in New Rochelle complete with mansion, underground research facilities was part of his inheritance.

Whoever he was was shrouded in so much mystery that if anyone wanted to find out anything about him, it would take two lifetimes of constant detective work and there would be no reason to do it.

There were three subterranean levels of research facilities under his mansion. All of it reinforced concrete. Days or nights meant nothing to Mr. Christian. Where he lived and how he lived were controlled by him. There was of course, heightened security. There was, of course, climate control. And there was life-sustaining, state-of-the art, medical equipment that allowed him to enjoy his activities without the slightest worry about his own health.

Below the massive stone mansion was an underground stream that was spring fed and seemed to never abate. It provided a large part of the cooling needed for his three hundred bitcoin servers. It provided part of the climate control for the entire structure, feeding in just the right amount of necessary humidity to keep his equipment in perfect condition.

Whenever he needed his two assistants, Toy Francisco and Stanley Burnett, his simply thought it and they appeared.

He needed his daily sponge bath, and after they completed their less than distasteful duty of sponging him down and drying him off and clothing him, he reclined in his enormous chair and spoke to them directly. When I say directly, I don't mean verbally. To Mr. Christian, that process was a complete waste of time. He spoke to them through their neural receivers, which were implanted as part of the hiring process.

Mr. Francisco was Hispanic. Mr. Burnett was African American. They were large individuals at six feet six inches each and solid three hundred pounds of muscle and intensity. They could have been twins. Each received an annual salary of one million dollars, paid up front, every January 1st. They didn't have to check because they knew the money was there.

But, their duties went far beyond the personal hygiene of Mr. Christian.

On the second subterranean level was the programming suite. Jonah Christian had not only mastered most of the major computer programs, but he'd improved them to such a degree that they were almost unrecognizable. He had a genius for understanding programming language and he used Artificial Intelligence to help him work at light speed to change these programs for his own use.

On the first subterranean level were the neural research labs. Not only was it state-of-the art, but it was also automated to such a degree that he controlled every aspect of the research from his central station through commands and non-verbal sound pulses. There were animals in cages that were used for his experiments. There was nothing about synapses and engrams that he didn't know or take advantage of for his own nefarious ways.

Automation was the key to everything Jonah Christian did. He had robots doing all the menial tasks throughout his mansion up to and including preparing food for him and his two assistants and one housekeeper. He had made discoveries in these labs that were far ahead of anything achieved in the best laboratories in the world. But, no one but him knew about his discoveries.

The achievement he was proudest of was the ability to alter and change human engrams. His research had discovered the way memories are stored as biophysical and biochemical changes and how to change the structure of these engrams by certain computer-aided sound frequencies. He could build up memories in your brain that were completely artificial. But, they seemed as real as anything you remembered from what had happened to you in your life.

Associated with these discoveries was his development of a new hypnotic-like state he created using Virtual Reality. He could use this on everyone he came in contact with and could turn it off and on at will. His two assistants knew they were subject to this hypnosis, but they did not object.

Chapter 12

Mase didn't know why he was so happy to attend his next therapy session because he had no desire to face his problem head on, at least not yet. He tried to lie to myself that he was going back to work, even though he knew his still had his problem. It hadn't gone away, but, neither had Lara. The thought occurred to him he was getting better, but it wasn't by helping himself, it was Lara. Oh, not necessarily by what she was saying to him or making him think about, it was her. But then again, he knew he had to get better before Vrain would let him come back to work.

He made it to Lara's office a little early. Paolo was brewing some fresh coffee and it smelled great. Mase knew he'd offer him some, and he did. He was his usual welcoming self, but there was a different look on his face that he was trying to hide, but Mase caught it and Paolo knew he caught it.

"You look well this morning Mr. Mason."

"I feel pretty good. The rain outside tried to make me cranky but it didn't work. That tells me I feel like working on my issues with Miss Deming."

Paolo was fumbling and shuffling papers on his desk and finally remembered he needed to reply. He offered Mase coffee again and Mase said yes, again.

When he brought it over to the detective, the concern on his face was taking over and his hand was shaking enough that a little of the coffee came out of the cup.

"I am so sorry Mr. Mason. I don't know why I'm so clumsy this morning. I'll get you a fresh cup."

"No, no, no Paolo. Don't worry about it. I'll take this one. I can use it."

As he handed Mase the cup, he stopped for a second and was about to say something but didn't and walked back to his desk.

"You OK, Paolo? You look like something's bothering you."

He didn't reply, but shook his head and twisted his face into a smile, which didn't work. Mase jumped on it again.

First, he stared at Mase and then he shifted his eyes to a slightly open room where Lara was conducting a therapy session. The door was open a crack, and he could see Lara's arms flailing away. She was wearing her VR headset again and mumbling incoherently. Paolo's eyes shifted back to the detective and then back to the room once more. Mase nodded at him just enough to show him he got it. He backed away slowly to his desk and focused on whatever bullshit he could find to keep himself occupied but always looking towards the room where Lara was. He checked the clock and went in to remind Lara of her next appointment.

I could hear him talking to her, but it appeared she was ignoring him. But he was persistent and she relented. Paolo left the room and closed the door completely.

"Mr. Mason, Miss Deming will be with you shortly."

Mase thanked him and waited and waited some more. Lara finally appeared in the waiting room and greeted him. He noticed the red pressure points on her head from where the VR headset was strapped. She seemed somewhat disengaged as she told him what would happen next after they entered the usual therapy room.

"Mase, I'm very sorry, but I won't be able to be your therapist any longer. I've been taking on too many new patients and the burden of scheduling and doing what's best for my patients prevents me from taking on any additional work."

He was caught by surprise. There was never a doubt about her engagement with him as they went through their handful of sessions, and, he thought they were making progress.

"Is it because of me? Did I do anything to upset you or cause any difficulty for you?"

"Not at all. It's just..."

She caught herself right then and stared out the window. Her face went in and out of confusion and puzzlement. He'd not seen that in her face before.

"I'm recommending to your Department that you be allowed back to work and that I feel confident that you are making the right amount of progress with your issue and that until you are sure yourself that you are handling everything well enough, that you go through drug testing and sobriety testing every three months."

He knew right then that she was just trying to get rid of him. He didn't know why, but he wasn't about to roll over and he knew damn well that his problem had not gone away and damn well that he'd made little progress.

"Lara...I was wondering if you would do one last thing for me before I leave."

"Certainly."

"You know that little meditation garden behind the lobby of this building?"

"Oh, yes, it's quite lovely."

"I was wondering if we could go down there for a short meeting. I promise I will not bother you any longer but I want to talk to you about something important."

"First of all Mase, you're not bothering me. In fact, I've enjoyed our sessions together and learning more and more about you. And, I consider it an honor and a pleasure that I was here to help such a dedicated public servant. No, you aren't a bother. I just..."

"Well, why don't we take a short fifteen minute stroll in the garden and perhaps we can end our work on a positive note. I hear that meditation is good for everything that ails you. Is that true?"

"It is. OK, let's go downstairs for a short while. I'll just let Paolo know that we're going down there so he can manage while I'm out."

Before she was about to talk with Paolo, her face went totally blank. It was as though she went into a catatonic trance. She didn't move a muscle and had one hand on the edge of the desk and the other hand on her right temple. Then, she snapped out of it and they went towards the door. Paolo gave Mase the look, the thank God someone's helping her look, following by a slight smile that meant he was happy but still worried.

The little Zen garden had a murmuring fountain/waterfall, a sandbox with a rake and Zen elevator music.

Lara and Mase sat on the little bench that faced the murmuring water. There wasn't much either of them could say, so he took his one and only opportunity.

"Lara, I'm not much good at things like this, but I want to be sure you hear it and understand it completely." He gently touched her hand.

She didn't move it or react, but her eyes looked at him with confidence.

"I didn't know what to expect when I opened up to you. But the one thing I knew was that I was scared to death. And when you looked at me and made me feel as though I wasn't beyond help and that I could be the one who could help myself, well, it made me feel like a human being again. And for that, I'm eternally grateful to you."

"No thanks are needed Mase, really. You are ready to face your issue head on."

"But, Lara, I'd be a complete asshole if I didn't let you know I see you are in some kind of tight spot right now. Don't forget, I'm the wonder boy detective, remember? And, I want you to know that I'm here to help you with whatever it is, no matter what it is, no strings attached."

Lara stood up and so did the detective. She gave him a hug and left. And there he was, wondering what the hell he had just done.

Chapter 13

Lara walked slowly into the elevator that would take her to the seventh floor. The door closed behind her as she leaned up against the back stainless steel wall. It felt cold against her thin silk blouse. She stared vacantly at the panel in front that had the floor buttons. She felt paralyzed and unable to lift her arm and walk to the buttons.

A tear fell slowly down her left cheek. Her perfect makeup with the slightest hint of Indian Pink rouge was about to be ruined. The tear hung on for dear life at the edge of her jaw. It stayed and stayed and stayed and then as it was about to fall, Lara lifted her hand and caught the tear on the tip of her thin long index finger. She looked at her finger with the tear and realized where she was.

She pushed off from the back elevator wall and moved slowly forward to push the button that would take her to the seventh floor. As soon as she pushed number seven, Muzak from the speaker instantly started with a slow jazz version of 'Gimme Shelter', no words, just sounds. Apocalypse Now ran fast forward in her mind and as each floor dinged on the progress panel on the top of the elevator door, she remembered that the smell of napalm in the morning was loved by warrior gangsters wearing uniforms and hate and evil and it came to her as she reached number seven that those were the same gangsters that killed her husband Carl, or did they?

When the door opened at number seven, the glaring fluorescent light filled her mind and the space she was in. She was drawn into her office waiting area and then directly into her office. She closed the door behind her with careful firmness. The VR headset that was resting on the desk beckoned her as she eased her way into the chair behind the desk. She stared at it and then gently set it on her head.

Just then, two men came into the office. They were well dressed and very large. Paolo's attention was immediately taken by these two giants who sat down in the waiting area and stared straight ahead. Paolo addressed them.

"Good morning, gentlemen. How may I help you?"

"We have an appointment with Miss Deming. No help is needed by either of us."

"I'm afraid Miss Deming has no additional appointments this morning. You may have the wrong day. What are your names?"

"Look at your schedule. You will see our names and appointment."

"I'm the one who makes all of Miss Deming's appointments and you are not scheduled with her this morning."

"Look at your schedule."

"Very well, if you insist." Paolo was into his placating mode of reception, and by the size and intensity of the two very large human beings, he knew it would be the only way to convince them.

When he looked at the schedule that he himself had created, there were the two gentlemen scheduled for 10:30 AM. He couldn't believe it. He knew for certain that he did not make that appointment, but, there it was. There was nothing he could do now.

"My mistake gentlemen. I will inform Miss Deming that you have arrived for your appointment and she will be with you shortly. May I get you some water or other beverage while you wait?"

The one who talked said "No, we won't be waiting long enough to drink anything."

"Mr. Burnett and Mr. Francisco to see you..." said Paolo as he was gently pushed to the side while the two men walked in silently, gracefully and with intent. Mr. Francisco closed the door strongly.

"Miss Deming, we're here to replace your current Life Insurance Policy with a new one." He took off her current VR headset and replaced it with the new one they brought it. She smiled meekly at them, but when the new one was put in place, a look of pleasure enveloped the rest of her face and she rested back in her chair.

"As you can see by the words scrolling by, *There is More To Life Than Living*. That is how you will recognize your new Life Insurance Policy."

"What does it mean?" Asked the therapist.

"It means just what is says. Life is more important. And now, through our auspices, you will have your own personal access to on-demand immortality."

"Immortality?"

"Why yes Miss Deming. In fact, we are quite certain that your life will never be the same. In fact, Miss Deming, you are now and will always be, immortal. Give it time. You will see. Good day Miss Deming."

The men left as abruptly as they had arrived. Paolo gave them a lukewarm good bye and took a deep breath and rushed into Lara's office.

"What was that all about?" was the unusual response to his boss. He was shaken and confused and scared. Lara didn't answer him but waved him off and stared into her headset.

Chapter 14

Vic Mason must have passed at least twenty bars on the way home, but didn't stop at even one. He couldn't. It was a Lara. That was all he could think about. Everything about her, whatever it was took his mind to unknown places and there was nothing, absolutely nothing he could do about it.

The 27th Precinct was straight ahead. How he got there was a mystery. It was like some unseen force pulling him toward a place he didn't want to go. He had business there, no point in denying it, and it wasn't bullshit; it was business.

Not a single person looked at him as he went past his desk. All his stuff had been neatly put inside the drawers and the desk was immaculate. There wasn't a speck of dust anywhere. Whatever their intentions, it made him sick. He found a cardboard box in the break room and put his stuff inside of it. There wasn't much there, a couple of notebooks, a used pack of gum, some pens, and a picture of Gina and Mia. He'd almost forgotten about them and he hated that. *Did they even remember him? Did they even care? Probably not.*

Apparently, someone had notified Vrain that Mase was taking his stuff. He came out sheepishly and was trying to act nonchalant.

"What the hell are you doing?" He said one half tone above a whisper.

He decided not to answer because it didn't matter and finished packing and was about to leave when Vrain grabbed him by his arm and dragged him to his office. It felt like he was pulling a man who had given up.

"Sit your miserable ass down and tell me what the fuck is going on with you."

"This job isn't for me and you know it. It's time. It's just time."

"It's just time! What the fuck does that mean?"

"Look, I don't want to go through this. Why can't you just let me do what I want to do and leave it. You know as well as I do that no matter what I do, I'll never be able to work here. It won't work. I still have my problem and it's not going away."

"Your therapist says different. She says you're working hard at facing it and your entire attitude about it had changed. She says you're ready to come back to work as long as you keep working on it. It never goes away completely, but if you face it and work on it every day, you'll be OK. That's what she said."

Mase was in no mood to talk about Lara, especially with him. He couldn't have known what had happened, the way she affected him, the way her eyes looked when she talked to him about his problems or anything. She had an aura, a field of silence around her, a once in a lifetime person who when you meet them, you can't ever be away from them and he was being pushed away from her by her for some crazy unknown reason. It was killing him. She was deep inside him now, everywhere, and she wouldn't leave. Until he got her back, he couldn't work or live or laugh or dream. There were no more dreams. There were no more reasons for doing anything.

Vrain paced around his office. Mase stared at the floor to see if he could find a way out of there. They didn't speak. Even the clock on his wall made him sick. So, he started counting the seconds, and when he reached one hundred, he left. He didn't say a word as he left, taking his stuff with him and leaving Vrain rubbing the back of his head.

Captain Vrain looked out of his third-floor window. He watched his protégé walk across the parking lot. Mase glanced up and saw his boss shaking his head and probably thinking, '*What a waste. If that's what he wants, good luck, the stupid son of a bitch. He's a fool and I was a bigger one for backing him up every step of the way.*' Then he saw Mase toss the cardboard box into the nearest dumpster.

Mase felt like wallowing for a while, telling himself how lucky he was to get rid of all that bullshit, and for them to be out of his sight forever. What he needed was a good stiff drink. As he walked back to his apartment, he changed his mind and took the D Train to Coney Island, where he ate three hot dogs and drank a root beer at Nathan's. He thought about the many times his dad took him to Coney Island and convinced him to eat clams on the half shell which he first found disgusting but after a while liked them a lot with the cocktail sauce and the little oysterette crackers. His dad would tell him, "Laddie, these little jewels will put hair on your chest."

He walked around the decaying area that used to be so much fun. When he couldn't take that any longer, he took the D Train back to his apartment. He had no memory of being in Coney Island, but then he saw the mustard stain on his shirt and vaguely recalled being there.

Chapter 15

He called the room "The Template". It was cavernous, well lit, spotlights high on the surrounding walls and Jonah Christian sitting comfortably in a well-padded chair towards the back. Monitors were placed throughout the room with Jonah at the controls. The color of the lighting reflected the mood he was in, whether red for angry, blue for calm, black for thoughtful, or green for positive.

"Please sit down, gentlemen and thank you for coming." He had installed his synthetic mouth before Burnett and Francisco came in. They'd seen him many times without his mouth and never reacted to it. Their programming always kept their emotions well under control; they were emotionally centered and never reacted.

After the two men sat down and the red lights came on, Jonah switched on the two biggest monitors in the room. The quality of the video was perfect even though it had been recorded from their lapel cameras just a couple of hours before.

"Gentlemen, as you notice, your meeting with my beloved started well. It went smoothly and according to our plan. Everything you did, you did perfectly, and for that, I applaud your efforts. But, as you will see, the balance of the video did not. And I'm not pleased, because ..."

Stanley Burnett interjected, "Because a plan cannot be altered. If it is altered, it has not been executed well. If it is not executed well, it can't be a plan."

"Thank you Stanley. And do you know why it wasn't executed well, Stanley?"

"Because ..."

"A simple yes or a simple no is all I need, not an explanation which, no matter what it is, would be futile and a waste of my very valuable time."

"Yes." He reached out his right arm as far as it would go after he attached a metallic wired glove. Jonah Christian said "Good", as he furrowed his brow starting a large and very painful charge into the glove. The pain was excruciating, but only one small twitch and shudder was all that was shown by Mr. Burnett. Toy Francisco squirmed a little in his chair but made no outward sign of the consequences of their actions.

"And you, Mr. Francisco, you did what you were told to do by Mr. Burnett, so today, there are no consequences for your actions. But, as you know, I pay each of you $1,000,000 per year for your services. And that money is always paid up front so that you never have to worry about anything, financially, that is. Now today wasn't a good day for either of you. But, I know, and you both know that I will not tolerate this type of ineptitude again. Do you both understand?"

Burnett whispered "yes" and Francisco nodded his head quickly.

"I've thought about your encounter with my beloved and I've concluded that perhaps I haven't expressed how important she is to me. And that importance, gentlemen, requires the utmost gentility and sensitivity to Miss Deming's emotional state and her physical well-being." At that second, the lapel video zoomed into Lara's eyes. 'Miss Deming's eyes indicate stressful anxiety and gentlemen, we cannot have that ever again or Level 9 consequences will occur, which I would hate to see for you two valuable employees. You are important to me, of course, but you can easily be replaced if she is ever in any way made to feel anything but love from you or me. You are my extensions. You are me unless you can't implement every minute aspect of my plans, no matter what they are. Understood? Good. Now, let's proceed, unless you have questions." The two aides stared at Christian, unblinking, blank in every way, exactly as he expected.

"Please gentlemen, you may leave now to enjoy the fabulous dinner our chef has created for you. And, once you have relaxed after your meal I will call you back here and we will proceed with the next part of my plan." Jonah Christian moved his opened right palm towards the large metallic door that opened to the dining area. Toy Francisco and Stanley Burnett stepped quickly out of the room. The door closed silently behind them.

A few seconds later, Jonah Christian put on his VR headset and reclined back into his comfortable chair and smiled hard with his artificial mouth. He ripped out the mouth and threw it on the floor. It lay at his feet and smiled back at him.

He connected his best program generator, the one he developed personally to create his own environment, his universe, his better than actual reality. He used non-verbal commands as he pushed forward with his newest and best creation; the mauve and purple world of Anthonia. If you saw it, you'd probably say immediately, this is fantasy. But it went far beyond a play world of knights and dragons and maidens in distress. It was a three-dimensional space, in ultra-super real ultra-high resolution HD, with neural programming built into it.

With the right headset, and with this program, and with Jonah Christian in whatever identity he was using, you knew you were there. It was that real. After all, what is reality but what your senses tell you it is. Our senses feed our brains until we believe what they're feeding us is real. Well, he made it take over your senses through mind control. Today, the balance of the program's creation would be centered on the evil force that was intent on taking Lara away from Creighton LaVelle.

He was almost finished when he felt the buzz of a scheduler that indicated it was time for him to make some money.

Chapter 16

"Remember Tommy, there's more to life than living." Said the voice on the screen.

The Call of Duty match ended in the complete domination of young Tommy DeAngelo. He had dominated every gaming tournament that he ever entered and had never known defeat like this. It was over in less than ten minutes. Tommy didn't know what hit him, and the loss was stunning. He took off his headset and walked downstairs to his parents' bedroom and sat in their chair, in the dark, crying.

His mother Angela woke up to the sobbing she heard and was surprised.

"Tommy?"

The sobbing continued without an answer until he stopped and angrily told her, "I lost. I lost".

"I'm sorry honey, don't worry about it. Just go back to sleep and forget about it for now."

Tommy's dad Lou stirred a bit as he heard the end of the conversation.

"What is it Angela? Who are you talking to?"

"It's nothing Lou. Tommy's upset because he lost a video game, that's all."

"A video game? Go back to sleep will ya. This is crazy." Lou flipped himself over to his left side and put the pillow over his head. His last comment went unheard under the silencer pillow. "Video game? Jesus Fucking Christ Almighty."

Angela and Lou never spoke to Tommy again, because Tommy walked quietly upstairs and took three Tranqs and a tall glass of Lou's favorite Gin.

"Don't forget the note Tommy," was whispering in his ear as he wrote "There's more to life than living", on a blank sheet of printer paper and taped it to his video screen.

#

Jonah Christian took no prisoners. He didn't appreciate Tommy's arrogance let alone his gaming skills. He was good, but not good enough. This game was just a warm up pitch in the bull pen. His newly upgraded program was more than a Bot. It was AI guided play in its final stages of development. Not only was it inhumanly fast, but, it calculated every move that could be made by an opponent and the best strategic counter move instantaneously to win the game. Speed, accuracy, and mistake free play now put Mr. Christian in the forefront. He could take on anyone and come out a winner. Too bad for Tommy. Too bad for Angela and Lou.

***

In the mind of Jonah Christian, suicide was simply nature's way of thinning out the weak. All he was doing was helping nature do its job. What could be wrong with that? After all, he was fluent in death, theft, anonymity, hate, and genius. After programming Tommy for his suicide, Jonah Christian went to his programming center and spent the rest of the evening refining his suicide program. It was good, but not good enough. It was the crying business that had to be eliminated. He was at his best when he programmed, especially when AI made keystrokes unnecessary. BroBitchSandMan was working.

***

He had compiled a list of two thousand and eighty gamer tags, enough for a while. BroBitchSandMan was a little too long, but it encompassed his reason for gaming. Foremost, to make as much money as possible from as many suckers as he could find. It was becoming more difficult each day to find those gamers who had money, enough money to lose and not care. They were still around, but they were getting harder to find. He'd become distracted because of Lara Deming. Gaming had to suffice for now, but soon and without doubt, it would only be Lara, just them, in his three dimensional world was in the works.

***

Jonah had been cultivating a big sucker in the Middle East. The Sheik he'd been working on was on the line. He wanted a one off game with this spoiled brat of a son of a King. *This guy was in deep. It was so obvious as to be laughable. But, this one had to be coaxed slowly. He was ripe for picking. The good news was that his birthday was coming up. First flatter him as much as possible in Najdi Arabic, ask him how many virgins he had today, and sound unsure about playing him since his skill level was a lot higher than anyone else, my own included, which kissed enough of his ass to make him smirk. The big change today was that he was feeling extra proud of his recent Moon and Star Gaming Tournament achievement where he beat every single challenger.*

"Listen, BroBitch, I want to play you one game. You can pick the game, the time, the stakes, everything. Just one game. That's it. The sky's the limit. What do you say?"

Jonah Christian knew all the nuances of making a pause pregnant. It had to have length and depth. So he waited and waited.

"I know you're there BroBitch. I can hear you breathing." Said the Sheik.

He knew he had to be patient because this would be the heavyweight championship of the world. Everyone would be watching. But it had to be worth it.

"Let me sweeten the pot. One Billion Dollars in Bitcoin. Untraceable Bitcoin."

"I don't know Sheik..." mumbled BroBitch.

"I'll make it sweeter. If I win, you won't have to pay me one dinar, not one single dinar."

"Let me think about it. It is tempting, but..."

"Tempting?" Squealed the Sheik in dismay.

This was exactly where he wanted the Sheik. But, because of his reputation around the world as the best video gamer anywhere, BroBitch played it for all it was worth.

"Maybe." And then he disconnected the feed to the Sheik. He wanted to make him wait as long as he could to make sure everything would be in place for the largest take he'd ever make.

#

The neural research lab was at its heart a den of statistical probabilities. The research was Jonah Christian's speculative calculations, fueled and managed by his version of AI on engram chemical composition. Encoding memories in engram cells is controlled by large-scale remodeling of the proteins and DNA that make up cells' chromatin. This remodeling, which allows specific genes involved in storing memories to become more active, takes place in multiple stages spread out over several days. Changes to the density and arrangement of chromatin, a highly compressed structure comprising DNA and proteins called histones, can control how active specific genes are within a cell.

So, his most recent queries centered on how to reconfigure chromatin's histones through sonic waves and pulses and, of course, how to compress the time needed for the reconfigurations. The statistical summaries were encouraging enough that he made Toy Francisco his first subject.

He summoned Mr. Francisco and put on his headset. After a few wavelength pulses, he asked Mr. Francisco if he remembered being a white dolphin in the north Atlantic. Mr. Francisco relayed to Jonah every part of his journey through the icy waters and how he battled other dolphins in the war of survival.

Jonah Christian thought it was funny to leave the memory intact in the mind of Toy Francisco.

Chapter 17

When Mase arrived at his apartment, he couldn't help but think about the absolute mess he put himself in, and why he was throwing away his career, and, most of all, why he didn't give a shit about anything any longer? He walked around in his underwear and looked around at the apartment he'd probably get thrown out of soon. It'd been a pretty good place after the divorce. He didn't have to clean it if he didn't want to. He didn't care what it looked like, nor did anyone else. For a brief minute, he thought about what Lara would think of it. She was unbelievably beautiful! Then he straightened it out, which he never did, and pictured Lara pointing around the dump to guide him. *Pretty stupid to even think about it.*

After he threw out the trash and straightened the furniture and washed the dishes, he checked his emails to see if, by some miracle, Lara tried to contact him. She did not. But, there was a weird message that looked like Spam and before he deleted it, he read it. "I'm advising you, Mr. Mason, to cease and desist. More to follow." Probably a crank, but maybe not. His detective's eyes scanned every part of the message. It was clean and somehow made its way through his virus protection and email filters. He decided to save it to review later.

He wanted a beer really bad. But then he did something he never thought he'd ever do. He took one beer from the six-pack and carried the rest of them down to the trash. Why? Lara! He had told her he would work on his problem because he knew it was the right thing to do, for him, that is. But, it was also the right thing for her. He drank it down and felt a small ripple of clarity that quickly left.

Then he noticed another email had just arrived. It had a fake author and a mile long subject line. The message said, "Do yourself a favor and check under your front door. There are more where that one came from." He archived it as he did the first one.

Sure enough, there was an envelope, a regular letter sized light blue sealed envelope with his name printed on the front. He grabbed the corner of it and carefully opened it without touching it with his hands. He knew there wouldn't be any prints on it, but just in case...

He opened it carefully and found a long strand of blond hair that reminded him of Lara's beautiful golden locks. His jaw tightened into a grinding sound that sounded like a mill.

He put the envelope and the letter in a Ziploc bag in case it would be necessary to analyze it. He thought about the possibility that the entire thing was a cyber hoax. *Why would anyone go to all that trouble to threaten me? What were they threatening me about? Why me?*

Was Lara safe? That question kept rolling around in his mind as he spent the night staring at walls and shaking his head. *I'm not a cop anymore. I threw in my chips. But I could follow up with Lara in the morning and find out if she was safe. That's what I'd do. I'd follow up. That's exactly what I'd do.*

Then he thought about cases that he'd had where just the smallest delay cost lives. He wasn't even sure if this fell into that category. *Should I call my precinct and ask them to do a welfare check on Lara?* He couldn't ask for that since all he had was a threatening letter and a strand of blond hair. He wasn't even sure the hair was real. It could have been from a doll or a wig or...

It took a lot of coordination of people and computers to pull off that stunt. But, it also had that stalker feel where someone's brain gets disconnected with the love of a beautiful woman or man, and then everything else takes second place.

He didn't feel sympathy for this guy, or was it a guy? This could easily be a woman. If Vrain hadn't ended his employment, yet, his pass codes would all still be in place. If he just wanted him to sleep it off, everything would be the same as it was before he'd walked into Vrain's office and blew his stack. He must have looked like an idiot, firing off stupid words that meant nothing. He'd seen him do it before.

Logging on to his computer proved futile. He got blue screen after blue screen. Someone had fried it, so he tried his cell phone. It was the same. There was a pay phone down the street, which still worked because he'd seen pushers and hookers using it all the time. When he got to it, he realized he had no change in his pockets. Who needs change anymore? Everything was closed. It was 2 AM. He went back to his apartment and realized he'd locked himself out with no key. He climbed up the fire escape in the alley and crawled into his bedroom window, fell into bed and slept like a baby.

Chapter 18

Lara lived at The Standish Arms Condominiums on East 73 St. near 2nd Avenue. Everything in the stylish condo reflected her love of modern furniture. Everything had clean lines, geometric shapes, and neutral colors, mostly bright white. There was a mix of leather, metal, and wood. The living room featured a large white linen sofa, a beige coffee table, and a large white entertainment center.

It was late in the evening that Thursday night. She'd left work early and decided it was a 'me' day and put on her most comfortable lounging outfit, a blue silk combo that was pale enough to highlight her beautiful complexion. Everything fit in its place, including her. But something wasn't right. She felt a chill down her spine that felt as cold as death.

Lately, and she didn't know why, a strong feeling of dread and doom filled her life. She had always been a logical, fact-based professional that never let unknown feelings take over her thoughts. These feelings could eventually be identified and dealt with. But, it's a lot easier to deal with them when they belong to someone else, not her. This was something she hadn't dealt with since the horrific death of her late husband, Carl.

Carl Deming had been the true love of her life. Everything he stood for and everything he did showed what kind of man he was. As an international investigative reporter, he followed the clues, no matter what they showed, to the very end. Whenever the most difficult international crises materialized, his editor called Carl because he knew that the actual story would eventually be uncovered.

When he started in New York at the Village Voice, no one, least of all him, thought his career would take off the way it did. When he uncovered union graft on the docks of New York, he was threatened and bullied and knocked around until they thought he'd relent. He did not. In fact, he dug in even deeper.

Lara and Carl had been taking the same photography class at NYU. It wasn't long before they finished the class and took photos of each other throughout the day and evening. They were married six months later. Lara's income was substantially higher than Carl's, before he became a newspaper journalist celebrity. He freelanced from then on and sent most of the money to Lara for safe keeping.

In November, 2018, Carl got a tip from an informant in Lebanon. He said he had proof that a coup was about to take place in Beirut and that it would cost Carl $50,000 to get in on it. Carl decided not to tell Lara because he didn't want to put her in any danger. He knew that if it was true, this story would be a blockbuster and he would be in on it at the beginning, middle and end. That was exactly how he liked it.

He arranged the payment out of his own funds, if and only if he could validate the claim. He knew the informant well and vice versa. So, Carl left for the Middle East, telling Lara very little. They had always honored each other's professional freedom to work unencumbered. She knew the life of Foreign Correspondents was frenetic and unpredictable. They set up their own way of contacting each other, and neither of them ever missed a chance to talk or write to each other. Mutual respect, love, passion, and ideals set in motion, for both; Lara helping others in a very personal self-help way, Carl helping the world understand the ebb and flow of global politics. They both lived their passions to the hilt.

They were supposed to talk with each other on November 18. That didn't happen, and Lara worried. Not a word came from Carl for days after that. And then, the day that changed their lives forever, and the headline that was seen across the world. November 23.

A photograph appeared on the front page of every newspaper around the globe; A bullet-riddled naked man hanging by his neck from a twentieth-floor window of an abandoned office building in Beirut. His eyes had been gouged out and he had been castrated. He hung there for three days.

Condolence telegrams by the hundreds came to Lara's home, and they stayed in a heap on the bedroom floor. She was inconsolable for weeks. His body bag arrived at JFK, and was met by Carl's parents and his sister Vivien, along with Lara. There was a family plot in Patterson, New Jersey where Carl was laid to rest with little fanfare. That was the way Carl would have wanted it.

Now, Lara dozed on the sofa in her living room. The gloom and despair she felt all day entered a dream. Carl was everywhere in the dream. He was as alive as if he were actually there. Many strange episodes of their life together and some that weren't, like living mosaics forming a large tableau of Carl's life, whether they were true or not. If somebody had been in her living room, they would have heard her moan longingly for her lost Carl. The dream continued on for a dream eternity.

She woke up in anguish and sweat all over her body. She went straight for the shower, dropped her silk lounge wear along the way and stood in the water's coldness for what seemed like forever. She cried, but the tears became a stream of water. Finally she turned it off, dried herself with an oversized thick white towel, and found a flannel nightgown that clung to her, just like the memory of Carl.

Immediately, she put on her VR headset and watched for more clues, because Carl was in there. He was always in there and all she had to do was push the little white button on the side and he would appear in the flesh. It was Carl. She knew it was him. It had to be him.

Chapter 19

Mase had no reason to believe that Lara would see him. He had to go because he had no choice. The thought crossed his mind that he himself might have just become a stalker.

First, he thought he'd try the helpless angle and look for sympathy. Then he thought about the brutally honest approach. Then he thought about the chance meeting somewhere quiet that would give him the opportunity to look into her eyes one more time. Those eyes! He kept thinking about those eyes. No chance!

The phone rang. Never thought he'd hear from him again.

"Feel better yet?"

"Define better."

Vrain thought about what he would say next. At least Mase didn't hang up, which for the experienced Captain, was a small opening.

"Better, as in cooling off."

"Not a chance in hell."

"How about a temporary change of scenery?"

"What the hell does that mean?"

"Like helping the boys at the 17th. They're short-staffed right now and have a couple of murders they need help with. I asked them if they'd like to borrow you for a few weeks."

"And..."

"Well, beggars can't be choosers."

Vrain could hear Mase chuckling on the line.

"Well, they really must be in a hole to want me."

"That's exactly what I told them."

Vrain paused as Mase chuckled again and thought.

"Look Vic. Nobody wants to see you throw your life away, least of all me. You're the best detective we have and beyond that, you're a good guy. Sure you've got problems, bad problems, but who doesn't.

A change of scenery will do you good and give you a chance to get your feet back on the ground. Stay away from the booze and try it. Whaddya say?"

"Guess it's better than living on the street."

"So?"

Vrain waited. No answer from Mase.

"Report to Captain Thomas."

"Curt Thomas?"

"Yep."

"Good man. I've always liked the way he treated his people, as opposed to an asshole like you."

"Fine. Report to Thomas at 9 tomorrow."

"OK."

"Great to have you back, Vic. Oh and by the way, we grabbed your stuff out of the dumpster when you walked out. Carlo's got it for you when you return to the 7th. I sent your badge and gun to Thomas. He'll give it to you tomorrow."

"What made you so sure I'd do it? I mean come back."

"Why? From one asshole to another, you're a cop through and through. Even though you're the biggest fucking pain in the ass, I've ever known!"

Vrain ended the conversation.

Mase felt better than he had for a long time. He checked his refrigerator even though he knew what he'd find. Nothing. But, on the bright side, he'd be able to buy food again.

Why did he always want to eat Chinese food when he felt good?

Then he wondered if Lara liked Chinese food. Was it those little cardboard containers that made it taste so good or those fucking chemicals they put in it? Questions like that are not meant to be answered. A rhetorical question is like sex with someone you don't actually like. They're just there.

Lara is someone I love. I not only love her, I care about her. But now is not the time to go OCB. Steady, boy. You're amongst the great employed again. So, be a good boy and go to sleep and wake up like a god damn daisy. And, don't forget to set your damn alarm clock.

He found an almost empty bag of chips in his pantry and slid down the rest of them into his parched throat. Tap water would have to do. It did.

Computers weren't his thing, other than they occasionally made life a little simpler. He thought he'd play a little video poker before he went to bed, but the damn thing was still blue. *Could that strand of hair belong to Lara? Was that even possible?* In his work, almost anything was possible. He'd check with Paolo in the morning to make sure everything was fine.

There wasn't much to do and besides he had to get his clothes ready for the morning. Nice to be working again. He knew he had to stop drinking or more problems would come his way. Anyway, after a while he wanted to show Lara more than anybody else that he was working it out. Maybe, just maybe, she'd take a liking to him. He knew they were very different. She lived a higher lifestyle and hung out in fancier places. He was just a guy who played video games and hung out in dives and ate cold leftover Chinese food out of his refrigerator. Not much in common there. But, when he talked with her in the Zen garden, he felt something. He saw something in her eyes, well-hidden, but there. He knew it. He felt it. It had to be there. All the signs pointed to it. But, now he knew it was up to him to make something of it or it would disappear as if it never existed.

Chapter 20

Getting to work on time was never a strong point for Vic Mason. But, Thursdays had always been lucky for him, so he got to work early, much to his surprise. He met Captain Thomas and was greeted me with an equal amount of friendliness and wariness.

The middle-aged Captain wore his uniform with pride and his office reflected everything you want a cop to be. He showed off his team with pride and honor. For the cops who had died in the line of duty, pictures and plaques covered his walls. His family portrait was directly behind him on the old wooden hutch that held mostly mementos from his distinguished career. Mase smiled as warmly as he could because he wasn't sure how he would take him in his current state of lost and found.

"Sit down Mase. Thanks for helping us out."

"Well, nothing better to do I guess."

"I'm not going to ask you how you are and all that bullshit. I'm just glad you can help us."

"I hope I can."

"I know you can Mase."

"Thanks Curt. Whatever you need. I've had a little trouble, as I'm sure you've heard."

"Yeah, I've heard you've been on a roll," Said the Captain waving his hand down. "But, haven't we all."

Mase wandered his eyes around Thomas' office, hoping he'd drop the subject sooner rather than later, not that he didn't want to hear what he had to say, he just wanted to get back to work. All the schmoozing was already getting on his nerves.

"Yeah, well, you know how life is." Said Mase.

"Boy, do I. Could I tell you some stories. But, no time right now. I want to get you going ASAP. Let's go out to your desk." The captain stopped himself and turned around towards the hutch. He reached into one drawer and pulled out Mase's badge and weapon, and handed it to him with little fanfare. Mase reached out and took them from the Captain, with the same amount of fake indifference. "I guess you'll need these. Let's go meet some of the boys. We're a little thin right now. Everybody's talking about their mental health issues and so they're taking a lot of 'me' time which has put us behind on our active cases, not to mention our cold ones. I don't know what all this talk means about mental health. We're all nuts to a certain degree, aren't we?"

Mase twisted his mouth into a smile and nodded his head as they walked out into the office area where the detectives called home. He recognized Charlie Tedford sitting at his desk and talking on his phone. He'd worked with Charlie for a while when they were patrolmen together. Charlie had a weight problem, and it looked like nothing had changed, not to mention bad teeth, thinning blond hair and a pug nose. He was younger than Mase but looked much older. He was always sweating, even in the winter. Still was.

As he passed by Tedford, Mase tapped him on his back and Tedford raised his eyebrows at Mase and nodded while he kept talking on his phone. He looked like he was glad to see Mase, and the feeling was mutual. There was no one else on duty.

Captain Thomas walked over to an empty desk located against the back wall directly under a large round clock. He could hear it ticking as he approached the desk... It was loud, and Mase wondered if he could take it.

After a while, Charlie came over to his desk and sat down next to it. He still had that smile that lit up a room.

"Heard about your troubles. Sounds pretty rough."

"Not rough enough."

"You hear about the Barlow murder?"

"I'm sure I will in a second."

"Liked to think he was God's gift to video game gambling. Wasn't."

Mase continued to put his things away in his desk. He didn't look directly at Charlie, but he didn't have to.

"You still gaming?" Asked Mase.

"Once in a while. It calms me down after a long day. But...I know my limitations."

"Nice to know things like that." Charlie put his hand on Mase's arm to stop him from moving things around on his desk.

"Look man, I'm sorry all these things happened to you. I really am. But, and I hate to admit it, I need your help. I'm trying to tie a nice neat bow around the Barlow case, but things keep popping up and I can't get it done. You could really help me by taking it and wrapping it, which, if anyone can do it you can. K?"

Mase stopped what he was doing and looked Charlie right in his face and took a long breath.

"Sure..."

"Here's the file. I can fill you in if you need any additional stuff."

Mase opened the file carefully and read it as Charlie got up and smiled at Mase.

"You talk to the grieving widow yet?"

Charlie laughed and said, "She ain't grieving, at least I didn't see it when I talked to her. Pissed that her ex-husband stopped paying her child support and left her in a big hole. She's still there and still pissed. I'll text you her address and I can go there with you so she won't freak out."

"Nope. I'll go myself. You know I have a way with women?"

"First I've heard."

Mase stood up, towering over the much shorter detective, to shake Charlie's hand.

"Yeah, me too."

As he went through the file, he kept thinking about Lara.

Chapter 21

The East River Greenway was Lara Deming's favorite jogging path. The views along it were wonderful; especially the river flowing strongly, wide, unstoppable. When she rested for a few minutes, the moist air and breezes renewed her strength and she was off and running again.

It was a pleasant morning as she was getting her last mile in, when she spotted a friend sitting on a bench. Thalia Markham had known Lara since before she married Carl. They'd attended aerobics classes together and had many of the same friends and acquaintances.

Thalia had a blank look on her face when Lara stopped to talk with her. They hadn't seen each other for a while. It took Thalia a minute before she realized Lara was there.

"Oh, hi Lara. Didn't see you." Said Thalia.

"Daydreaming?"

"Sort of."

"What's going on?"

"You hear about Bryce?"

"No. What happened?"

"Oh, Lara. It was horrible."

"What happened?"

"He killed himself. Jumped off of the Manhattan Bridge."

"What?"

Lara gently sat down next to Thalia. She couldn't believe that Bryce Kaplan killed himself. Lara and Bryce had gone out together for about a year until Bryce found another woman. He'd gotten into drugs and online gambling. They'd lost contact with each other.

"I just heard about it. It was on the news this morning after they identified him as the jumper. How sad is that, Lara? I mean Bryce Kaplan, of all people. He was always such a happy guy and a good friend to both of us. How could this happen?"

Lara didn't answer her friend. She could see the Manhattan Bridge from where they were sitting. All she could do was shake her head gently and hold her friend's hand. They both wept together, choking back their tears and hugging each other.

Chapter 22

Sheikh Al-Habib's gaming room, in the small Arab kingdom of Zakar was lavishly furnished and equipped. Whatever the 24-year-old son of the king wanted, the son of the king got.

The tiny kingdom was awash in oil money. It seemed that they sometimes had to find things to spend their money on because that was all they had to do. The kingdom was nothing more than a few giant sand dunes surrounded by more sand. The small city of Maqin on the coast was a skyscraper showcase; tall, empty, silent spires poking up from the sea of sand and wind.

Besides unlimited supplies of oil and money, the Kingdom was now in the spotlight for the #2 gamer in the world. He seemed unbeatable in every game he played, and the victories were always lopsided. He had lightning fast reflexes, a keen mind for strategy, and a 'never give in' attitude.

The Sheikh's father stopped by as the Sheik trained.

"They say," said the king, "they say you have the mind of a great warrior."

He didn't answer his father's comment because he was too deep in the game he was playing. His father walked up behind him and put his hand on his son's shoulder. The Sheikh never lost his concentration as his father's hand stayed gently where it was. All the King could hear were the beeps and shots from the game. He thought how different modern warfare was. No insurgents, no destruction, no family dramas, just clicking and moving. He smiled to himself, tapped softly on his son's shoulder and left shaking his head.

The King was proud of his son's accomplishments in the world of gaming, but he was secretly ashamed that his son was doing nothing with his life but gaming, gambling, and girls. The last one was fine, but the other two weren't.

After the King left, the Sheikh's game ended and he motioned with his chin to one of his aides to close and lock the door. Training was about to level up, in a big way.

Sheikh Habib motioned with two fingers to the oldest of the aides. Two very young girls were brought in. They couldn't have been older than thirteen or fourteen at the most. Their gazes never left the floor underneath their brightly painted toenails. As the aide brought them to The Sheikh, one tear formed just below the left eye of the taller of the two. She bravely kept the weak smile on her face as she lifted it to look at Sheikh Al-Habib. He carefully looked her over, up and down, and in the middle, where his eyes rested on the perfectly round little breasts that pushed through her silk robe.

All he said was "Leave," and everyone exited backwards through the door. He reached out his hand to the young girl and she reached out to his. He drew her towards him and the training went to a higher level.

He took the girl back to her mother, a laundress for one of the lower level leaders. When they came into the house, the mother was beside herself with thanks to Allah and the Sheikh.

"Allah is here. Allah is one. Sheikh Al-Habib, you have brought honor to our lowly house. Allah has blessed us for this." She kissed his ring and he left. When he was gone, she slapped her daughter across her face, stripped off her clothing and washed her in scorching hot water until her skin was raw. As she dried her with a long white towel, she hugged her and apologized, and told her to go to bed.

At night, the girl dreamed of white horses racing across the sand dunes. The Sheikh dreamed about killing the only person who could defeat him, and he didn't even know his name or what he looked like. The death of this ghost would be as painful as he could make it. After he defeated him!

Chapter 23

On 33rd Street near Queens Boulevard, Mase found the low rent dump of Kristina Barlow, ex-wife of Jerry Barlow, the late Jerry Barlow. Mase could see the trash piled up around the apartment building where she lived, so he already had a pretty good idea of what he'd find.

Her apartment on the third floor, 317, was a walk up. He side-stepped piles of dog shit, used condoms, and hypos. He doubted himself for even going there, but Captain Thomas wanted to close the case and put a bow on it.

As he walked up to the graffitied door, he saw a heart drawn in blood with a large x through it. "Micro Boy Never Loved Kristina".

He was about to knock on the door when he heard an argument loud enough to be heard where he stood. It sounded like a woman and a young child, probably a girl. The words were hard to make out, but not the feelings. Maybe it was a good thing he was there. The dispute was rising in volume. He knocked hard on the door. No answer at first, so he tried again. Then, just as he was about to knock a ghost of a woman opened the door at the same time.

"What d'ya want?"

Mase already had his badge out when she opened the door. She stopped, glanced at the badge and froze in place, not stunned but surprised.

"My name is Mason."

"So?"

"So I'd rather not talk out here. Can I come in?"

"Not really. I'm busy."

Mase had his foot next to the door in case she tried to close it before he came in. She hadn't opened the door very far, but Mase could see the little girl standing in the kitchen, crying.

"Were you Jerry Barlow's wife?"

"What's it to you? He's dead, so who gives a shit?"

"Certainly not Jerry." Said Mase.

"I guess not."

Kristina seemed to calm down a little. She could see Mase wasn't a threat, so she slowly opened the door, turned her back on the detective, and walked into the kitchen.

After she cleared a few dirty dishes off the kitchen table, she motioned for Mase to sit. He brushed off a few crumbs on the chair and sat down. The little girl wouldn't stop crying.

"What's her name?" Asked Mase.

"Kathy."

"Kathy." The girl ignored him. He searched his pockets and found a long forgotten candy bar. "Kathy. Would you like this candy bar? You can have it. It's OK. Here."

As he held it out to her, she stopped crying, picked up something on the floor and threw it at her mother. It bounced off the wall and shattered. Mase recognized it right away as a crack pipe.

"Kristina. You know they can take your kid away from you for having stuff like that around the house."

When Kathy heard what Mase said, she walked over to Kristina, sat in her lap, and hugged her.

"Probably be the best thing for all of us. Don't you think?"

"Not my call. But I know one thing."

"What?" Kristina's eyes were watering.

"When my mom died, it was then and still is today the worst day of my life."

"You gonna call child welfare?"

"I'm not here for that."

"That's what you say, but I can see that look on your face."

"What look?"

"Like all cops. They think they're smarter or better than everyone else."

"Look, all I want is a little information about your ex-husband. That's it. Just answer a few questions, truthfully, and then I'll leave. Deal?"

"Depends on the questions."

"Do you know if anyone had a beef with Jerry?"

"How much time do you have?" She snickered. "I mean you pick anyone he knew; they all had beefs with Jerry. He wasn't always the way he became, but when his gambling got way out of hand, he owed everyone money and didn't like paying. I mean everyone...including me." She lit a cigarette and offered Mase one. He declined.

"You know if anyone had threatened him?"

"We hadn't talked to each other for a couple of years. But, you know, you hear things on the street. And believe me, I heard things. Seemed like everyone had a beef with Jerry. It was pretty bad, actually. I mean they were coming to me for money until they saw the way we live here. That's all I know detective. That's it."

"What was it like when you two were married?"

"A big fat zero. That's what it was." Kristina took her last drag on the disappearing cigarette, as Kathy stroked her hair. It wasn't much of an apology to her mother, but it's all she had.

They both stared at each other in silence. Then Kristina spoke.

"What you said. Is that true, about them taking Kathy away from me?" Kathy shook her head quickly and violently.

"I can tell you one thing, Kristina. They will if you don't do something fast. I won't blow the whistle on you, but someone will. You know that, right?"

"I know." She nodded slowly.

"Look, I may come back to get more information and if I see you have done nothing to help yourself and Kathy, I'll have no choice but to blow the whistle. And it's not good when a cop does that. They take it pretty fucking seriously."

Kristina nodded sadly, stood up, and walked Mase to the front door.

"Here's my card. Call me anytime. Even after I'm done with this case. I can probably get you the help you need. I've gone through the same shit that you're going through. It's tough, believe me. I know. But it can be done...."

Mase waved goodbye to Kathy as he left the apartment. He thought about the strength of most mothers and how they'd do anything for their children. But, he also knew the uncontrollable pull of addiction. Which one would win? He knew it was a tossup, at best.

Chapter 24

The dull, muted ring of his cell phone barely woke him up. It was under the covers as he fumbled around for it. It kept ringing. He didn't recognize the caller ID, but something told him to answer it, so he scraped out some words.

"Hello."

"I can't find Kathy."

"Who?"

"Kathy's gone. I don't know where she is."

"Who is this?"

"Kristina Barlow. Kristina Barlow. Yesterday. Remember?"

"Oh, yes. What's going on?"

"I told you. I woke up and my daughter's gone. She's gone. I'm telling you she's gone."

"Hold on," Said Mase. He got out of bed and stood up. "What do you mean, she's gone? How could she not be there?"

"I don't know. I woke up, and she wasn't here. I went outside and looked around and she wasn't anywhere to be found. Can you come here now and help me find her? I need help Detective."

"I'm leaving now. I'm getting some help, so you'll be seeing a couple of uniformed officers soon. Don't worry Kristina, we'll find her."

"Please hurry Detective. I'm scared. I'm really scared. Kathy's everything to me. Hurry! Please, hurry!"

A warm, mist-like rain was falling when Mase arrived. Two patrol cars marked the area with their spinning reds as a small crowd started milling around the scene. Some of them had umbrellas; some seemed to enjoy it. Mase was recognized by one of the patrol officers. His name was Randy Singleton. Mase knew him as a good, journeyman cop who followed procedure, usually the right way. He seemed a little annoyed, so Mase went over, shook his hand, and asked him what had already happened.

"Kinda far from home, ain't y' Mase?" Asked Singleton.

"Kinda. You find the kid yet?"

"Not yet. How..."

"The mother's the ex-wife of a homicide victim I'm investigating. She called me, I called it in. That's it. You pissed about something?"

"The mother's out of her freakin' mind. Junkies can't handle shit like this?"

"Could you?"

"Wouldn't know. Don't have kids."

"You OK with me talking to her?"

"Sure, help yourself. Maybe you can make sense out of her. I couldn't. I've got three men searching the area, but so far nothing."

A Crises Care employee was sitting with Kristina in her apartment. These situations are hard for most cops to handle, but in this case, Mase flashed his badge and walked over and sat down next to Kristina. At first she appeared catatonic, but when she saw Mase, her eyes opened immediately.

"Please find Kathy, detective. Please..."

"What happened?"

"I fell asleep and when I woke up, she was gone."

"I'm not gonna bullshit you, Kristina, but I'm going to ask you a question and I want you to answer it honestly. Were you high?"

Kristina slowly nodded at Mase and closed her eyes. Every part of her face twisted in pain and guilt. He knew this was no time for games so he patted her gently on the shoulder and the Crises Care aide asked him to leave. He thought *if I'd just called in a child abuse complaint, they would have taken the girl away and she wouldn't be going through all of this. I know how this is going to turn out. It's totally on me.*

He returned to the street. They'd called in a canine unit to help with the search. One dog seemed to get excited and was barking wildly some distance away. Everyone heard it. But then, nothing. The search continued.

An hour passed. Nothing good happens at night, especially when a child's life is in the balance. After looking and waiting and crying, the search was temporarily ended; the dogs were brought back, Kristina was brought in for further interrogation and Mase went home to think about everything.

He asked Singleton to keep in touch and offered his help. Singleton didn't think there was anything else he needed from Mase. All the way home, Mase went over and over what had happened until it formed a knot in his stomach. He thought about a beer and that's when it happened, he remembered something. The original report after Jerry Barlow had been murdered said something, something about his shrink. If he could find out who the shrink was, maybe it would lead to something, maybe not.

Did HIPPA rules apply to dead people? Patient privacy and murders make little sense. How many shrinks were in New York City? Better talk to the DA after I get the full list. What did that have to do with finding the little girl? Maybe all of this was connected. The volleyball in his stomach wouldn't move and once again the thought of a cold beer took over. *Don't do it, boy. You'll wind up in the gutter again. Lara is watching. Oh yeah, Lara. Why didn't I find out if she was OK? You're slipping, boy. Get yourself together, and quick. Your two weeks are almost up soon and then it's back to the 7th.*

Then he thought about Kathy... it wouldn't go away. He turned his car around and went back to Sunnyside. It was almost 3 AM. He couldn't leave Kristina there, alone. *Keep looking and don't stop until you find her. She's all alone.* He could see the light was still on in Kristina's apartment. She'd left it on or were they still waiting for Kathy to return. It was just a light, nothing else. He kept staring at the window. A silhouette appeared on the shade. It moved back and forth. Mase got sick and vomited in the street. He wiped his mouth and started searching everywhere again.

First, he wandered around on foot and then in his car. There was a small park nearby. Maybe she went to the park. Kids, like his own kids, love parks, especially when they go there with the other kids.

There was a crescent moon low in the western sky. Mase got out of his car and started walking around. There were shrubs and a sandbox and a slide. The swings were moving by themselves in the wind. It had picked up and now all of the swings were pendulums, marking time, counting lifetimes of kids coming and going, living and dying. He sat on one swing and listened. Maybe Kathy was close by, listening, hoping her mother would come, and maybe she recognized me. He thought he heard small children laughing in the night, little children, like Kathy. Nothing...

He drove home to his apartment and threw himself down on his bed.

Chapter 25

A few long days had passed with no word about Kathy. A missing child is the most agonizing experience anyone can ever have. It's never ending torture that scrapes a mother's mind until it bleeds. No matter how you think about it, there's no answer, only pain. Kristina was now being held on a child endangerment charge, which was probably the best thing for her. She was on a suicide watch in her cell. Mase knew her mind was in full bleed mode.

Now, even though Kathy's picture was on every news report and newspaper headline, nothing new came from it. The public was stumped. The cops did whatever their training taught them to do. Mase walked into the 7th Precinct and headed to Vrain's office. Everyone was working and nothing had changed. His old desk hadn't changed. Then he went over to Chuckie Carlo's desk and sat down next to it for a few seconds.

"What kind of mood is he in?" asked Mase.

"Same."

"Anything I need to know about before I go into the fires of hell?"

"Some." Carlo moved a few things aimlessly around his desk. "We can talk after. He's waiting for you. I mean just get it over with."

Mase went over to the open door and walked in. Vrain was looking out of his window.

"Captain?"

"Sit down Vic."

The tone in the Captain's voice was somber. Maybe he was just playing with Mase and he was actually glad to see him. Vrain didn't turn around for a long time.

When he finally did turn around, the eye-to-eye contact was brutal. Vrain kept silent and Mase kept his cool as long as he could.

"Spit it out Cap." Said Mase.

"I'm not gonna sugar coat this one bit. You fucked up, again. You were at the Thompson Street Hole in the Wall last night and you were drinking. One of our men saw you, Vic. You can't keep doing this and expect to work here again. As it is, the brass wants your ass gone. They think you're an embarrassment to the team and only bad things will keep happening."

Mase stared at him for a while and didn't say a word.

Vrain pulled up a wooden chair so it faced the detective head on. He spoke in a much lower tone.

"Look, son...we've been through this too many times. Too many higher ups are out to get you and there's nothing I can do. I'll hold your spot for you but not for long. Do whatever you have to do to fix this, or you're done. Do you understand what I'm saying?"

Mase's head dropped. He mumbled a few words, but the Captain couldn't quite make it out. It sounded like "Kathy", but Mase finally said his parting words.

"Yes, I understand."

"Good." Vrain tapped him gently on his knee. "Now go take care of this."

***

Mase left and went directly to Lara Deming's office. It wasn't so much for him, but he had wanted to check up on her but had gotten side-tracked with Kristina Barlow.

Kathy was all over his conscience. An old cop had once given him advice when he first started out as a patrol officer. His name was Cornell, Harvey Cornell. Good cop. He said, 'Vic, you're gonna have to make instant decisions as a cop and they won't always be the right ones. But, and I know you didn't ask me, but if there's one piece of advice I can give you, it's this. Your emotions are important, but they're only a guide. Let common sense and the safety of people you've been hired to protect be the basis for every decision, no matter how lousy the decision may feel.'

Funny he should have thought about it right then, especially because it was too late for Kathy, for Kristina, and for himself. He had failed miserably, and it pissed him off to no end.

When Mase arrived at the office, the lights were off and the door was locked, and it was 10:30, well within working hours. The frosted glass entry door looked like a mirror that didn't work right. He was about to tap on the glass just to see if there really was no one there. He saw his own reflection distorted and wavy. The hallway fluorescence buzzed more distortion at him until he couldn't look at himself again.

He tapped with one knuckle on the glass. There was no response. He tried it again. No response, again. His sixth sense was tapping on him, clicking in his brain and annoying the hell out of him. He could easily open the door, but he knew that these buildings all had security alarms set up in every office, not to mention cameras everywhere, which he saw blinking at him just down the hall.

He tried tapping once more. There was no response. He left, looking directly into the security camera. *So, he wasn't satisfied, so what. He wasn't a cop now, anyway.* He went home, left a message on her office phone and returned the next day. Maybe they were taking a mental health day.

***

East 71st Street was crowded. Fashionable women in expensive tight fitting outfits walked with purpose and determination as if only they were important. But, every one of them looked the same way. Young men, some wearing suits, some in fashionable casual clothes, focused on themselves via their smart phones, social media, games being played, stupid inane jokes by people they hardly knew; all of this as they walked. Everyone had a tattoo or piercing, even the guys in suits.

He picked up his walking pace to keep up with the rest of the pedestrians. He was taller than most of them and could see over most of their heads. He spotted something in the crowd behind him. Someone was following him, and he was good, very good. So good in fact, that as soon as Mase spotted him, he disappeared from sight. Mase now knew he was on someone's screen.

Chapter 26

Paolo Manteo unlocked the office door precisely at 8:30, the same way he'd done for the past six years. He turned the key slowly this time because he was hoping. Something was wrong with Lara and he hoped it would all change back to the way it had been. Lara, strong-minded and always self-confident and professional, had been his anchor after a troubled life in Spanish Harlem. He always told her how much he appreciated her for what she'd done for his life.

Everything looked OK as he entered the office. He took a deep breath. Lara had texted him finally, the night before and told him she'd be in at 8:45, just like always. The office had been shut down for a few days. He was glad because he needed a break, but he was worried about his boss. She wasn't the same and it worried him.

Paolo went about his usual straightening up, dusting some of the furniture, checking the schedule for the day and making coffee. Lara always liked a fresh cup of coffee at the start of her day and he knew exactly how strong she liked it. He'd have it ready for her.

He focused on the round wall clock to the right of his desk. Timing the brewing of the coffee was important, so Lara would have the perfect cup to start her day. He started it brewing at 8:40.

Lara came into the office exactly at 8:45, just like she said she would. She wore her navy pants suit that fit her perfectly. A white silk blouse and her favorite gold chain balanced everything perfectly. So far so good, thought Paolo. He held his thoughts and emotions in place as he greeted her. She smiled but looked tired. He could see slight puffiness under her eyes despite the makeup. She walked towards her office silently and Paolo noticed two strands of hair that had fallen out of place that must have gone unnoticed. Paolo's concern grew because the old Lara would never have allowed it.

He smiled gently back to her and brought in her fresh coffee, steaming hot. The sunlight was bright and the steaming coffee was highlighted as it lifted around the desk. Lara stared at it for a few seconds and finally thanked Paolo.

He placed a sheet of paper with the day's schedule, including conference calls and consultations with other behavioral therapists. It would be a busy day because she'd be playing catch-up after her hiatus.

"Good morning Lara." Said Paolo.

She stared out the window as one stripe of sunlight gleamed intensely on the gold chain with the small gold heart in the middle of which was a yellow diamond flickering gold flashes at the room. She moved her right hand to it and clasped it for a second.

"Good morning Paolo. I apologize for the last few days. I just needed a little time for myself. Even therapists need mental health breaks."

"Of course. No problem at all. In fact, I enjoyed the time off myself and so did Tibbles."

Lara finally gave a genuine smile and looked relieved.

"I'm sure he did. I know how cats are when they miss their owners and finally get to spend quality time with them."

"Do you have a cat?"

"Not now. But I had one when I was a child. Her name was Tilly and she was a feral cat that adopted me. We became great friends over the years. She was very possessive. I'm sure Tibbles is the same way."

"Absolutely! Glad to know you're a member of the Cat Lovers Association."

"I am." She smiled again and looked down at the schedule. She took out her VR headset and put it on the desk next to the coffee. Paolo didn't like that move. He'd grown to detest that contraption. It seemed to take hold of her when she put it on.

"Thank you Paolo. You can close the door behind you so I can focus on reading my patient notes and get back up to speed on my clients. And, thank you for being so understanding. You're awesome."

When Paolo returned to his desk, Mase was sitting in the waiting room. Paolo was taken by surprise since he knew Mase was not on the schedule and, in fact, was no longer Lara's patient. He knotted his brow as Mase walked up to him.

"Good morning Mr. Mason. How can I help you?"

"Good morning Paolo, nice to see you. Can I see Miss Deming for a minute? It's important."

"I'm afraid that would be impossible. She's extremely busy."

The expression on Mase's face tightened up and his lips puckered up in a not very pleasant way.

"Paolo. Answer one question for me."

"Certainly, Mr. Mason."

"Is your boss's personal safety and well-being important, to you, Paolo?"

"Certainly." Paolo fidgeted in his chair.

"And how about your own personal safety and well-being?"

"I don't understand what you're getting at, Mr. Mason. And I certainly don't like your tone. It sounds like a threat."

As Paolo rose out of his chair Mase encourage him to sit back down.

"Now Paolo, I know we're friends and I know friends understand friends, just sit there like a good friend and keep your mouth shut. I'm seeing Miss Deming and the reason I'm going in is because she's in grave danger and so are you. Do you understand me? Don't answer just nod." Paolo nodded. "Good, now, Paolo, just go about your business and I'll just be taking up a few minutes of Miss Deming's time and you don't have to worry about anything. Are we clear?" Paolo nodded again. "And don't worry about announcing me to your boss. I'll take care of that when I see her. Thanks."

Mase went into the office, slowly and quietly, catching Lara with her headset on. He walked over to her and gently removed the headset. She was taken aback by the sudden removal of it and by the appearance of Detective Mason.

"Good morning, Lara. I apologize for my abrupt interruption."

"You should apologize. You have no business being here. This is a private office and you're no longer my client. It's...it's..."

"It's not right, which I know. But, I've been very worried about you. I have the feeling that you're in big trouble. Are you, Lara?"

"I'm not. Now, if you don't mind, I'm very busy this morning and I'm going to have to ask you to leave immediately."

"Oh, I will, but not yet."

Mase put on the VR headset. Lara tried to snatch it out of his hand, but he easily brushed her off. He watched it for a few minutes and was completely baffled and surprised.

"Is this a game?"

"No, it's not a game. This is a client who needs my help and you have no business interfering. Give it back, Mr. Mason, right now."

Mase sensed Lara pulling away into some inner world. The closeness he had felt between them the last time they'd met was no longer there. He left with loss in his heart, but a growing fear of what was becoming of the beautiful therapist that had tried so hard to help him.

***

When he got home, the phone rang late. It was Genevieve Carlo, Chuckie's mother. She was frantic, which wasn't her at all.

"I haven't heard from Chuckie at all. He always calls me to tell me what's going on and to just talk. Always! He won't answer his phone and no one seems to know where he is."

Mase told Genevieve that he would go and look for him immediately and that he'd call her as soon as he found him. He probably met some girl and got too occupied, you know how it is. Genevieve was skeptical.

When he arrived at Chuckie's apartment, the police were already there in full force. He could see the body of his friend, covered in blood, on the living room floor. They wouldn't let Mase into the room, with the 'you're not a cop' excuse that pissed him off. They were adamant about keeping him out, and they did. He watched from the hallway, as Captain Vrain appeared. He'd just notified Chuckie's mother and felt as awful as he looked. He didn't say anything to Mase as he passed him and carefully entered the crime scene.

"You call the M.E.?" Asked Vrain of the two officers working the scene.

"She's on her way. Probably ten or fifteen minutes, max."

"Lab boys finished yet?"

"Nope."

Chapter 27

"Miss Deming?" The image on the headset asked.

"Yes, this is Lara Deming. How can I help you?"

"My name is Christian, Jonah Christian. I'm the person who sent you the VR set you are wearing now."

"When can I talk to Carl again?"

"I'm not sure I know what you're talking about Miss Deming."

"I want to see, I mean talk to Carl again. I know you know where he is. He's alive, isn't he? I've talked to him."

"Whether a person is alive is up to them. I certainly am in no position to verify if one person in this crazy world is alive or not. But, I know one thing. I am alive, but barely."

"I need Carl. Where is he?"

"If, and I mean if, if I can find Carl for you, I must get your assurance that you will help me with my current situation. You see Miss Deming, I have a complicated problem."

Lara tried to remove the headset, but her hands were not in control. She tried everything to remove it, but whether she lost control or didn't have the will power to gain control of hands didn't matter. She was paralyzed and unable to act on her own.

"Look at me Lara. Look at me carefully. What do you see?"

"I see a young man. But I can see that it's not you."

"Well, who is it then? For a second it was Carl, and then it was a young man, much younger than you sound. Who are you?"

"I'm a person in desperate need of your help."

"How do you think I can help you?"

"Let's see. Where should I start? First, my self-image is a disaster. I hate the way I look and my ability to interact with other people is pathetic. There's more. Shall I go on?"

At that point Lara felt a buzzing in her ears that made her feel disoriented and dizzy. Then, just as quickly as it started, she felt fine again. In fact, she felt better than she had in a long time. The conversation took on a more positive tone.

"I see." Said Lara. "I think the best course would be for you to schedule a visit here. I can transfer you to my assistant and he can get you set up for a visit with me."

"Thank you Miss Deming, but that's entirely unnecessary. You see, I'm unable to leave my home, for any reason. That's why I sent you the VR headset. That's how I communicate with everyone. It's much more effective for me and how I live. But, I still need your help and I'm positive that you are the only one who can help me."

"Why does your voice sound the way it does?"

"I'm not quite sure I understand your question."

"Well, for one thing, it doesn't sound real. I mean it sounds artificial, even though we're having a conversation. I don't feel I'm actually talking to a real person."

"Your perceptions are spot on, Miss Deming. You are correct."

"Then who am I talking to?"

"You're talking to Jonah Christian, a real person."

"Where are you?"

"I'm right here; right in front of you. We can even shake hands. See?"

Lara found herself inside the image she was viewing. She was shaking hands with the person who called himself Jonah Christian. But, she had changed as well. She was almost herself, but not quite. She didn't feel real. Wherever she now was and whatever she was doing, felt wrong. How could she be two dimensional now and shaking hands with someone who wasn't there? She was mystified, but in a new and pleasant way. She felt great. She accepted where she was and how she got there even though she didn't know how it happened.

He was now Creighton LaVelle, the name sounded familiar, a medieval knight on a sacred mission. There was a campfire in the middle of a dark forest. The crackling sound of the fire was the only sound Lara could hear. Creighton LaVelle was as handsome as he was mysterious. His armor was golden chain mail that reflected the firelight. He stood in front of Lara who was now Cornelia Summerlyn. There was something very familiar about his face.

He'd just rescued her from the Floating Castle of Anthonia. It had taken him three weeks to pass every obstacle that was placed between him and the fair maiden. This was the final obstacle. Securing the maiden and destroying the Castle. He was being stalked by the seven immortal archers of the man who had kidnapped Cornelia, The Black Knight. He carried the Mace of Death, a powerful weapon stolen from the gods. Owning it gave you immortality, and your every wish would be granted.

***

Lara Deming awoke in a sweat, in her bedroom at home, with the VR headset beside her. She heard someone pounding on the door of her apartment. Apparently, she'd been screaming at such a high pitch that two of her neighbors had been awakened by it and were worried. She lifted herself out of her bed and went to the door.

The neighbors were about to call the police when she opened the door. Two women dressed in nightgowns were standing there and sagged in relief that she appeared to be OK.

"Mary, Cassie, what is it? What's going on?"

"We heard you screaming so loud that we thought you were being attacked. Are you OK?"

"I think I'm OK. I must have had a bad dream, I guess." Lara scratched her head in foggy confusion.

"Must have been one helluva dream for you to scream that loud." Said Cassie. "Mary was just about to call the Police. Good thing you opened the door."

"Come in, come in, please." Said Lara, opening the door as wide as she could.

"No thanks. It's late. We just wanted to make sure you were safe. That's all. Get a good night's sleep, Lara, and no more nightmares, OK?"

"OK. Promise." Lara meekly smiled, waved at them and closed the door slowly. She wondered if she should have closed the door. She heard Cassie and Mary faintly mumbling as they closed their own doors. The air in her apartment felt thick and unbreathable. Lingering images of unknown people wandered pathetically around in her mind. She walked into the bathroom and closed her eyes at the image in the bathroom mirror. Maybe, if she kept them shut long enough, the image would disappear. It didn't.

Chapter 28

There's something eternally sad about a rainstorm in Manhattan. Maybe that's why the native-Americans sold it so cheap. The rain fell in sheets that coated the windows in Lara Deming's fashionable apartment. She thought about the rain as she stared out of her sliding balcony door facing the East River. Mostly, she thought about Carl and how wonderful he'd been to her and how dedicated he was to the truth. The thought crossed her mind that maybe the truth wasn't all that important. Maybe people were more important than the truth. Maybe all the truth she spouted to her clients was less important than who they were as people.

The pelting rain attacked her windows and streamed down like pain from a wound. She tried to turn away from the door, but each time she did, she returned to it. What good would it do her to keep watching it fall and drape the world in sorrow? It was useless. The sound of it frightened her. She frantically covered her ears with her hands as her eyes widened in terror. There was little she could do. These things have to pass.

She wanted to run out into the street and never return. There had to be a way out. She knew that if she stayed there, for some unknown reason, it would be the end of her. What could she do? Where could she go now?

Call a friend. Reach out to someone. Ask for help. The usual stuff she dispensed in her job if someone faced an immediate crisis. *Was she in a crisis? Maybe a glass of wine. That wasn't the answer.* She panicked, ran into the bedroom, and saw the VR headset on her bed.

When she picked it up, she held it in her arms, close to her body. She lifted it gently to the side of her head and caressed it.

Whispers came from her soul.

"Carl, don't leave me...Carl, I love you."

As her words dissolved into the night's darkness, Lara fell asleep; too lonely, too tired, too anguished to stay awake. The headset blinked for hours as she slept. It finally shut off and went dead. Lara dreamed of the best days of her life with Carl, and only Carl. He was in her heart and a part of her. He would never be taken away from her memory. But was it a memory, or had she really talked to him? She knew she had talked with him, seen him, felt him. He was so close that she could touch him. He was her, every part of her. They were one person.

Lara woke up suddenly. She thought she heard a sound in the living room. She didn't hear it again until she woke up 5 hours later. She pushed away bedding and got up slowly out of her bed. It was chilly in the apartment, so she threw on her robe. The robe didn't help. It had been an Irish robe that belonged to her mother. With soft green lace at the end of the sleeves and silk brocade along the length of the front, it was all she had left of her mom. Everything else was in a taped up cardboard box in her closet.

As she tied the robe around her, she walked slowly into the living room. The morning sunlight had barely lit up the sky. The rain had stopped and she could already hear the sounds on the street below; people talking, garbage cans being pulled along the concrete, cars beeping in the distance. She was glad something finally made sense.

She pulled the curtains back from the balcony door. The sound of the sliding rings along the metal rod was reassuring. When she turned around, she was terrified to find a man sleeping on her couch. His back was to her, so she couldn't see who it was. He was breathing heavily. She turned on all the lights and the man awoke and turned around. She was shocked to see Vic Mason rubbing the sleep out of his eyes.

"What are you doing here, Detective Mason?"

Mase shifted his body around on the sofa and sat up. He was half asleep and leaned back on the soft little cushions. A smile came to his face as he rubbed the top of his head. He felt like he was eight years old and his mother caught him doing something stupid again.

"Well, would you believe me if I said I was homeless and I needed a place to sleep tonight?"

"No, I would not."

"Would you believe me if I said I've fallen in love with you and couldn't bear the thought of being separated from the love of his life?"

Lara's answer came out a little slower but was still a firm 'No'.

"How about door number three?"

"Only if it's the truth."

Mase sat up straight, put his large hands together in his lap and spoke worried words directly at Lara.

"Lara, I believe you are in grave danger."

"Oh, come on Vic. That's been tried on me so many times that I can't even count them anymore. Please."

"It's not something I'd be kidding about, believe me. I wouldn't be here if I didn't know it was true."

"You're not telling me everything, Vic. I can hear it in your voice and see it in your eyes."

"That's correct."

"Why?"

"Because I don't know everything yet. But as soon as I do, I will."

"Must be nice to know everything. How does it feel?"

"Wouldn't know. Haven't gotten there yet."

"Thought you were out of a job."

"They called you, didn't they?"

"Uh, huh." A small smile crossed her lips. Her bemused look lit up the room.

"Then you know I've been a bad boy?"

"Want some coffee? I need some myself."

"Sure, got any eggs? I like mine scrambled."

"I like mine..." She patted him softly on his knee and he followed her into the kitchen.

The dawning sunlight streamed through the kitchen window; the kind of sun you only see in the morning when your eyes need a fresh start. Perfect sunlight, crisp, focused but not intrusive.

Mase wasn't surprised at how good a cook she was. Even though she still looked a little distracted, the scrambled eggs and toast were perfect in every way. And the coffee was hot and strong and effective.

"That's the best damn breakfast I ever had."

"You're a liar... but thanks."

"I'm not sure how this whole thing is going to unfold." Said Mase, staring at his coffee cup.

"What are we talking about here Mr. Mason?"

"Why so formal Miss Deming?"

"Why? It's simple. Right now, we're two people with problems. Sure, everyone's got problems and we're no different. But, the demons you're battling come from a personal place. Mine are coming from my past."

"I'm talking about your life, Lara. It looks like someone is trying to do something crazy to you. Sure, I'm crazy about you, but that's not for now."

"What's for now?"

"Keeping you out of whatever danger is coming at you. I wish I could tell you more, but all I can say at this point is that there's no question in my mind that you are the focal point for something bad. I promise you I will get to the bottom of it, but in the meantime, I've got to keep you safe."

"Look Vic, I appreciate your concern, but I'm fine, I'm fine, really I am. I think that right now we both need to go about our lives like we always have and let things take their natural course."

Vic stood up and paced slowly around the kitchen. He took his dirty dishes to the sink and started washing them by hand. Lara admired his domestic skills with a wry smile.

"Not bad Mr. Mason. I can see you've done this before. There's a dishwasher right there. You could just put them in there, you know."

"I think more clearly when I go domestic."

"Maybe you should mop the floors and vacuum the carpet so you can think even better."

"You could hire me as your housekeeper."

She was standing behind him as he turned around and pulled her close to him. He kissed her and she closed her eyes. Her arms went around him tightly. The kiss lasted longer than both of them were expecting. She released herself gently and cleaned the table.

"I've got to get ready for work Mr. Mason."

"I'll call you during the day so I can keep tabs on you while I go see Captain Vrain and beg for my job."

"I've talked to him. All he wants is for you to take your life seriously and get healthy. He's a good man and only wants what's best for you. He really cares about you, you know."

"He does. Sometimes I wish I wanted what's best for me too. But, I've got to make him believe that I'm starting my life over right now. I think I can make him believe that, but he's a wily old son of a bitch with great radar. If he sees any blip on the screen, the missiles will fire, and I don't think I can take any more missiles right now."

"Just be truthful to him. But, most importantly, be truthful to yourself."

"Will do."

Mase put his shoes on and hugged Lara gently before he left.

Chapter 29

When Mase left her, something stirred in Lara. It was half thought and half longing. Before she took her shower, she plugged in the VR headset to recharge. It came to life quickly. For the first time in a long time, Lara felt like a woman. She wouldn't jump to conclusions, but she knew the feeling, and it was worth the wait.

She was almost ready for work. Her makeup was put on as flawlessly as she'd always done. Her silken hair was combed and brushed into a new arrangement that she'd never done before. This happened automatically. It was as if it was a new Lara. She stared at her image in the foggy bathroom mirror and knotted her brow in surprise. Who was that woman staring back at her? What made her put her hair up like that? It was put on the opposite side of her finely chiseled face. She never put her hair up like that. But she liked it and it was getting late. The day ahead was going to be busy. And it had been a long time since she actually looked forward to her job.

The morning still felt fresh as she put everything she needed into her purse. She felt as though she was forgetting something as she opened the door to leave. What was it?

As she was about to close the door, she remembered. It was the headset. She ran back into her bedroom and reached for it. It was hot to the touch. She couldn't hold it in her hands, so she left it there, unplugged. It blinked away in the empty bedroom as she left to go to work. It kept blinking and speaking to the empty room.

"Cornelia. Cornelia. I'm here. Don't worry. Cornelia, come back."

She grabbed her cell phone and left for work. As she strode with her usual long stride out onto the bright sunlight of 71st Street, a feeling was building of both joy and dread. She bought a single red rose from 'Angel's Flower Emporium' and held it gently in her right hand as she caught the 2nd Avenue bus to her office. The faces on the bus were disengaged as usual, some reading The Post or The Daily News, but more were reading their cell phones to stay disengaged.

The bus ride lasted fifteen minutes, a bit faster than usual. She smiled to herself as some riders left to go to their jobs. Do people really want to go to work or is it simply that they have no choice? A handsome young man in a tailored business suit passed by her on the way out and smiled at her. Do people smile like that because they see a beautiful woman or are they being courteous because their moms told them to be courteous? She smiled back because she knew she'd never see the man again.

When her stop arrived, she sprang up and left the bus quickly. She'd been on buses where the driver would shut the door on you because you were too slow. She wasn't going to let that happen today.

Paolo was walking into the building just as she was and they greeted each other warmly. That feeling was still in her mind, but she knew she had to keep it at bay if she was going to have a good day at work. She'd had too many unsatisfactory ones lately and that could not continue. Paolo and Lara took the elevator up to the office together and began to get things arranged for the day ahead; Paolo quickly dusting the furniture in the waiting area and making coffee, Lara arranging her desk and files for the day's schedule.

She promised herself that she was going to have a good day. Her patients counted on her and she needed them. *Focus on them, Lara. That's what you're supposed to do. So, do it.*

When the work day ended, Lara felt great about her sessions with her patients and Paolo took a deep breath that everything was getting back to normal. They both left together and went their separate ways.

Out of the corner of his eye, Paolo noticed Lara went a different way than she normally went. At first, he thought it was odd, but then he dismissed his little concern and convinced himself that she had a date or was perhaps going shopping. He knew she loved her shopping, especially Bloomingdales. He shrugged his shoulders and went home satisfied with his own reasoning.

Lara had called her friend Thalia Markham and asked her if it was OK to visit her at her apartment on 59th Street. Her friend told her she was always welcome at her home. She was glad to hear Thalia's sympathetic voice and the way she always made you feel special and welcome. They'd known each other for many years and each of them was always available to the other, no matter what the situation was. Thalia sensed a bigger problem in Lara's voice than Lara was making the visit out to be, a social call and nothing else.

Thalia had been a successful graphics designer in one of the most successful graphics design companies in the city. Her apartment was decorated simply but elegantly with some of her own creations gracing the beautiful furniture laid out in a modern but elegant way.

As soon as Lara entered the apartment, Thalia read her face. It read like a mystery with too many red herrings. After a brief greeting, she offered Lara a martini, which she gladly accepted.

They both sat down and looked at each other in that knowing but slightly concerned look. When you've known and trusted a friend for a long time, the usual formalities are unnecessary.

"Mind if I couch surf with you for a couple of days?"

"No problem. Wanna tell me why?"

"Not really."

"Explanations are not needed in this house. You're welcome here for as long as you want. No questions."

"Thanks. I just need a little time for myself and my thoughts. Sometimes the walls in your own home close in on you and before you know it you're bouncing from wall to wall. Know what I mean?"

"Actually, I do. It happens to me more than I want to admit. It's a weird feeling. I mean you think you're losing your mind, but it's not that at all. It's...Well, like what happened to Bryce. I can't bear to even think about it, really. Those damn video games. I hate them."

"I know. No need to explain. And I promise not to be weird either, OK?"

"Deal. How about some dinner; I'm starving? How about you?"

"Well..."

"I'm on it. How does garlic rosemary chicken sound?"

"Wonderful. Can I help?"

"Let's get at it."

The two friends ate heartily and spent the rest of the evening in careful neutrality, talking about unimportant things that women talk about over the phone because it's fun just to talk. They joked a bit and talked art and politics until it was time to sleep. Thalia set up the couch with beautiful linens and down pillows sheathed in satin pillowcases. Lara had thoughts about death and longing until nothingness took over and she slept.

Chapter 30

Sleep came quietly to Lara as she enjoyed the comfort of her bed and the feeling of safety in her friend's apartment. Getting to sleep had been difficult recently so, the easy way into it felt good. She woke up briefly, tossing around to find the most comfortable position. She found it and dove deeply and quickly into the soft comfort of the evening.

Thalia sensed her friend was still upset about something when they left each other to sleep. She heard low talking in the living room and thought it might have been Lara talking on her cell phone. After a while, the talking stopped, and she dozed back into sleep, thinking that Lara had done the same. It remained quiet.

Thalia woke up at one in the morning and went to see if Lara was doing OK. Lara was moving around on the couch. She was restless; the cover being thrown on the floor and her face twisted into deep concern. She was mumbling incoherently and then seemed to go back to sleep. Thalia didn't wake her, but pulled the covers over her so she would be warmer. She felt cold.

Thalia tried to sleep again until a piercing scream jolted her out of her bed. She ran into the living room and saw Lara sitting up on the couch and trembling as if something horrible had appeared to her. She couldn't stop shaking as Thalia sat next to her and hugged her with soft calming words.

"It's OK! It's OK...It's OK."

"I must have had a nightmare, I guess." Said Lara. "Wow. It was a bad one."

"What was it about?"

Lara closed her eyes and tried to remember. Whether she did remember or not, she kept it to herself. Thalia was concerned enough to stay with her until she stopped shaking, which she did after a short while.

"I'm good now. Go back to sleep, honey. I'm fine. You know how bad dreams can be. You can feel like they're actually happening and there's not a lot you can do. They just keep going. But..."

"Yeah, but the look on your face..."

"I feel like a child, and my mother just came into my room to sing me a lullaby. No worries, I'm fine. Go back to sleep, because that's what I'm gonna do."

Thalia looked back at Lara as she went back into her bedroom. She could see the concern still on her friend's face, which she hid professionally with a smile and a wave towards Thalia, indicating she should keep going.

Thalia couldn't go back to sleep. She worried and dozed in and out of sleep. When she glanced at the clock beside her bed, she saw it was after four in the morning. Something made her get up again to check on Lara and when she slipped on her robe and quietly opened the door to the living room, she was surprised to find that Lara was gone.

The bedding on the couch was folded and put in neat rows and there was a little note left on the coffee table.

"Thank you for being such a good friend. Got to get ready for work. Call me."

When she arrived home, she started her usual get ready for work routine. Put on a pot of coffee. Lay out the work outfit. Turn on the shower to get the hot water moving. Set out the makeup. Everything was put in its proper place and then, she saw the headset. It's red light blinking.

She stood frozen in her steps as she gently touched the headset. It felt warm, like it was alive. But, it couldn't be alive. That wasn't possible. The bedroom filled with steam from the hot shower water. She'd left the bathroom door open. It was like a steam bath in there. She waved her arms from side to side to clear the steam away from her path. It was so thick with steam that she bumped hard into the doorway and bounced back. She turned off the water. Her forehead got bruised, but it didn't seem to matter to her. She went to her bed and curled up gently and put on the headset.

In an instant, something clicked in her brain. It was like a switch being turned on and she was immediately transported once again to the forests of Anthonia. It was familiar but strange in its beauty. Oddly shaped trees that had thick blue branches covered in heart-shaped scarlet and purple leaves. Each tree appeared to be more than alive; each one had its own personality. There was a soft breeze blowing through the leaves. It smelled like perfume and was warm and soft. She was taken by the strange and unnatural beauty of everything around her.

As she peered into the lavender sky, she saw diamond like gems suspended in the sky. They weren't stars. Each gem glistened and sparkled together, like ornaments placed there by an enchanted hand.

The deep blue forest welcomed her and guided her way along a bright orange path that stretched far ahead and through the shimmering trees. Along the path were small animals that she'd never seen before. One little creature had two long teeth in front that helped him walk. He made funny hops that looked like a child jumping with a pogo stick. Another one flew through the blue tree branches and when he landed, he looked like a baby tiger with stripes that went straight across his body and then circled his tail like a snake. He would change into a multi-colored bird with long and feathery rainbow wings the moment he would take off and fly.

A voice came through the undergrowth. It said, "Cornelia, we are here. We will take you."

She knew it was talking to her. She was Cornelia Summerlyn once again. She walked toward the voice and suddenly four golden stags with extremely long antlers appeared. They walked slowly towards her and surrounded her. She was enthralled by their huge stately manner. They stood still as one of them spoke; their antlers seemed to come alive.

"We will take you to a place of wonder the likes of which you have never seen before." The antlers grew and grew and grew until they created a crystal carriage behind them. It was so beautiful that she smiled in blind judgment.

The door of the carriage opened and Cornelia seemed to float into it with no effort. Then the four golden stags trotted forward as if the ground wasn't there. They glided forward and in a soundless motion the forest slid past the mesmerized Cornelia, scattering all the strange little animals away as they went past.

As they followed the path along a murmuring brook, Cornelia was mesmerized by what looked like champagne in the brook, not water. It bubbled and flowed and reflected the moon, which had now become a red spotlight in the sky, when suddenly a loud screeching sound came to her from every direction. It was so loud that she could barely stand the pain of the piercing noise. She had to cover her ears with her hands to make it stop. It kept ringing and it wouldn't stop.

Chapter 31

Captain Vrain's unit had been drained, so at that point he had no choice but to bring Vic back to his Precinct. He thought the best he could hope for was that he wouldn't drink on the job and pick up some of the slack around the almost empty office. Cases were piling up. The Brass was all over him, again.

A pile of case folders was stacked up on Mase's desk. He wouldn't admit it to anyone, but he was glad to be back to work. He missed it. So, he opened each folder and created three piles. Now, later, and don't waste your time. Vrain watched him getting organized and finally pulled the shade down in his office and kept to himself.

He liked the expression on Mase's face. It had sober focus with the old Mase determination. He was as hopeful as it was possible to be with someone like Mase. His best detective was unpredictable, quirky, but completely dedicated to getting justice served, no matter what.

As Mase plodded through each folder, little things that most detectives would have ignored would catch his eye and these would go into his top drawer. He didn't want anyone to see what those were. He needed a little bit of time to mull them over and assign his own particular meaning to them.

As he worked through the files, he kept looking at Chuckie's old desk. It was completely devoid of anything, no calendar, no pencils, no photos of his parents, nothing. Old memories flew into his mind and left just as quickly. Mase wondered if anyone would remember him after he died. No amount of wanting could keep a memory intact forever. Time was the great destroyer of thoughts about people you've known.

If you think about someone long enough, something important will pop up. It has to. He remembered a lot of things about Chuckie, but the most important thing was 'stay with it'. That was his favorite saying. He stacked the rest of the manila folders in neat stacks.

A simple thought crossed his mind. He wanted Vrain's take on Chuckie's death. When it happened, he wasn't able to dig in because he had been suspended. Now, he wanted the official explanation because, none of it made any sense. So he walked over to the Captain's office and tapped gently on the glass window of the door. All the shades were drawn.

"Yeah? What is it? I'm busy." Growled the busy Captain.

"It's Vic. Got a sec?

"I'm busy as hell. Come back later."

Mase ignored the words. Vrain knew Mase wouldn't go away and he kind of enjoyed having the pain in the ass back on the team, whatever was left of his team. The half-smile on Mase's face was that same familiar look that usually meant Mase was on to something. But, like usual, it would be something far from the normal.

He walked into the office with mute determination and dropped like a dead weight into the worn out chair in front of the captain's desk. He stared at the Captain until Vrain finally looked up from the piles of paper on his desk. He wasn't a good paper pusher, but he did what he had to do.

Vrain held the pencil he was using as if he was ready to play a game of darts, and Mase was the target. He jabbed it in the air at the tall Detective with five o'clock shadow.

"How many times do I have to tell you I'm busy for chrissake? Busy. Understand?"

The half-smile on Mase's face morphed into intense focus. And he finally spoke, ignoring everything Vrain had just said.

"What really happened to Chuckie?"

Vrain dropped his pencil. It had obviously caught him by surprise.

"Chuckie?"

"Yes. Chuckie. Can you tell me why someone as smart and in control of his life would kill himself? It makes no sense."

"You know what else makes no sense. Why, with all those unsolved cases sitting on your desk, would you ask me about a closed case? Chuckie committed suicide and that's that. It was embarrassing enough for the department. I know he was a good friend of yours, but for chrissake let it rest Vic, OK? I've got enough IOU's with the Brass to last a lifetime and the last thing they want to be reminded of is Chuckie Carlo and his fucking mental problems, OK?"

"Cap, I know you don't believe that, and neither do I."

Vrain stood up, stretched his back, turned around and went over to the window. It was a typical, end of fall day, with small clouds rushing to the west. He held his right hand on his lower back as he meditated on the street below.

"Y'know Vic, I never realized how much god damned paperwork came with this job. Papers and papers and papers. It never ends." Vrain rubbed his back in small circles. "It never ends."

"Look, I don't want the official report. I want your take on what happened to Chuckie. That's all. And don't worry, I'll take care of all those open cases, but what happened to my friend is important. I owe it to his family. I owe it to Chuckie and I owe it to the force. I owe it to you and me because I know how much you loved Chuckie Carlo as much as I did, and still do."

"You know you're a god damn pain in the ass Vic. You know that, don't you?"

"Yes, sir."

Intermittent shards of sunlight broke the dull cloud-filled sky and entered Vrain's dusty old office. When Vrain sat back down in his old wooden swivel chair, one of the sun shards glanced across the right side of the captain's face and into his mouth. He spoke hesitantly through the ray of light.

"Off the record, Vic...It was one of the worst days of my life. He was a good cop, but and an even better human being. He never had a bad day; always smiling, always helpful to everyone, never a bad day, jeez! That should have been his name, Never a Bad Day Carlo." He glanced down at all the messed up piles of paper and looked as sad as anyone Vic had ever seen. Vic felt the same way. Vrain moved a few of the sheets around in an aimless pattern of meaningless squares. He stopped and looked at Mase. The eye contact was powerful and piercing. "Keep your mouth shut, Vic, but find out what the fuck really happened, will you? I know in my heart that Chuckie Carlo would never have committed suicide. Find out, OK? Just find out. Now get the fuck out of my office before I fire you again."

Vic smiled broadly. It was the one thing he wanted to hear, and now he was prepared to find out.

"Yes sir. Thank you, sir."

Vrain stared stupidly at his paperwork and waved at Vic like he was swatting a fly.

Chapter 32

Mase dreaded the fact that he had to meet with Chuckie's parents, Orlando and Genevieve, to get more information. He'd known them almost all his life and loved them almost as much as his own parents. Orlando worked at the Fulton Fish Market and Genevieve stayed home taking care of Orlando and making sure Chuckie kept himself on the right path, which turned out to be a simple job until the end.

Mase knew he'd be starting from scratch. There was a reason this happened. But, the facts just didn't add up. Why would an upstanding and happy person just decide to kill himself? It made little sense.

There were tears and hugging and apologies from Mase that continued forever. He wanted to help them, but he knew that was impossible. The best he could do was to promise them he'd find out what really happened. They didn't want this stain on Chuckie's life to be permanent. The last thing we all have when we leave this earth is our reputation and what the world really thought of us. Chuckie was too good to have done this and Orlando and Genevieve wanted to clear his name.

As they sat in the living room and drank a little Chianti, Mase thought about the years he'd known his best friend and all the adventures they'd gone through together. Mase gently reminisced with the Carlo's but didn't want to be too much of a burden. It was obvious they were still in mourning. When he asked them if he could spend a little time alone in Chuckie's room, they agreed but looked puzzled. He also asked them if they still had his cell phone and if they knew his password. They gave him both, and he went into the room and closed the door behind him. Orlando and Genevieve hadn't touched a thing. Chuckie's room was now a shrine to their boy.

Mase stood in the center of the room and looked around. Chuckie always played video games at night when he would visit his parents, and followed his beloved Mets every day. Mase looked at the closet door and opened it to find everything the way it always was. When he would stay overnight at his parents, he kept some clothes there for work; Six suits and a couple of sports jackets that he used for work. On the right, neatly hung on wooden hangers were his Met's T-shirts and jerseys, each separated from the other so as not to wrinkle them. Mase smiled at Chuckie's little museum of the Team that went nowhere most of the time. It never stopped Chuckie from being a fan.

Mase sat on his bed and looked at his Mets alarm clock shaped like a baseball. He checked his watch to see if the clock matched it. It did.

Nothing popped up as something out of the ordinary. Mase kept looking around and all he could see was his friend's room and how it was now a Chuckie time capsule. He gently laid himself down on Chuckie's bed and stared at the ceiling, hoping to hear his friend's voice one more time. He could hear Genevieve and Orlando chatting in the living room. Then he checked his own phone for messages. There weren't any, but then remembered he had a couple of old voice messages from Chuckie.

Maybe, he thought, if he just heard his voice it would link to something in his room, something that ...

As he stared at the ceiling, he noticed a very thin little wire on the overhead light fixture. He squinted his eyes to focus on it, and then he stood up and was almost able to reach it with his six foot four-inch reach. He pulled a chair over to it and gently pulled it out slightly until he saw it was connected to a small microphone and camera. He put it back into place.

When he listened to Chuckie's message, the sound of his voice must have made it all the way to the living room. Genevieve and

Orlando heard their boy and ran to the room. They saw Mase standing on a chair.

Genevieve looked surprised and asked Mase what had happened and that she thought she was going crazy because she heard Chuckie's voice. Mase stepped down off the chair and apologized.

"I had an old voice message from Chuckie and I was listening to it. I'm so sorry for scaring you like that."

Orlando asked him why he was touching the light fixture and Mase told him the bulb was loose and flickering so he tightened it. That was it. He figured it was time to leave, but he asked them if he could stay for a little while longer. They only agreed because Mase had been so close with them and Chuckie.

"Would you mind very much if I had Chuckie's phone analyzed by our forensic boys? Oh, and also the hard drive from his computer. We won't mess with it, and I promise I'll return them and put the hard drive back."

"Well Vic, if you think it's necessary, I suppose it'll be alright."

"I'll be through here in twenty minutes just as soon as I get the hard drive out. I appreciate you cooperating with me. I just don't want to miss anything that might be important, that's all."

"We know that Vic," said Genevieve, "and we know you'll do your best. You're the one person we trust."

"Thank you, Mr. And Mrs. Carlo. I'll be done shortly."

After they closed the door to let him finish, Mase took the hard drive and pulled the wire and the listening device out of the light fixture with the end of his shirt, in case there were any usable prints on it. He put it in his pocket and turned off the light in Chuckie's room as he gave it one more steel-eyed look like he was taking a mental snapshot of it. He gave hugs to Genevieve and Orlando and told them he would be back in a few weeks. Genevieve patted him gently on his cheek as he walked out the front door.

Chapter 33

Mase was on the way to meet Lara at Chaisin's deli on 1st Avenue in a downpour that wouldn't stop. He sometimes wondered how everything in the city somehow withstood all of those torrential washouts, and it always amazed him that it did. Then, as he approached the deli, the darkness became a multiplier of the rain and soaked the detective to the bone.

Everyone on the street ran to where they were going and when he finally got to the deli, Lara was there waiting for him in the covered doorway. He stepped out of the rain and into the doorway with her and kissed her gently on her cheek. She stood stone-faced as the rain dripped down her wet hair. They stared at each other for a minute.

"Hungry?" asked Mase as he touched her on her arm and waited for an answer.

Lara shook her head and kept her arms close to her body, which shook from being cold and wet.

"I'll take that as a yes. Let go in and warm up. I'm starving."

Chaisin's was one of the most popular eating spots on the east side. But, the rain had kept the customers away and the place was almost empty. They chose a window table where they could see the rain and the pedestrians and the taxis flaring water everywhere.

Lara seemed distant and distracted. Her eyes glanced from the table, to the rain, to the menu, but not to Vic Mason.

"You know what's good here?"

"Everything?"

Mase laughed and said, "Yes. How did you know?"

She refocused her eyes and looked long and hard at the kind and thoughtful eyes in front of her.

"You know I know everything," Said Lara as she forced a tiny but sincere smile.

"I do, actually."

"Good. Then we can proceed."

"Proceed? With what?"

"The menu."

Mase caught himself looking disappointed and ended it with a recommendation.

"It's all about the pastrami in this place. I don't know what they do to it, but, it's definitely the best; better than the Carnegie, actually."

"And a cream soda?" Added Lara as she folded the menu and placed it thoughtfully on the table. Now, Mr. Mason, let's talk."

"Oh, I see, we're back to Mr. Mason. What happened to Vic?"

"That was in my pre-fantasy era?"

Mase stared intensely at Lara and reached across the table to touch her hand. She liked it enough to remain touched, but, that would be another time, not today. She reached for a tissue in her purse and dabbed at her eye.

The server brought their two huge pastrami sandwiches that were too high and too large for any human mouth. Lara looked dumbfounded at the sandwich and wondered how she was going to eat it.

"How the hell are you supposed to eat this?"

"Let me show you. You hold it with both hands like this. And, then, you start at the top. Then you nibble away until you've sculpted it down to a manageable size. See, watch."

Mase started eating and Lara copied him, step by step. She nodded her head in deference to her new eating teacher. They both ate vigorously until they couldn't eat any more.

"And now, Mr. Mason?"

"Now you put it down for a quick second and lift your bottle of cream soda and take a sip, not just an ordinary sip but a savoring sip like you do with a good Cabernet. See; slosh it around in your mouth to savor its perfect complement of flavor."

Mase took an exaggerated sip and sloshed it around his mouth like a gourmand who knew his stuff. Lara thought it was the funniest thing she'd ever seen. She laughed hard at his antics, which she knew were performed to help her change her mood.

"You know your Dr. Brown, Mister Mason, don't you?"

"Well, thank you Miss Deming. I try."

He reached over the table and held her hand and looked at it. It was delicate, beautifully shaped, with long tapered fingers. He looked hypnotized at its perfect shape. She eased her hand back and folded both hands under her chin. She rested her head on them and tried to close her eyes for a moment. She ran thoughts through her mind that seemed anonymous and troublesome. Her face changed.

"Hey, hey. None of that Miss Deming."

"I'm sorry Vic. It's something I just have to deal with. That's all. It has nothing to do with you. You're a really nice guy."

"I've been called a lot of things in my life but never 'a really nice guy.'"

"Never?"

"Never."

"Well, that's too bad, because you really are, you know."

"Let's make a toast." Mase lifted his cream soda bottle and Lara did as well."

Lara held up her right hand and lifted her bottle with the left and clinked Mase's bottle.

"To you and your battles ahead," Said Lara.

"To you, finding your way ahead," Said Mase.

Mase paid the bill and Lara walked out into the interminable drizzle. She was about to walk away alone when Mase scurried up next to her and put his arm around her arm and walked with her.

"I'll walk you home,"

"That's not necessary Vic, really."

"I have to fulfill your analysis of my personality."

"I can make it home without any help."

"I know that. But, I have to."

"Well, didn't you say I was a really nice guy?"

"Yes..."

"Well, this is what nice guys do. So, let me make my mother proud of me and let me walk you home, OK?"

"I thought chivalry was dead."

"OK, well maybe it is dead. But hope isn't."

They walked amid the bustling pedestrians on 1st Avenue, Mase holding Lara's arm, Lara staring at the ground and saying nothing. Vic was worried.

Lara kept mumbling the word 'Chivalry' under her breath. When the words stopped, Lara kept moving her lips and pursing her lips and leaning her head slightly to the side.

"Ever play Chivalry: Medieval Warfare?"

Lara ignored Mase. It was like she was some place far away. They walked at a faster pace until they reached her apartment. Her eyes moved back and forth, and she unhitched herself from Mase's grasp.

"Thanks for dinner Vic. I enjoyed it."

When she let herself into her building, Mase was left out in the cold, wondering what had just happened. There was a moment as he headed to the subway station on 72nd Street, where the detective in him took over. He nodded his head as he went down the stairs into the dark, fluorescent tunnel leading to the subway train. He didn't realize it, but he kept nodding as people looked at him and he looked back at them. He smiled courteously at them but kept nodding his approval of something that started to make sense.

Chapter 34

When Mase left Lara at her apartment, something kept poking at him and wouldn't stop. It wasn't anything he could point at directly, but he definitely had a feeling about what was going on.

Then he thought about Lara and her dilemma.

He'd worn her VR headset that one time in her office and he didn't like the feeling at all. As soon as he put it on, everything felt different, ominous, and claustrophobic. He couldn't put his finger on it, but it was not a pleasant feeling.

What was all of this? It had bits and pieces of a clue, but he couldn't put his finger on it exactly. But, he liked that rush he was feeling, and it wasn't whiskey. Whenever he felt like that, it meant that a picture was forming that would eventually give him the answer he was looking for.

***

Mase also knew that straight logic would work best on the cases he was given and whatever was going on with Lara, she was being pushed into another realm beyond her control.

A shot of whiskey might help his clarity but was discarded by his new puzzle. Detectives are supposed to solve puzzles. Detectives must stay above the puzzles and not get emotionally involved. He knew exactly how he felt about Lara, but somehow he would have to detach from his emotions. He started thinking about the best ways to do that.

This was all cyber security at its core, but what was it. He knew his own limitations with the world of computer programming, so he was certain that the best way through this was to get the right help. First, he'd check with the Computer Crimes Squad to see what

Forensics had found on Chuckie's home computer and phone. There had to be something there. He knew it but didn't feel it.

When Mase got to the office, he went directly to Forensics, to the one person who knew all the latest digital science and forensic work done on computers. Then he sat down in the chair next to Faron Highsmith and looked at him. It caught the technician by surprise. He looked at Mase and kept writing his report that was overdue.

Finally, he put his pencil down and talked to Mase. "You want something Mase?"

"I need help. I'm working on this case that is baffling to me and as everybody knows I don't work well when I'm baffled."

"If I remember correctly, when you get baffled you do your best work."

"Somebody made that up."

"So you're telling me you're not a superstar like everybody says you are?"

"Far from it actually; can you help me or not?"

"If you ask nicely."

"How about if I get on my knees and beg you in front of all these people?"

"People might talk. You know how people are."

"We couldn't have that. Could we?"

"Guess not."

"Boys here ever get Chucky's computer hard drive? I left it to be analyzed?"

"Yeah, we got it. All done."

"Find anything?"

"Not enough."

"What the hell is that mean?"

"It means exactly that. There's a lot of stuff in his phone and a lot of stuff on his hard drive but none of it makes any sense. Someone,

someone who knows what they are doing has messed around with Chucky's phone and his hard drive. Now, what does that mean? It means that whatever is on those two devices needs to be put together in a way that we have no means of doing here in our lab. It also means that you're going to need more help than we can provide. In other words, this case goes nowhere until you get someone who can put the pieces together."

"Someone?"

"There's only one person I know of that can do something like that and I'm not sure even he can do it based on what we've seen on Chucky's devices. We know Chucky didn't do it."

"I think I know who you're talking about. You're not talking about The Putz, are you?"

"He's the only one."

"I've dealt with them before. He's hard-core, man. And he costs a lot of money, money we don't have, money I don't have."

"You want me to call him? He owes me a little favor that I might cash in on if you're OK with that?"

"He's the biggest pain in the ass I've ever worked with, and I've worked with a lot of 'em in my life. He does things his own way, and it isn't always the right way."

"And you do?"

They both stood up and shook hands. Mase smiled and patted his coworker on his back and thanked him. He went back to his office and sat at his desk staring at the clock on the wall. He thought it was interesting that that particular clock sometimes looked friendly and welcoming and other times it looked like a horror show. Today it was a horror show. He could see Capt. Vrain's office light was still on. He wanted to go in and talk with the captain, but he decided against it and just went home instead. He was thinking about how he would deal with The Putz otherwise known as Sherman Weiss. He didn't particularly care for this man, but he knew he was the best in the business. To know him, was to not love him. But, for this case, he was the right man.

Chapter 35

Jonah Christian was being attended to by his two 'Assistants'. He demanded the best and usually got it, even though it annoyed him to be served. It was a symmetrical existence, always one of them on one side and the other on the other side. Every day, the routine was the same. He was lifted gently out of his enormous bed and escorted into the bathroom, where he was bathed by the two helpers.

After the bath, he was dressed with extreme care, making sure that each garment was carefully handled, that it was the one Jonah wanted and that all the colors complimented each other. Jonah needed the right color for the day. The two men were always on the lookout for swings in facial expressions, language intensity, or voice modulations that showed a different mood than when they started.

Today, they detected a look of focused serenity on Jonah's face. This new look had been evolving over the past two months. They'd seen it before, on occasion, but never for long periods of time. Today was serenity by obsession.

Once the boss was bathed, dressed and fed, his artificial mouth put in place and his grooming completed, they set him in his Tech Room and waited for further instructions. He dismissed them, but they stayed within range for the entire day. He required twenty-four-hour attention, even when he slept or went to the bathroom. It didn't matter. They had to be available whenever they were needed.

The Tech Room was spotlessly clean, acoustically soundproof, air purified constantly, and more than anything, it was a cavernous haven for the genius who created it entirely with his mind, money and maniacal attention to detail. Even if he was just a wealthy man who needed toys, it was still the most technically up-to-date computer nerve center that any man or woman ever dreamed of.

His identity was unknown to rest of the world, only to his two helpers, and he worked tirelessly to change his identity every day and sometimes every hour, in the unlikely event that someone was ready to discover who he was. To make it even more difficult to find him, he now employed Artificial Intelligence to reinvent himself hourly. He was so good at it that sometimes even he forgot who he was.

He was well rested, clean, focused, except for his new obsession, and preparing for his biggest gaming event, the one that would put him at the pinnacle of video gaming wealth creation; for Jonah was a gambler, although he disliked that term. It was what it was, and Jonah Christian was the best in the world. These gaming events came infrequently, but when they did, he prepared for it like he was a hybrid Muhammad Ali/J.P. Morgan getting ready for the biggest event of their lives.

His hands were flexible, fast, precise and fluid. But his mind was the instrument that coded on the fly and used facial muscles to incorporate AI as the game proceeded. If you were his opponent, his deep fake skills, along with his technical genius, never let you see the real Jonah Christian.

This was a practice day. It was always the same routine. Play two rounds of Keep Talking and Nobody Explodes and three rounds of Crawl and assess any weaknesses in his opponent and, in him, using his statistical analysis program, and create his strategy, in a code of course, in his mind. Not only were his skills far superior to anyone, but his creativity, his lack of a conscience and his ability to convince any opponent that he was just a regular guy who got lucky once in a while.

After precisely two hours of challenging practice, he meditated for an hour and called Toy and Stanley to bring in his lunch of two poached eggs, a lightly buttered croissant, and a cup of decaf espresso. He walked over to his work center and dismissed his two helpers. It was now time for his hour of spoofing. This was done in a darkened room with Viennese waltzes playing in his earbuds.

For Jonah Christian, to spoof was to live. No IRC! What was there to chat about? It was his world. No one else in the entire world could be with him.

Payday was coming soon and he had chops to flex, to the world. Nothing else mattered. The online gaming community was easy money, but for Jonah, it was more than that. They were a goldmine of information about those few high rollers that couldn't help themselves; the more skilled the high roller, the easier the take, which was always substantial. For these gamers, he could become whatever they wanted him to be. Jonah was completely tapped into this community, knowing the latest gossip about the highest rollers, about whom their wives were screwing or who their husbands were doing. Every bit of this type of information was valuable for Jonah, and he used it well.

Today, he was Childish Harold, the sixteen-year-old high school dropout who never lost a game of Mortal Combat. He bragged and bullied every other gamer until he forced himself into an ugly reputation of unbeatable skills. He even challenged people he'd never met online, as long as they called him Master Harold. That was Jonah, today.

Childish Harold was a crying infant avatar. He could shed tears or blood depending on his mood. Today he was crying blood.

Chapter 36

Sheik Ram Habib had the gaming world at his fingertips. He had mastered every asymmetrical multiplayer game out there, including Dead by Daylight, Crawl, and Evil Dead: The Game and Keep Talking and Nobody Explodes. Not only was he more skilled than most players out there, but his obsession with gaming put him through daily skill workouts that pushed his mind and body to the limits.

For the past few months, his father had been showing signs of a growing dementia. Within the family, calls for The Sheik to accede to the throne were increasing. He knew eventually he would, by necessity, have to take over the entire family's business, but not now, not yet. He had one more goal to achieve.

As the entire gaming community knew, there was one anonymous player who was far and away the most skilled player in the world. No one knew his real name, or where he came from, or anything else about him for that matter. There were only the whispers and chatter that persisted every day, in any and every meeting of gamers. Who was this person? When would he show himself, and why was it such a secret? Unless Jonah Christian would decide that one day he would let the world know, he would remain as visible as the wind.

The Sheik was at the highest skill level of gaming. His hands, his reflexes, his eyes and his ears were leveled up as high as they could go, and he knew it. And he was egotistical enough to brag about it to whoever would listen. It was true; he was a fantastic player, maybe even the best. But everyone knew that if he wanted to be truly considered the number one player in the world, he would have to go through the one player out there that was considered the best.

Sheik Habib had been approached through various channels that a match between him and Jonah was being considered. Habib was thrilled, but knew that it would have to come from Jonah himself. The Sheik had the money, but Jonah had the reputation, and that was what he wanted more than the throne of his country, or anything else. But his patience finally paid off when Jonah contacted him and the deal was struck.

The grounds for the online match were simple but immense. If Jonah won the single match of Rainbow Six: Siege, the Sheik would pay him one billion dollars in crypto cash, the exact method of payment to be determined prior to the match. If the Sheik won, Jonah would declare to the world gaming community that the Sheik would be considered by him to be the best player in the world. That was all the Sheik wanted before he would take his country's throne and retire from online gaming.

Both players were ruthless in their own ways. They knew it about each other. The match would happen in about two weeks, depending on Jonah. The Sheik despised Jonah's arrogance and control. He never took a back seat to anyone in his life. But for now, he had to deal with Jonah. He would wait and defer as long as he knew the goal was within reach. Besides, he believed he could win. What he didn't realize was that there was much more at stake. He expected Jonah to make more demands before the match. He didn't know what they would be or how much they would cost. But he knew he would agree to them, no matter what.

***

The Sheik's feelings made no difference to Jonah. In his own way, Jonah had anticipated everything. Nothing would be overlooked, especially the treachery that the Sheik was known for. Jonah knew that the best law of protection was to make absolutely certain that his anonymity was locked down safely with as many layers as possible.

In his mansion in New Rochelle, the stage was being set for his upcoming match with the Sheik. Jonah was the master of Artificial

Intelligence integrated with gaming programming skills, his python programming skills, and his ability to erase every step he made along the way. There was no way he could lose.

When Jonah was at his best, he was completely focused on the task at hand. If he was in that zone, he was unbeatable. However, there was one minor distraction. He had put a lot of work into his new Fantasy program, The Golden Shield of Anthonia. It was the only way he could get Lara Deming's attention and keep it. After he had infiltrated her personal data because of her connection with Jerry Barlow, he became infatuated with her after seeing her photos. Jonah always made sure that he understood his targets before proceeding with the inevitable. In Jerry's case, it wasn't so much the money that he was owed by Jerry, as much as the message that needed to be sent. The gaming world always needed reminders; welching had certain consequences. In Jerry's case, an example had to be made!

Jonah, being a scrupulous perfectionist, studied Jerry's background enough to know all about his family history and his problems, and his occasional visits with his Therapist, Lara Deming. When Jonah came upon her photo, it was as if he was hit by an emotional stun gun. He knew at that moment that he had to have her. But, it was more than that, much more than that.

Jonah knew that his deformity would stand in the way of any attraction, so he decided on the next best option because he simply had to have her, to own her, to make her dependent on him in any way possible. Maybe, if she got what she really needed, she would give in to his obsession. Jonah had a plan. It was a plan that needed stealth and mind control through subliminal messaging and that's exactly what he accomplished with The Golden Shield of Anthonia, a quest for the Hero, Creighton LaVelle, to defeat the Black Knight and destroy the golden shield. Lara became the princess, Cornelia Summerlyn, being held captive by the Black Knight. What Jonah accomplished in a short amount of time was nothing short of astounding.

Using Deep Fake technology along with other Artificial Intelligence programs, he was able to implement faces on the three characters that were exact lookalikes for the people she knew. The face of her late husband Carl became the face of Creighton LaVelle, the Black Knight became Vic Mason, and Lara became Cornelia Summerlyn. Within the actual programming, he, Jonah, became Carl and all that Lara loved about him.

Jonah had infiltrated all of Lara's patient's records, including Vic Mason's. With his men visiting Lara's office and their observations about how Lara had reacted to Mase, he came to the quick conclusion that she was having feelings for Mase and that he had to do something about it. So, Jonah made Mase the villain in the game, the Black Knight, and along with subliminal messaging within the game's programming, could put Mase in a terrible light. The Black Knight would kidnap the beautiful princess Cornelia.

It wasn't easy to create such a complex program, but in this case Jonah had no choice. He simply had to have her, no matter what it took to accomplish that. He wanted her mind. He wanted control. His deformed face would prevent any physical attraction, but he wanted her any way he could get her. He would be the reincarnation of her late husband, Carl. After studying everything about Carl, including his journalistic achievements and other personal documents, he put all of that knowledge into the character of Creighton LaVelle.

There was one more intriguing aspect to the reality and the fantasy of Vic Mason and the Character of The Black Knight. He would monitor Mase but not get involved with any rough stuff. If he let Mase do his thing and be himself, Lara would see him as she always did. But, now, with The Quest for The Golden Shield of Anthonia, he would become the arch villain in her life.

Chapter 37

When Mase returned home, there was a package waiting for him. It was smallish, wrapped in plain black paper with just a shipping label, no return address. He said hello to Mrs. Merkle on the first floor and she returned his greeting with her usual frowning smirk, which meant hello in Merkle talk, the closed language of busybodies. Unfortunately, they weren't a dying breed. A newer group was in the wings, as represented on the second floor by Agnes Townsend who was also was sweeping away the invisible dirt from in front of her apartment in case any tidbit of gossip might be overheard. Mase was holding his package as he walked by her, which he knew would create a comment.

"I see you got a package there, Mr. Mason; birthday present?"

"No, Miss Townsend, it's not a birthday present. Have yourself a wonderful evening."

"Mmm."

Mase pulled off his jacket and placed the package on his kitchen table. He was hungry but not hungry enough to cook something, so he grabbed a can of green beans and poured it into a dirty bowl that was still in his sink. He started eating it with his fingers while changing into his old blue jogging clothes. Once in a while, he would jog around the block to fool himself into thinking he was keeping himself in shape. Today wasn't one of those days.

He took the package to the living room, turned on the latest sports review shows on his TV, and took the wrapping off the package; saw that nothing interesting was on, so he turned on his Xbox to play some Halo Infinite. But just as he played, he remembered the package sitting next to him on the sofa. So he stopped playing and reached over to open it.

A Meta Quest 3 was in the box with a brief note attached to it. All the note said was, "*Mr. Mason, thought you might enjoy a new toy to wile away the hours. When you wear it, you'll be able to see Miss Deming and she has a message for you. Enjoy."*

***

Every instinct in his detective brain told him not to put on that headset. After the first one in Lara's office, he knew something wasn't right. He'd played thousands of video games in his life and after that headset; he felt different enough to be concerned. He debated with himself and felt he was strong enough to deal with whatever was in that device, besides, time, valuable time, was passing. So, he decided to take a chance. When he put it on he saw her likeness, but not the real person. She was dressed as the maiden called Cornelia Summerlyn. When she sees his avatar, which is called the Black Knight of Anthonia, she screams in fear. Someone had gone to an awful lot of trouble to make a point. What that point was, he had no clue.

He was concerned with the fact that Lara was being used by someone for some unknown motive. But, he would find out more about it tomorrow, he thought, as he removed the headset and tried to play some Halo Infinite, but lost interest quickly. At that point, he felt weird and just laid down on the couch to rest. He felt himself dozing off, which felt good. His mind ached and his body seemed to collapse on the sofa as sleep crept in.

A weird dream took over his mind as he found himself in a large, black granite castle that floated in the sky. Everywhere he looked, black granite, large images of dragons, and statues of what looked like mythological creatures. The dragons moved as he walked by them. There were more dragons on the marble staircase that spiraled through the castle. He walked up the staircase and when he arrived at the top landing; he heard a woman crying in one room.

As he approached the metallic gray door that stood at least twenty feet high, the sobbing got louder and louder. He was dressed as a knight with shining black armor that felt like skin. It was part of him, and he didn't know why. The door opened automatically as he stood in front of it. He walked into the room to find a beautiful woman who looked like Lara Deming lying down in a huge canopy bed with white lace hanging down around her. Her left arm was covering her eyes as she moaned in tearful misery.

Everything remained silent except for Lara's crying. The sobbing got louder and the expression on her beautiful face had morphed into pure terror. He couldn't understand why she was so frightened of him. When he took one step toward her, she recoiled back as far as she could go on the bed, pulling the beautifully embroidered blanket over her head and screaming for help. There was no help for her because it was just the two of them in the castle. How did he know that? Why was Lara dressed that way, and why was he this evil-looking knight?

When you're in your own nightmare, you can't know why you're there. You simply continue on with it until it ends. But this one felt so real that it took on a reality all its own. He had to leave the room and return to the main area on the ground floor of the castle. He moved without the slightest idea why.

Each of the dragons that he passed hurled fire from their mouths and roared. But, as soon as he passed each one, they stopped. Were they on motion sensors? It was all so real, but none of it made sense. When he reached the ground floor, he looked around. What he saw was evil, but also beautiful. Everything looked perfect, like it belonged exactly where it was and had always been there. He knew he was alone with Lara, but why?

Just then, a loud noise woke him up out of his nightmare, or whatever that was.

"Hold on, hold on. Just a minute."

He shook his head to release the cobwebs, yawned and opened the door only to find the smirking Miss Townsend, right arm extended, holding Mase's car keys.

"You dropped this right there, right there, mind you." Pointing to the area in front of Mase's apartment door, "I thought I'd bring them to you before some unscrupulous person stole them and your car all at the same time. Aren't you glad I found them for you? Aren't you? Huh? Huh? Aren't you?"

"Yes, Miss Townsend. Thank you very much. That was very thoughtful of you. I really appreciate it. I really do."

As Mase tried to close the door on Miss Townsend, she had stepped forward enough that she was about to ease her way into his apartment. But Mase quickly closed the door, preventing her from peering in and entering.

"Thank you Miss Townsend, thank you so much. Thank you. That was very nice of you. Thank you. Have a blessed evening."

He threw the keys on the coffee table and went to sleep in his bedroom. The note in the package wouldn't leave his mind alone. He wanted to sleep but just couldn't. The words on the note took on a voice in his head. He kept hearing the words repeating in what seemed like an endless loop.

There was no point in trying to sleep because he knew it wouldn't happen. He knew his own mind. The detective in him was taking over, which meant that sleep became a lower priority for his brain. The nightmare he'd just experienced came back in fractured fragments. He couldn't remember all of it except how awful he felt when he saw Lara crying and that apparently he had caused it.

He walked back to the living room and noticed the headset and the box and the blinking red light. When he sat down to examine it, an overwhelming urge came over him to put the headset back on his head. It was such a powerful compulsion to put it on that he saw his hands move involuntarily towards them to pick them up. As they moved closer and closer to the headset, he jumped up and back to get away from it.

He'd felt nothing like that before. Not only didn't he not like being controlled, but he knew something had happened when he wore that headset and saw the images in it. Whatever had happened, it wasn't good for him and it would not be good for Lara.

The connection between this experience and the one in Lara's office was so obvious that he almost didn't make it.

Chapter 38

Mase brought the box and the note to the lab. No prints, of course.

The decision to visit Sherman Weiss was easier than he thought. The man was a jerk, but he was an honest and brilliant jerk. They'd worked on cases before.

He was called "The Putz" for a reason. His personality grated on everyone, but in cyber forensics and anything tech, he was the man. Faron Highsmith said he'd call Sherman because "The Putz" owed him a favor. Before Mase left to visit Weiss, he checked with Highsmith, who verified that the call was made and that "The Putz" would help him with his case. So Mase took a deep breath and drove out to Far Rockaway where the man lived. Weiss still lived in the projects because spending money never appealed to him. He kept whatever he made.

The old man buzzed him up and when he got to the eighth floor, the smell of urine and frying garlic in the hallways was almost too much to take. Mase took small breaths to mitigate the nausea that was about to take over. He knocked on the metal door and Sherman opened it cautiously.

Weiss looked older than he really was. Too much sitting, too much glare from old computer screens, and way too much thinking about programs and hackers and all the other minutia of cyber forensics. His back was a mess, his eyes were always swollen, and his bad breath was enough to peel the skin off your face. But, that was Sherman Weiss, five feet one inch of laser focused intelligence dedicated to the proposition that all men were not created equal in his realm of cyber technology.

The difference in height between the two men was staggering. Weiss strained his neck to look up at Mase and almost fell backwards doing so.

"Oh, it's you." Sneered the old man.

"Bet you never thought you'd see me again."

"One can only hope, Mr. Mason."

Mase looked around for a place to sit. There was none. Every square inch of Weiss' apartment was covered in laptops, hard drives, wires, electrical connections, printers, monitors, you name it.

The old man moved an old laptop from his recliner and motioned to Mase to sit down.

"What brings you all the way to Far Rockaway this afternoon, Mr. Mason? There, I greeted you with courtesy. But that's it, and make it quick. I'm a busy man."

"It's simple. I need your help. That's it. You know I wouldn't be here if I didn't."

"God forbid you cops ever fixing your own messes. What would our taxpayers do, of which I am unfortunately one?"

"I'm a taxpayer also, you know. And I'm not thrilled about working with you either, but as you know, sometimes we have to accept our limitations and seek help elsewhere. I guess you're elsewhere."

"Thank you for your honesty, Mr. Mason. What is it you need from me?"

"People are being murdered, manipulated, and mind-controlled by someone who knows how to do these things without being detected. Don't know if it's a man or a woman or a kid. All I know is that we have to catch him before more people are killed."

"What else?"

"I'm pretty sure they've also started on me and someone I know. However, and this is the kicker, all of what I've just told you is sheer speculation. All I've got is a hard drive from a dead colleague, his cell phone, and a VR headset that was sent to me loaded with some kind of video game that has me in it playing the villain. Here."

Mase pulled the items out of his jacket pocket and held them out for Sherman Weiss. The old man looked at him with a deadpan look that Mase had seen before.

He knew it for what it was, a request for money. The old man sat in his chair, not moving, blinking, or anything resembling a response. Mase continued.

"Highsmith said you owed him. I'm here to collect."

There was a slight pause and a faint smile on The Putz's face.

"I owe nothing to anyone, Mr. Mason. In this line of work, we defer to our colleagues who have helped us. And when we defer to them, there are certain courtesies that are extended which, under most circumstance would not be extended if I make myself clear. Do I make myself clear to you, Mr. Mason?"

"Perfectly, Mr. Weiss."

"OK, Mr. Mason, I'm glad we understand each other. So, why don't we start again, from the beginning?"

"A few weeks ago, my drinking got the better of me. I was politely asked by my supervisor to seek help from a trained therapist, which I did. In the process of working on these challenges, the therapist somehow got herself in a bit of trouble."

"Get to the point, Mr. Mason."

"She was given a VR headset. The headset must have had some kind of programming in it that trapped her into thinking that her murdered husband might still be alive. Why she was given this headset is still unknown. I don't have that headset, but I was given the one I've brought with me today. I believe there are similarities and connection between both headsets since the one I have came with a note referencing the therapist."

The Putz handled the headset for a while, looking it over for any anomalies. He handed it back to Mase.

"What I can tell you about this headset is that it's the top of the line. It has high downloadable content capabilities and a high FPS. So, it's intended to handle the most complex programming."

"FPS?"

"FPS: Short for frames per second, FPS are a measure of how smoothly a game runs on a device. Higher FPS means smoother gameplay, while lower FPS can cause lag or stuttering."

"What's the difficulty factor in someone, say a hacker or video game programmer, creating a program using deep fake technology to add real-life face images incorporated into the actual game itself. I mean, is this easily done or does it take a lot of skill?"

"If this was done just in the past couple of weeks, it would be extremely difficult. Almost impossible, unless ..."

"Unless what?"

A new expression appeared on the old grouch's face. It was as if his mind had just engaged in something he didn't expect, and when it did, the thought of it brought new interest, the kind that people live for. He didn't answer Mase immediately. His nodding head reflected an inner conversation he was having. Mase didn't interrupt his thinking. But when the old man lifted his right index finger in the air, he knew The Putz was interested, which was exactly what he was hoping for.

"Leave your stuff with me and I'll have something for you tomorrow. Can you live with that, Mr. Mason?"

"Well, I was kind of hoping you could speed it up a little."

"Speed up what?"

"Speed up whatever the hell you're going to do with these items."

"If you can't wait one more day, then I can't help you. Good day, Mr. Mason."

As he handed the headset and hard drive to Mase, Mase wouldn't take them. Instead, he relented.

"What time tomorrow?"

"Come here at 10:30, sharp. You're not the only job I have you know. Believe it or not, I have to earn a living so I can afford to live in this palace."

"I'll be here."

"I'll call you if there's a delay, but I don't think there will be. Can you give me a number to call in case I need to contact you?"

Mase gave him his number, stood up and shook the old man's hand. He was frail looking and quite thin, and he smoked too much. Mase gave him a wry smile.

"Mr. Weiss, I notice your expression changed as I was telling you what happened. What was it that caught your attention?"

"Something unusual."

"Like what?"

"Well, there's been a lot of chatter lately about some strange things that are going on in our little tight-knit community. It's under the radar, but something new is going on and nobody seems to know exactly what it's all about."

"Don't those things happen all the time? I mean, you know, gossip shit that people sometimes make up just to kill time."

"Not this time."

"Well, what is it?"

"No time right now to talk shop with you, Mr. Mason. But, when you come back tomorrow, I'll have more information for you and I'll be able to tell you what all the whisperings mean. It may or may not be related to your current situation, but your description of recent events seems to show something much more than just a video game."

"Any advice on what I can do to help you find out what's going on?"

"My advice is to stop playing those stupid video games, and that's not just advice from an old asshole like me to a millennial in their prime."

"Then what is it?"

"It's your life, man!"

The visit ended abruptly as the old man waved Mase away so he could resume his nerdy preoccupation with technology. So, Mase left, scratching his head and wondering what the hell he'd gotten himself into.

Chapter 39

At headquarters, Mase began his review of the last four weeks of cases that needed follow-up. The office was still just about empty, too many detectives home sick. This would be a good time to look for certain key indicators that might hint at any connections. His mind was racing because this was no time for overthinking.

Before he got started, he thought he might call Lara to check in on her. When he called, Paolo said he was holding the fort down because Lara had taken the rest of the week off. She said she was OK but needed a little time off and that she'd be back Monday. So, Mase tried to call her, but she didn't pick up.

The last thing he wanted was for her to think he was stalking her, which he probably was, but his growing feelings wouldn't shut off. Sometimes, he had a tendency to fall too deep and too fast and then bad things happened. Then, there was the drinking, which constantly followed him all day, every day.

Put all of that together and what do you get? A red flag shit show.

He knew that the best thing for him was to dive into the backlog and let his mind wrap around the impossible and while he was studying the cases let his instincts take over. They always worked, even when he was out of it.

Three cases stuck out. Two were suicides and one was murder. The two supposed suicides were Chuckie Carlo and Bryce Kaplan. The murder was Jerry Barlow. Chuckie, Bryce, and Jerry. What did they all have in common besides death, the hard way?

So, he wrote their names on a blank piece of paper and looked for any connections. Why did he pick those three? He didn't know except that at that moment he was relying on his never failing instincts. He just let it flow as he stared blankly at the paper.

Just then, Vrain walked by and asked him what he was working on.

"There are nine cases. But I'm working on three right now."

"Which ones?"

"Chuckie, Jerry Barlow, and Bryce Kaplan."

"Chuckie and Kaplan killed themselves. Don't waste your time on suicides unless you know for a fact they weren't. Do you?"

"Not for a fact?" Answered Mase.

"We work with facts here. Don't waste time on speculation. We're too short-staffed and can't afford to leave the actual murders unattended. All I'm saying is, use your time wisely, that's all. You know I trust you, Vic. Do what you think is right."

"I will Cap. Thanks for the advice. I appreciate it."

Mase snapped his fingers when he finished his conversation with Vrain. Then he snapped them again. He called Paolo.

When Paolo answered, Mase asked him if he'd ever heard of Bryce Kaplan.

"You know, Mr. Mason, I'm not permitted to give out any information. What is it exactly that you want to know?

"I appreciate the need for patient privacy, but I'm asking if you ever heard that name mentioned in your office."

After a slight pause Paolo said, "Yes, I've heard the name Bryce Kaplan before."

"Do you mind telling me in what context?"

"I think Lara had dated Mr. Kaplan for a short while. She had mentioned his name maybe twice, in passing, you know, going out for drinks or having dinner. That's all. I never heard his name again, so I assumed it was over. But, to answer your question, yes I heard his name."

"Did she ever mention anything else about him? You know, anything unusual or out of the ordinary? He committed suicide recently."

"Oh, my god, really?"

"Do you recall if Lara mentioned anything about him, like he was unhappy or anything like that?"

"I can't recall anything like that. I remember one thing, though. She said he was younger than her and was always playing video games. Oh, and that he was always smiling. That's about it."

"Thanks Paolo, you've been a big help."

"No problem, Mr. Mason. Any time."

The conversation ended and Mase snapped his fingers a few more times, showing that his gut was right. He knew it. He knew it.

Then he looked down at the paper and wrote two more names down on it. "Lara" and "Me". He drew lines between Kaplan and Lara, between Barlow and Lara, and then between himself and Lara.

He whispered to himself, "It's Lara."

All he had to do now was figure out why. He was leaning towards obsession. He knew how strong his attraction to her was, so any man would probably be attracted to her. What other connections were there?

***

Mase went to see The Putz the next day. It was raining, of course. He arrived at the specified time. Mr. Weiss was a stickler for being prompt. That he was old, and a techie was more than an anomaly. It was a testament to his brilliance.

He knocked on the door, but there was no answer. He tried again, but still no answer.

"What the hell do you want?" Yelled the old man from inside.

"It's Vic Mason. Remember, we have an appointment."

"Wait one goddamn minute. I was in the bathroom. Hold on."

When he opened the door, he looked at Mase with a kind of worried look on his face. Mase thought it was odd because the old man never looked worried. His general demeanor was agitation, not worry. The Putz greeted him with the usual.

"So, what the hell do you want from me? Can't you see I'm busy?"

"You said you would look at the VR headset and hard drive that I left with you. And you said to be here at 10:30, which is now."

"Sit down, Mr. Mason. I want to talk to you first."

Mase noticed that Weiss' brow was furrowed, and he was measuring his words as he spoke.

"There's a big player out there, and he or she is causing a lot of commotion. No one knows who it is, because; well, because his skills seem to be higher than any of us. And by us, I mean all the people like me who do this for a living. Whoever this is, they're causing a lot of problems everywhere. Unfortunately, no one has even touched it yet. So, that being said, you have a big problem, Mr. Mason."

"How so?"

"Who is Lara Deming?"

"Why do you ask?"

"Just answer the question, goddamn it."

"She's a therapist who helped me and now I'm trying to help her."

"She's everywhere in the program I'm analyzing for you."

"You mean you're not finished yet."

"I mean I'm still looking at it. I've never seen anything quite like it before. Whoever put this together really knows their shit, and that's not all, by a long shot."

"What have you found out so far? I mean there must be something you can tell me that will at least put me on the right track."

"Just from what I've been able to see right now, Mr. Mason, I would say your friend is in big trouble. Whoever went to the trouble to put all of this together, he has an obsession with Miss Deming that borders on the psychotic."

"When you say trouble, how much trouble? I mean can you tell me are we talking her life, or what?"

"That I can't say yet, but I'm getting closer. Just to let you know, I've put all of my other projects on hold. The reason is simple: This is a whole new world for me and I'm fascinated by it. And I'm good enough at this stuff to put the pieces to together. But, unfortunately, it will take me a while longer."

"How much longer?"

"Can't say yet. Maybe a few days, maybe a few weeks. This programming is so complex and new that it's like learning to speak a new language."

"But didn't you say she may be in danger?"

"Yes, I said that."

"A few days may be too late to save her. Can't you speed it up a little?"

"No, I can't. It's a two-headed monster. He's interwoven Artificial Intelligence and his own program. That's a new standard I've not been exposed to before. But I am moving as fast as I can to help you and your friend, but you're just going to need a little patience."

"Patience?" Mase stood up, looking angry and losing what little patience he had.

"What about the hard drive I left with you? Have you looked at it?"

"It has the same digital footprint as the headset. I can tell you this. The person who programmed the headset is the same person who sent messages to the owner of this hard drive, no question. No question."

"When should I circle back to you?"

"Knowing that your friend is in danger, I'll work on it as hard as I can. It's hard to speak a new language when only one person in the world knows the words."

"Should I come back tomorrow?"

"Can you come back around midnight tomorrow? I'm hoping I can at least crack a few of his codes in this monster."

"I'll be here. And, thanks Sherman, I really appreciate what you're doing. This is unbelievable."

"If I were you, I'd get your friend to a safe place where she's won't be exposed to any of this stuff."

"I will. Thanks."

Mase left in a hurry and started calling Lara. She wouldn't answer.

Chapter 40

Two stately white horses with golden manes pawed at the soft ground. They made no sound when they moved. Creighton LaVelle had planned for this day. He could see in the far distance a purple castle floating in the air. It was atop a reddish black cloud that was stationary in the sky but put out beams of yellow flashing lightning bolts that boomed loudly and often.

Cornelia Summerlyn had been taken by the Black Knight in the middle of the night from her father's castle. One of her father's servants saw the abduction and said the Black Knight was holding a large golden shield. On it was inscribed a code in a foreign language. He told the servant he wouldn't be harmed and that all he wanted was Cornelia.

Lord Summerlyn summoned Creighton LaVelle. LaVelle had been courting Cornelia for some time and was known for his bravery and intelligence. He took an extra horse for Cornelia. He was that confident that he could save her, but it wouldn't be easy.

There would be many obstacles ahead that would make the rescue that much harder. Then, he would have to deal with The Black Knight himself. Lord Summerlyn reviewed the best path to Anthonia on a large, detailed map in the Great Room in his castle. It was woven into a tapestry on the wall to the right of the enormous fireplace.

Lord Summerlyn was an old man. The stress of losing his daughter to this evil knight was taking its toll on him, and his frail body shook as he pointed to the map with his ivory and gold cane.

"I've traveled these roads many times through many wars and I know the best path for you to take and the steps you'll need to take along the way. I know you probably think that these are just the words of an old man, but believe me when I say this, follow this path and you will succeed. Don't follow it and you and I shall never see

192

my daughter again. Here, I've written detailed instructions for you
to follow. New and strange impediments may arise, but if you follow
my instructions to the letter and use your God-given common sense
for the rest, you will make it through and save my daughter."

The handsome LaVelle listened carefully to every word. He knew
this new knowledge would keep him alive and that the path that was
indicated was so dangerous that only a few had made it through.

First, you had to travel through a steep mountain pass known
as the Torrent Run. It edged along the side of the tallest mountain
range in the country, Mt. Quinston, a mountain so haunted by the
ghosts of men killed there, that they say when the wind howls
through it passes; it's the voices of the men who died there. One slip
and you're in the torrent below, a boiling river of doom that no man
had ever come out of, alive. Then there were the Dagger Caves of The
Blind Giant, who is said to be immortal and will eat anything that
enters his cave. The problem is that you have to go through the cave
itself to get to Anthonia. There is no other way.

And the last obstacle before you get to the floating castle is the
Fire Swamp, a quagmire of red volcanic acid that dissolves anything
that falls into it.

Lord Summerlyn emphasized each of the obstacles by hitting
each spot on the map with his cane. Each time he hit a spot, it was
louder and louder and his voice became more intense and louder as
he spoke.

"These are not ravings of a senile old man. You must follow my
directions explicitly. If you take one wrong step young man, it will be
curtains for you and all of us. Do you understand what I'm saying?"

"Yes sir, I do. And thank you for your guidance. I will follow your
instructions exactly as they are written."

"And remember one thing. You must retrieve the Golden Shield
at all costs. The shield gives The Black Knight his power. Remove the
shield and The Black Knight is defeated. Remember that. The Three

obstacles and the Shield. Follow my instructions and bring back my daughter."

"I will, sir. Three Obstacles and the Golden Shield. Yes, sir."

The two shook hands vigorously. Lord Summerlyn put his hand on Creighton's shoulder and spoke his final thoughts to his only hope for reuniting with his daughter.

"When you get to the castle, you must remember one thing. The Black Knight is a liar, a very accomplished liar. Don't believe a word he says. Let your powers of observation and your keen intelligence lead you to the truth, for the truth is ever present. However, it is sometimes hidden behind well-spoken lies by evil people who only want something they shouldn't have. Remember that and you will succeed."

**

With Cornelia's white horse in tow, Creighton LaVelle began his journey. The instructions were kept safely in a black pouch that hung around his neck. He had studied it carefully before he left, but in case he forgot any of the details, he had it with him.

It would take him the better part of the first day to reach the first obstacle, Torrent Run. He knew that once he spotted Mt. Quinston somewhere along the northern horizon, the actual journey would begin. He camped in a lonely cluster of trees that had strange yellow flowers.

At night, he thought he heard laughing, youthful voices laughing from inside the trees. The green moonlight was bright enough for him to see that the flowers were laughing. As the gentle breeze blew through the trees, the laughter rose to a loud crescendo.

"Don't go, don't go. Go back!"

The laughter continued, but now with the message, the chanting of 'don't go' kept ringing in his ears. It wouldn't stop. He knew he had to leave this place now and travel at night. No point in remaining there because he couldn't sleep through the laughing and chanting. The stars above were crystal blue. With the laughing trees behind him now, Creighton LaVelle rode through the night. As the sun rose to his right, it was reflected off the snow atop Mt. Quinston, up ahead, not more than a few hundred meters away. He was almost there.

The horses were getting nervous at the sound they heard. It was the sound of thundering water booming through a small canyon. The closer he got, the louder the sound of the Torrent River. He needed to find the little bridge over the river that would take him along the side of the mountain, which would then lead him to the Dagger Caves, his second obstacle.

He found the bridge, which swung wildly in the wind created by the raging river and the shape of the little canyon. The horses didn't like being led across the bridge by Creighton. He was leading them by foot to show them they could do it. After a few stops, one slip by Cornelia's horse and one gust of wind that almost pushed him over the rope that was used for holding on, they made it.

He had to calm the horses first, and once they were relaxed enough to move forward, they moved along the very narrow dirt path, wide enough for only one person or horse. Creighton connected the horses with his belt as he led them along the precarious road ahead.

They were coming to the end of the path when he noticed that a small section ahead was missing. It looked as though it had eroded and fallen into the river. When they reached that spot, Creighton took a big chance. He would jump across it slowly, hold on to his horse's reigns and show him how he jumped over it, hopefully giving him the confidence he needed to jump as well. He hoped that would give Cornelia's horse the confidence to jump as well.

Amazingly, it worked. They'd made it. He could see the Dagger Cave ahead; a large round opening in the next mountain. As he approached, he noticed that all around the edges of the opening, large dagger points protruded. They looked ominous and frightening!

He took his time now, even resting with his horses near a large greenish gray boulder with sparkling flecks of silver all throughout its surface. He remembered the written instructions but took the scroll out of his pouch to read it one more time. It said, "Cover the eyes of your horses and rub your hands over the surface of the green boulder until it is covered with the silver particles. They will protect you in the Dagger Cave. Approach the cave slowly, as if you had no fear of it. The daggers come out only if you show fear. And stay as quiet as possible as you travel through the cave. The Blind Giant lives in that cave. Your silence will protect you, unless he awakens. If he wakes up, hold both palms up toward the Giant. There are special vibrations given off by the silver particles that the Giant finds annoying and painful to his ears. He will let you pass."

Creighton followed the directions thoroughly. The sound of the wind through the cave opening was like a low humming. At first, he thought it was the Blind Giant, but it was the wind. He tiptoed along slowly and deliberately. The horses seemed much calmer now. The darkness inside the cave was lit by enormous emerald-like crystals embedded in the walls. They gave off enough light to see the narrow path in front of them.

He heard a loud snoring noise and knew immediately that they were about to pass the sleeping Blind Giant. They had to be silent as they made their way through the dark maze in front of them. The horses were getting jumpy. They could smell the awful stench of the sleeping behemoth.

They were directly in front of him now, Creighton slowing down to quiet the horses and taking small steps forward, hoping that the giant would not awaken. Each step got them farther away past him. They were almost free now; just a few more steps. And then, without a warning, the giant awoke and was angry. He stood up and said, "Who goes there", in a loud and thunderous voice that shook the entire cave.

"Who goes there, I said?"

Then Creighton remembered the instructions. *"Hold up your palms toward the Giant. It will protect you. He will feel the painful vibrations and allow you to pass."* Creighton stood there and held up his silver dusted hands. The Giant put his hands over his ears and started wailing, twisting in agony, knocking over boulders and bumping into the walls of the cave. Creighton seized the opportunity to run, and he ran with the blindfolded horses.

It was darker now, so dark that he had to slow down to feel his way forward. He caught a whiff of fresh air, just a slight odor but enough to know they were getting closer to the exit. He felt the ground vibrating, large booming thumps that seemed to get louder and closer. Was the giant chasing them now?

Then, he heard that deep heavy voice swearing and yelling at them and the vibrating ground feeling like minor earthquakes, each one worse than the one before. Then he saw the faint light ahead, and he knew they were almost out. But, the giant was getting closer.

Creighton removed the blindfold from the horses, jumped on his horse and held the reins of the other. The giant was almost on them as the large opening to exit the cave was directly in front of them now. The giant was taking huge strides now, panting, still cursing at them, and just before they were at the opening, the giant took one last lunge at them and as he did so; he stumbled and grabbed at Cornelia's horse, but just missed. They were out and safe because Lord Summerlyn had told him that the giant would never leave his cave under any circumstance. Obstacle number two was overcome, leaving Obstacle number three, which Lord Summerlyn said was the most treacherous and deadly to get past.

They could still hear the angry giant yelling even when they were far from the cave. The landscape after the cave was of verdant valleys filled with herds of animals he'd never seen before. When they rested, they found the grass was lush, giving the horses the nourishment they needed for the final stage of their journey.

When the dawn broke and they all awoke, Creighton knew what lay ahead, a fiery quagmire that would be a way out or certain death if they failed.

The ride to the Fire Swamp was uneventful. The horses were well rested and fed, and he was ready for what was in front of him. They proceeded with confidence and daring, but they had no idea what they were about to see.

Suddenly, the wind stopped, the birds were no longing singing and flying. They approached a small wooded area with dark red trees that looked more like large hooked spears, each one pointing in different directions with sharp limbs covered in hooks and spikes.

The path they were on led them through the red trees. As they entered the woods, the horses became nervous again, and it was all Creighton could do to keep them calm enough to continue their journey. As they moved along the path, the strange trees bent towards them, with the occasional limb scraping them as they moved.

He scanned the woods as he attempted to control the horses. There were no animals anywhere. It wasn't a place for the living. But Lord Summerlyn had warned him that no matter what, do not leave the path.

Some of the trees changed color. They took on a darker brown tint, like they'd been burned by something. The smell of sulfur and the sting of acid came rushing through now. The horses sneezed and coughed as they plodded along, still jittery and scared, still trying to turn around to go back to the beautiful valley they'd just come from.

Creighton wouldn't allow it. They must stay on the path no matter what.

Creighton could see a yellowish haze coming through the strange trees. The haze was more like a fog, thick with no visibility. *Stay on the path Creighton. Keep going. Don't stop.*

They'd made it through, and as they left the strange forest, what he saw in front of him was beyond belief!

Chapter 41

Sherman Weiss slept fitfully all night. The VR headset was on the old man's head as he ran the program from it, feeling dizzy and weak. The entire program ran from the beginning in Lord Summerlyn's castle to Creighton LaVelle's approach to the Fire Swamp. It was exhausting.

The Putz had the feeling that the program worked with subliminal messaging, Artificial Intelligence, and superior programming skills all combined into a weird hypnotic fantasy that was intended to confuse and convince anyone who watched it, that it was indeed real. He had nothing to prove his theory, he just had that feeling. His gut never lied, so when he broke it down into its parts but couldn't find a way into it, he put a Sherman Weiss digital tripwire in it which would go off at a certain point and stop the program dead in its tracks.

That point was the Fire Swamp. It was the last level before you reached Anthonia and the Golden Shield which to Sherman looked suspiciously like a New York City Police Badge. Unfortunately, while he ran the program while lying in bed, he fell asleep smoking in bed. A small fire started on his mattress when he accidentally knocked over his ashtray. The fire woke him up right about the same time as the trip wire. Both events shook him awake and his heart raced so fast he thought he was having a heart attack.

He successfully extinguished the fire in time. However, the smoke alarm was triggered, leading several neighbors to notice the smoke and begin pounding on his door. He answered the door in his old worn out shorts. He calmed everyone down so they could shut off the alarm.

He didn't like anyone looking into his apartment, but he couldn't blame them for their reactions. He thanked everyone in his own way, which wasn't much, but everyone left when they were convinced that everything was OK. The fire department had been called, but they left after checking his apartment. Sherman Weiss was paranoid about anyone checking what he was doing. There was too much sensitive information lying about and he couldn't take any chances. But, the firefighters were satisfied that no threat remained, but they warned him about smoking in bed and reminded him it was a smoke free building, to which he thanked them courteously and promised to never smoke again and that he knew it was bad for him but dangerous for everyone in the building.

They patted him on his back and as they left and he closed his door and locked his three door locks; he flipped off the firemen like the true putz he was. He sat down at his desk and realized that he was lucky. But, without a doubt, he could feel the hold that the program had on him and that not only did the tripwire fail, but the adrenaline flowing in him from all the commotion of the fire, caused him to snap out of whatever the hell that program was doing to him.

Whoever created this program was a genius on a level he'd never been exposed to in his life. To envision this lethal video game and then to meld with AI and subliminal messaging, well, it was phenomenal. But it was so fascinating that he immediately went back to his computer to continue on with it. His first concern was the subliminal messaging part. He knew beyond a doubt that subliminal messaging works, and works very well, especially if someone has a weak mind or is in a weakened psychological state. He quickly researched a recent expert's opinion that reported, *"The duration of the effects of subliminal messages can vary. As a general rule, it will take 26 to 30 days to make permanent lasting changes to your subconscious. However, depending on the person it can take a few days to several months. Major changes usually take place after 3 months or 90 days. Sometimes it can even take up to 6 months to see permanent results.*

As for erasing subliminal messages, there's no clear scientific evidence on whether they can be completely erased. However, the mind is incredibly powerful and can reject any subliminal messages that could be potentially harmful. Ultimately, the longevity and impact of subliminal messages on conscious, rational decision-making are still subjects of ongoing research."

His optimism increased when he read that "the mind is incredibly powerful". Not that optimism was something he relied upon as a usual trait of his personality, but in this case, he didn't want anyone hurt by this insidious program and the truly evil programmer who devised it. And he definitely had a lot of work to do to fully understand this maze of digital programming before he could offer Mase anything concrete. He secretly wondered, *"How the hell did this guy do it?"* He was in awe, and, in fear!

Chapter 42

Sheik Habib employed three of the best gamers in the world to practice with. He had three more days before the championship match and he had to be sure he was in top form. He'd already gotten the concession from Jonah Christian that the game they'd play would be his choice, since it was a one-way bet for the championship. Since he was putting up the one billion dollar prize, it seemed right that it would be his choice.

If the Sheik won, Jonah would automatically announce online that the Sheik had won, and that he was the champion. If Jonah won, the crypto currency would be automatically released and he would be wealthy beyond his imagination.

The Sheik had chosen Resident Evil Village - Winters Expansion Level 1, but had the option to choose Sekiro: Shadows Die Twice using Sekiro Online within one minute of the start time.

Sheik Habib paid well for the three gamers to give him the best challenge they could muster. To show his skill level, he somehow played all three simultaneously, easily defeating each of them. Those three top-notch players were amazed at the Sheik's skill level. They gave their ratings, and that was that. The Sheik was ready for Jonah, but was Jonah ready?

Sheik Habib was slightly disappointed in the three online gamers. He wanted more from them, but he paid them off. The word spread throughout the online gaming community that the upcoming match would be the greatest match ever, as the anticipation grew and the betting was enormous.

Las Vegas and all the new betting websites were raking in millions every day. The buzz was amazing. The odds were slightly in the Sheik's favor, but for the real aficionados of online play, Jonah could not be defeated. They knew how good he really was.

***

Meanwhile, back in the Big Apple, Mase had a problem. He'd taken Sherman Weiss' advice to protect Lara. There was just too much evidence in his mind, pointing at the danger she was in. He felt strongly that he had to do something.

But, as hard as he tried to contact her, she just couldn't be found.

Paolo had told him that Lara went to a secret location for mind-clearing relaxation. He mentioned a few spots that she'd used in the past, but none of them panned out. Mase was getting nervous.

He asked Captain Vrain if he could get a search warrant for her phone records. He had no evidence that she was in trouble other than the words of an old hacker in Queens. It wasn't enough, besides Vrain needed Mase to clear out all the other cases that were still piling up.

"You've got too many cases piling up on your desk to be chasing women. Enough already! Forget the therapist and finish up what I need you to finish up. Now get the hell out of my office. I've got a desk full of shit, OK? Now!"

Mase stormed out, but his mind was still on Lara. He didn't want to tell the captain that he could solve three cases at the same time. It didn't matter. He was going to do what he wanted to do, which is how he always did things. He didn't care what the Captain thought.

As he drove over the Queensboro Bridge, his two-way radio was reporting a new crime scene, but the whining tires going across the steel grating of the bridge prevented him from hearing it clearly. He thought he recognized the address but couldn't be sure. He wasn't supposed to be working in Queens, so he ignored it and continued his drive to Sherman Weiss' apartment.

Maybe Weiss had more information, and while he was there, maybe he could get into Lara's phone records for him. It was illegal, yes, but necessary. Weiss would understand. Traffic was lousy, but he finally made it. He parked his car, locked it and ran up to the apartment. He was out of breath.

After knocking on the door as hard as he could to get the absent-minded grouch's attention, no one answered. He tried again, still nothing.

"Sherman, open up." Yelled the detective. Nothing.

More pounding on the door. Finally, the old man appeared, zipping up his pants and telling Mase to shut up already and can't an old man take a shit in peace?"

"For a minute... I thought you were..."

"Dead? Not yet. But soon... probably."

Mase walked in to the smoky stale air. The look on The Putz's face was concern coupled with just a hint of fear. Mase didn't like fear on the old man's face because he'd never seen it before. Exhaustion caused Weiss' eyes to blink and look bleary. He knew that Weiss had been up all night, probably working on this case.

***

Jonah Christian was all over his programming, leading up to his big match. He studied the practice games of the Sheik because the ego of the Middle East savant wouldn't allow him to practice in private. The reaction times to certain moves and the strategy were fairly common, but what set him above the rest was the ability to think on the fly and create diversions that were totally unexpected.

Unfortunately for the Sheik, these games were beatable if you had the means to react instantaneously, and Jonah did. By using his Artificial Intelligence programming, he could not only predict but respond to any move the Sheik made as soon as he did it. Would the Sheik suspect anything? Possibly. But Jonah was counting on one thing and one thing only. The Sheik believed, right to his core, that he was the best player in the world. And, perhaps he was, but Jonah knew the limitations of a human being's ability to think, assimilate, and react and he knew there was no way to be quicker and more accurate than a computer.

Jonah was waiting for his men to return, and while he waited, he did his practice by fine-tuning his program. It was easy for him. He knew he would beat the Sheik as long as his program worked perfectly and seamlessly during the game. Today, he was making sure it would.

He felt somewhat distracted while he programmed. A feeling was rising in him and he couldn't explain it or handle it. It was growing, and he didn't like the discomfort it was causing him. It distracted him enough that it was obvious. More than ever, his passion for Lara Deming was occupying his every waking thought. All the work he had put into tracking her movements, finding out about her past, looking relentlessly at every aspect of her health, her mental health, her likes, her preferences in men, her late husband's life and how she adored him, everything about her consumed him, and, he hated the fact that it had become his one big obsession. It had completely taken over his life. Nothing had ever had that effect on him. All the other things he was involved in diminished in importance, and that worried him.

As he was nearing the end of fine-tuning his gaming program, he kept looking at the time on the monitor. *What was taking them so long to get back?* Jonah contacted Toy Francisco on his two-way radio.

"ETA Mr. Francisco?"

"Entering the grounds right now, Boss."

"Follow our plan exactly, Mr. Francisco. How is she doing?"

"She's fine, maybe a little tired from the process of securing her, but other than that, no problem."

"Excellent, Mr. Francisco. Make sure her accommodations are perfect in every way. Was anyone there when the process was started?"

"Not a soul, sir. Clean in every way?"

"When she is all set up, I want you and Stanley to get my bath ready. I want to look perfect for Lara."

"Certainly boss. It should take us just a few more minutes."

Jonah's heart was racing. All the built up anticipation he'd experienced over the past weeks would finally come to fruition. The woman he had always hoped for, the perfection of her was now here with him. He loved her as he'd loved no one in his life, and the part that made it even stranger was that he'd never even met her, never seen her in person, only by phone pretending to be a person in need of her professional therapist services.

He was too consumed by Lara's presence to finish his programming, besides; it was as close to perfection as he could probably make it and knowing what the program could accomplish, that was enough. There was no way the Sheik could overcome the sheer instantaneous speed of it.

Jonah never wore his artificial mouth during the day, when he was by himself in his work area. It was too constricting. The only shortcoming was controlling his own saliva. Without lips, it's hard to manage the flow, especially when he was hungry.

So brilliant was this man, that this little invention of his, the artificial mouth, that it alone could have helped millions of people around the world and made him wealthy. But instead of sharing his brilliance, like everything else he did, the invention stayed with him, for him, and was always about him.

Before his men came to attend him, he put his computer system on automatic detection and response. Every one of his security features, his tracking programs, his vast network with its built-in spoofing mechanisms, were set to perform at peak levels for twenty-four hours a day.

He'd been completely distracted by Lara Deming; and somehow missed the minor interference indicator that flashed for less than a second on his main monitor.

Chapter 43

Jonah Christian's real name was Jonah Boyd and he lived in a rural area of New Rochelle, NY. He'd lived there all his life, inheriting the gated mansion from his successful investment broker father, Desmond Boyd. Very little was known of his family life, except that after his mother died shortly after his birth, his father remarried a much younger woman, a dark-haired beauty named Victoria Steplova, an emigre from Ukraine.

Jonah shut himself in for most of his life, graduating Princeton at sixteen, and that was all anyone knew of him, before and since. He inherited everything from his father, and no one knew what happened to Victoria. It's as though he wanted invisibility and anonymity, and succeeded masterfully at achieving both.

He expunged everything from his personal history; medical records, birth records, school records, government tax records. There was nothing anywhere that could lead people to his actual identity. He had no friends or acquaintances. Jonah Boyd became Jonah Christian and neither existed.

He now had the love of his life with him in his mansion. The room he created for her came right out of the video game he'd created to envelop her life and create a beautiful new life for her, and him. It would be Cornelia Summerlyn's life now, complete with all the trappings of a medieval castle, wealth, position, and security.

A mild sedative had been injected to keep her sedated for a short time. She would remain in her room until Creighton LaVelle would save her life and become her hero.

The room was completely sealed, climate controlled, filled with fresh roses and lilacs, and soundproof. By possession, she was his now. He was in full control of every aspect of her new life. Of course, he wanted her to love him, but he knew that the sight of him would not allow that. He chose captivity instead, settling for being in the same building, breathing the same air, eating the same food, reading the same poetry she was forced to read and listen to the subliminal messaging he put into her mind.

***

Mase followed up with Sherman Weiss about Lara's phone records. The Putz came through for Mase. Not that Mase enjoyed breaking the law by having someone hack into private phone records, it was just that getting a warrant, going through a cell phone company, and waiting for someone to analyze them would take way too long and he knew he didn't have one minute to lose. He also knew that Weiss was good enough to cover any tracks that might be left. The old man looked terrible when Mase arrived.

"You look like shit, man."

"I feel like shit, thanks to this goddamn problem you dumped on me."

"You get her records?"

"She was spoofed, of course, but there's always something there if you look hard enough."

"Here's the record of all the calls she made and received for the last three months. Here, look at it and tell me if you see anything."

Mase took the printout and stared at it but couldn't see a problem. He was glad to have the records so he could begin his search back at headquarters.

"I see nothing that pops out at me, but then again I wouldn't know what to look for."

"I could verify the phone numbers for most of the calls, but I checked her emails, and that's where I think I found something, not very much, but maybe something useful."

"The type of VR headset that is used here, like the one you gave to me to check out, that one needs a network somewhere, even a personal hotspot, something, to work properly. Whoever did all this used a Tor network."

"A

what?"

"It's a way to hide your original IP address. You route your message through several servers, making it nearly impossible to track. However, the last server he went through, I know that server, the guy who owns it I mean. He pulled up some records which I now have. It isn't much, but at least it's something. I'm still working on it, so why don't you work on those phone records and I'll keep working on the program. Come back tomorrow and we should have more information on how to proceed. Were you able to find the woman?"

"Not yet, but I'm working on it, and I hope these phone numbers will lead to something more definite. I've got a bad feeling about this, Sherman."

"I do too. You know, Mr. Mason, the sad thing about all this is that the person who created this unbelievable program is undoubtedly a programming genius, the kind of genius that comes around once in a lifetime. To think how much good he could have done, staggers the imagination. This is no small thing, Mr. Mason. What he's done here is staggering. It's a shame he's done it for the wrong reason, whatever that reason is. Who knows? Well, goodbye Mr. Mason and I'll see you tomorrow, hopefully with something more concrete."

Mase shook Sherman's hand and looked into the strained eyes of the old man. He never expected such a dedicated effort and was proud to work with him.

Chapter 44

The office was almost empty when he got there. The flickering fluorescence from the ceiling looked cold and menacing to the desperate detective, as the housekeeping crew moved in slow motion to kill as much of their time as they could. One of the older housekeepers, Felicia, smiled at Mase with her wide, one-tooth missing smile that never failed to get him to smile. She always talked about her son in Monterey.

Felicia offered to clean the area around his desk, her overly tight sweat pants revealing creases and other things that Mase didn't want care to see. Mase declined the offer for the moment, and Felicia smiled again. He moved all the papers away from his monitor and keyboard and went to work investigating the few phone numbers given to him by Sherman Weiss.

Nothing immediately popped up as he looked at them except that they were all the same New York origin.

He dialed the first one and no answer, hung up, and dialed again. No answer. He'd try it later. The second one answered the call even though it was already 9 pm. It was an answering service.

"Conrad's Computer Supply. You are calling after our regular service hours of 9 am to 6 pm. Please leave your message at the tone."

Mase hung up without leaving a message. He would visit them tomorrow. The third and last number wouldn't ring through. It said the phone was no longer in service, which caught his attention since it had been in service the day before when Weiss discovered it. He'd check on it tomorrow. Mase thought it was probably a disposable phone used once and then thrown away.

Mase tapped his pencil on the desk as he stared at his monitor. His tapping grew louder, the more he felt frustrated that nothing seemed to click yet. He kept tapping his pencil as the housekeepers glanced at him from time to time. The thought occurred to him that maybe Lara was home now.

When Mase arrived at Lara's apartment, he rang the buzzer to get in the front entry, but no one answered to let him in. *Where could she be? Was she in danger or just enjoying her private time on some beach somewhere or in a mountain cabin sipping some wine in front of a fireplace with a roaring fire?* Each question had the same answer. No, no, no. She was in trouble, and no one was helping her. But where was she? He left and sat alone in a bar in the West Village, turning a shot glass around and around on the bar.

The mirror behind the bar caught a look on his face. His eyes went down to the shot glass and back to the mirror. He paid for his drink and left without drinking it. It was a minor victory, but a victory. Lara would have given him a thumbs-up had she seen him. The thought that he was out of options pissed him off, so he went home to think about what to do next. He knew he couldn't report Lara as a missing person yet, since she told Paolo she'd be back in a few days. The only people in the world who worried about Lara at the moment were Paolo and him.

He played a few video games at home and checked in on a few of the gamer blogs. There was a lot of buzz about an upcoming match between two of the best gamers out there. One was some Sheik guy in the Middle East and the other was some guy no one knew about. He was just there. The buzz mentioned a big payoff for whoever won. Mase figured it was all hype to get the suckers to bet on it. The winners were usually the betting websites and he wouldn't be surprised if the whole thing was created just to get the sucker money flowing.

He played a few more games, turned off his computer, kicked off his shoes and flopped down on his bed with all his clothes still on.

Mase dozed off, woke up, dozed again. Then he woke up thinking of one phrase. 'Fire Swamp'. Those words echoed in his head and wouldn't stop. Suddenly, he felt a searing pain in his feet, as if they were being stuck in molten lava or acid. The pain was too much to take. It woke him up, and he jumped out of bed, hopping up and down and crying in pain.

When he looked down and saw that his feet were the same as they always were, the pain stopped immediately. It was all a nightmare. When he looked at his clock, only a few minutes had passed, but it felt like hours of pain.

Chapter 45

When Creighton LaVelle looked around, he knew without a doubt that he was in big trouble. The sulfurous smell permeated the light green mist that hung above the Fire Swamp. Occasional bubbles burst on the surface, popping lava spray everywhere. What hadn't burned to a crisp already would certainly incinerate quickly, including himself, if he didn't figure out something quick.

His horses were exhausted from their trek through the spiny woods, but there wasn't a spot to rest in or a place to hide. He checked the handwritten scroll of instructions Lord Summerlyn had given him.

"When you get to the Fire Swamp, say the following words, three times, carefully: "Long Live Anthonia". When you hear a voice answer, you say: "Anthonia will be free".

If you follow these instructions to the letter, a large winged dragon will appear and take you safely to the castle of The Black Knight. He is a fearsome-looking creature, but stand your ground and keep your horses close to you. Do not panic or retreat, or you will die immediately and all will be lost. It is all up to you. God Bless!

That was the end of the scroll. He rolled it up and tied the golden thread around it and put it back in his pocket. He was now ready to start.

***

A loud crashing sound brought Mase back to the present. He'd accidentally knocked his laptop on the wooden floor in his bedroom. The saga of The Black Knight had continued in his brain as he slept. It must have been planted there when he wore the VR headset. It felt genuine enough that he could smell the sulfur gas coming out of the swamp. He left his bed and went to the bathroom to wash away the imaginary smell from his face and nose.

The kitchen wall clock read 7:36 am. He wanted to visit the computer supply store that Weiss had identified as a supplier of the high-end software that was being used by the person who caused all this grief.

Vrain had left Mase a text message to call him right away. That was at 7:15. He texted him back he was working on a lead from one case he was working on. This was no time for stupid debates about bullshit priorities. Finding Lara and getting her out of harm's way was the only priority. This he knew, and he wasn't about to stop his search until he found out where she was.

***

Conrad's Computer Supply on West 28th St. had that look; the look of a place that saw little foot traffic, but kept their business going through online purchases and lots of repeat customers. It was obvious when Mase walked in and the person behind the counter looked surprised.

She was about fifty-five, slightly overweight, her hair was dyed a bright red, which matched her long artificial red fingernails. When the bell rang as Mase opened the door, Rose, the name on her name tag, looked up from the smart phone and decided right then that the tall, good looking man that just walked in was worth at least a smile.

Mase flashed his ID at the smiling face with thick makeup and nose ring. She didn't say a word.

"I'm investigating a murder, and I need some information from you. It has something to do with this case, so it's important."

"Yeah?"

"Yeah!"

The look on Mase's face was intense and unwavering in its intensity. Rose got the message and softened her recalcitrance. He handed rose a slip of paper that Weiss had given him; it had a date, and a time, and a particular piece of software printed in the weird lettering Weiss always wrote in.

"We get lots of calls Detective. Whaddya expect me to do, remember every phone call and who called? Come on. How am I supposed to remember every call?"

"I know for a fact that the hardware listed here isn't a common item that people ask for. It's expensive and I'm certain you would remember it, wouldn't you, Rose?"

"I might." She stopped and started playing with her smart phone again.

"Rose, is there someone in the back that can cover for you while we bring you down to headquarters for questioning, because right now you are wasting my time."

Rose woke up from her daydream.

"Look, detective. I'm just a poor working girl trying to earn enough money to pay my rent and eat regularly."

Mase pulled a twenty out of his pocket and handed it to the clerk. She looked around and slipped it in her purse.

"It was bought using a disposable credit card about a month ago, and sent to a post office box in New Rochelle. That's all I can remember, honestly. Oh, and I remember calling the person who was going to get it delivered to let her know it was going out for delivery."

"I don't think so, Rose. But, for now it'll have to do."

Chapter 46

"How many Post Offices are there in New Rochelle?" Asked Mase of Jinx Simmons, the catch-all assistant that had a way with computers and search engines.

"Two." Said the attractive brunette with the long eyelashes.

"Those lashes ever give you problems?"

"Only when I laugh."

"Thanks. Just wondering."

"Here are the addresses of the two Post Offices." She winked at Mase and he blew her a kiss.

"You're the best."

"You should find out some time."

"I don't know. Those lashes look kind of dangerous. I don't know if I could handle all that."

"There's only one way to find out...Mr. Mason."

"Oh, now we're getting formal."

***

As he drove to New Rochelle in the pouring rain, he couldn't help but think that he was making progress, not major progress, but enough to keep him focused on the name "Burnett". Jinx had printed out everything with the first name or last name of Burnett; one hundred and forty-seven. It was a long list, but he'd had worse.

Rose at the computer supply place had looked up the record of the purchase after Mase had put some pressure on her and found another twenty for her in his pocket.

He saw it. All it said was "Burnett", P.O. Box 49.

The two post offices were on Quaker Ridge Road and North Avenue. He went to the North Avenue one first. It didn't have any boxes. So, off he went to the one on Quaker Ridge Rd. Turned out that the Supervisor was off and no one had the authority to look at the records of who rented it.

There was an old style coffee shop across the street from the Post Office. Mase was hungry and frustrated. The atmosphere was friendly and old school. Booths along the front windows, seats with torn vinyl along the counter, one cook who looked like he should have retired about twenty years earlier, and a short server with curly blond hair.

It wasn't like she was very busy, but the server took her time coming over to serve Mase.

"Busy day?" Asked Mase, smoothing out his frustration.

"Can I bring you some coffee, sir?"

"Two eggs over easy, wheat toast, hash browns and coffee."

She took the order to the cook, who looked at it and placed it on the counter as he slowly drank his cup of coffee. Mase watched the scene from his booth and knew right away that he might or he might not ever get his order.

He watched a large Lincoln SUV drive up to the Post Office. He wasn't totally sure, but he could see that the large man who got out of the SUV walked over to a box on the wall that was in the same location as Box 49. It was too late to follow it, but he got a partial plate as the man sped off. He called Jinx.

"Can you run all the plates that end in T7? That's all I could get off the SUV. Late model Lincoln Commander, don't know the exact year, just a hunch. I'll be at the office in forty-five minutes."

"You're not asking a lot are you, sweetie?"

"I only go to the best."

"Thanks for the butter, but I ain't buyin' it."

"Who's your favorite detective?"

"Alright. Alright. I'll check on it. Don't expect a lot. It's not like I'm sitting here doin' my nails, for chrissake."

***

The bits and pieces were coming together, but not fast enough. Everything was still jumbled like one of those impossible jigsaw puzzles that lay scattered on your kitchen table with no solution in sight. He pictured himself sweeping his arm over the pieces and scattering them on the floor, but then he remembered he hated cleaning up messes.

Traffic was horrendous as he drove back to headquarters. He thought about the city of New Rochelle. He was getting that tingling sensation in his stomach that always indicated something good.

***

While he found himself stuck in traffic on the West Side Highway, he checked with Paolo to see if he'd heard anything from Lara. He did not. Then Mase called Sherman Weiss. The phone kept ringing. If he let it ring long enough, Weiss would certainly pick it up. Mase got no reply, thought it was odd, and made a mental note to call him at the office.

When Mase had finally arrived, Jinx was out to lunch, but she'd left him the information he wanted on his desk. He smiled.

Seven Lincolns with T7 on their plates, two were the right color, none had Burnett attached to them. Mase tried every combination of addresses, 'Burnett', and T7 he could think of and nothing fit. Then he tried different variations of the name 'Burnett'. Again, nothing worked. His frustration was growing as fast as the headache that started pounding in his head. A tall, cold beer sounded perfect right then, but he knew he was running out of time and that wherever Lara was, he was certain that she was in trouble.

He remembered Vrain once told him that no matter how bad things were going, there were always options and the only reason you think you're out of options is because you haven't thought about that one option that mattered. Mase thought about that as he stared at Vrain's closed office door. He would knock on Vrain's door, but he needed to call The Putz first.

He finally answered after multiple calls. The sound of his voice said 'don't bother me' but the words said 'we better solve this now or she won't make it'.

"Anything new?" Asked Mase.

"Fire Swamp."

"I saw it too. He must have thrown the whole bullshit fantasy into the subliminal messaging he put in the program. I saw it myself, and I woke up just in time."

"After this is over, see a good shrink to de-program yourself."

"I'll leave right now. Keep your door locked and turn off your Wi-Fi connections."

"Done."

***

"Sherman. Sherman. Open up. It's me, Vic Mason."

He kept knocking on the door. The last thing he wanted was any curious neighbors coming out into the hallway to see what was going on. He took out his set of skeleton keys and finally unlocked the door after a few tries with the wrong keys. He worried that the two or three safety locks that Weiss had on his door would make the entry impossible. But he got in, no safety locks. He had nothing but awful premonitions. And when he entered, he was right.

Sherman's body was coiled up on the floor in a pool of blood. His head was almost decapitated by the deep ligature he suffered. There was little evidence of a struggle, so whoever did this was a total professional.

He made sure not to touch anything in the apartment, hoping that when the lab boys came in, they'd find something, although professionals leave nothing.

The lights suddenly went out and a tremendous blow to the back of his head sent Mase into a spinning world of exploding lights and muted words of invisible demons.

When he regained consciousness, he found himself tied up and in an old warehouse. His head ached and his body felt paralyzed from lack of blood flow. Or maybe he was paralyzed, but then he could move his right thumb and figured it was just the tightness of the rope and the position he was in.

His feet were tied together, his hands were tied behind his back and the blindfold they had placed on his head slipped off as he rubbed the back of his head against the concrete wall he was leaning against. His head was still throbbing like a pounding sledge hammer was inside of it. As he shook it off, it hurt even more and he noticed that blood had trickled down the back of his neck and on to the floor.

He realized, even though his fog hadn't completely lifted, he did realize that he was in a warehouse, but not an ordinary warehouse. There was nautical debris everywhere; old anchors, rusted compasses, and mooring ropes. This was some kind of old naval repair area.

The thought kept bouncing around his brain that it wasn't luck that he was still alive. They easily could have done away with him if they wanted to. But they didn't, and that was the question he had to answer. But first he had to free his body from the ropes, and these weren't just regular ropes, they were nautical, thick, fibrous ropes.

Somehow, his brain engaged, and the thought came to him somewhere inside the aching pain that seared inside his head, to move over to the closest anchor he could find. The pointed, rusted tip of the anchor could easily cut through the ropes. But he was hog-tied and as numb as a dead man.

He tipped over on his side and slid inch by inch to the anchor. It seemed like it took him an hour to move six inches. He barely felt the floor under him as he moved slower than a snail. But he was moving.

Chapter 47

Mase had lost too much blood. He now felt weak and half-gone. The inch by inch crawling took more energy than he had, but he knew if he didn't make it to the anchor, the end would come quickly and he couldn't help Lara and put out of business whoever was doing all this. He struggled to get there and after what seemed like an hour of trying; he made it.

Now he had to squirm his way around to get the rope around his wrists to face the rusty tip of the anchor so he could rub the rope against its sharp edge and cut it loose: easier said than done. He shifted his weight a few times and finally, finally, felt the anchor tip against the rope. He slowly started to rub the rope against it.

Some of the rope strands were being cut, but it was taking forever and Mase had no idea when the people who put him there were coming back.

The rope was fraying when the anchor tipped from the sawing action and fell over and took the detective with it, spinning the detective on the wrong side. He was now in an awkward position that made him feel like a crab that fell on his back and his legs were flailing around.

A warm liquid was dripped on his wrists. It could only be one thing, blood. He took a deep breath. If he'd cut his wrist with the rusty anchor tip, he had just minutes before he would die. This was it. He used every ounce of energy to twist his wrists and move his arms in one last paroxysm of movement to get free. The movement hurt like hell and to make it worse, the anchor tip was now digging into his arm and wrist.

He grunted with his last effort and the rope was cut! Blood was everywhere, and he knew if he didn't stop the bleeding right then, it would be the end of Vic Mason. He quickly untied the rope around his legs, tore off a strip of his shirt and made a tourniquet to wrap tightly around the large slice on his wrist. Luckily, he didn't think the artery was damaged, but the wound was long enough that it took a few more minutes for the blood to stop running out.

He was standing now, woozy from the blood loss, but standing. He looked around the warehouse for a way out. The place itself was enormous. As he walked along the walls, he could see windows at the very top. One was partially broken but way too high for him to get out. He noticed the large metal door, with a metal bar across it that was a lever to slide up and down to open it from the inside. It was padlocked in the lock position. There was no way he was getting out through that door.

Behind a few empty wooden crates, he spotted a vent in the wall. It was metal, but thin metal. He bent down and felt a few of the metal slats that were closed. He could move them into their open position, which he did. Then he turned his back towards the vent and kicked it with his heel. They were bending, but not all the way yet. So, he kicked harder and harder until he kicked a few of them out. He knew right then that he could kick the rest of them out if he kicked like hell, like a stubborn mule pissed off at his owner.

Finally, most of the slats were out, and he could barely get through the opening. But, by lying on his back and pushing backwards with his legs, he wiggled his way out. He stopped for a moment as he stared up at the blue sky above him. It was the most beautiful sky he had ever seen! Never had he ever seen a sky that blue, that beautiful as the one he was looking at now. He took a few deep breaths and leaned up against the outside wall.

As he looked around, he could see the Brooklyn Bridge and the Williamsburg Bridge and the East River, in all their glory. He realized then that he was in the Brooklyn Navy Yard. Then he heard a car engine, and it was getting closer. He had no intention of taking any chances. He found a hiding place in between some abandoned equipment.

Panic took hold for a second when he realized that he might have left a trail of blood on the ground. He looked down, and sure enough he saw small drops leading right to where he was then. He tried doubling back on them so he could run in another direction. The drops were smaller now, but they were still there. They could easily follow the trail if they spotted it.

He went to the water's edge, looked down, and made his decision!

Chapter 48

Mase dog-paddled along the edge of the river until he found what looked like a security booth for a dock used to unload barges. He looked around to make sure he wasn't being followed and lifted himself up. He was a stinking, oily mess, like something out of a slasher movie. The security man had his legs up on the small counter and was busy ready The Post. When he saw Mase he almost fell off his stool.

"What the hell! Who are you?"

The man drew his gun on the detective; his shaking hand jiggling the gun he probably never used. Mase could see the safety was off and immediately held up his hands.

"My name is Vic Mason and I'm a cop. I need your help. Don't worry, I will not hurt you. Here's what I need you to do."

The man followed Mase's instructions. He even gave Mase his jacket to keep him warm while a patrol car came. He showered at headquarters and put on his old uniform that he kept in his locker. Captain Vrain got a big kick out of seeing Mase in uniform again.

"Still fits, huh?"

Mase took it well. He patted his own stomach.

"Still in good shape."

"Maybe you should leave it on, permanently."

Mase knew Vrain was kidding, and he laughed it off, but if he didn't get some answers for the Captain real quick, he might wind up wearing that uniform, permanently.

He gave his Captain an update on what happened and told him he'd solve multiple cases when he caught the guy who did it to him. Vrain had confidence in Mase and offered any help he needed. Mase said he needed a lab guy and one officer to accompany him back to the warehouse where he'd been kept prisoner. Maybe, just maybe, some little item, some small piece of something was left there to finally open things up. He kept thinking about Lara.

As soon as a nurse changed his bandages and disinfected the cuts and abrasions on his arm, Mase got in the patrol car and they drove off.

***

Vrain had gotten a search warrant for Mase so he could search the place without having to worry about breaking and entering. They had to use a crowbar to open the big metal door. Mase saw the hole in the vent. Nothing seemed to have changed since he was there not three hours earlier. There was his dried blood all along the floor to the rusty anchor that saved him.

The lab guy, his name was Paul Thomas, looked for fingerprint samples but many of them were old, probably ten years old by the looks of them. Mase pointed out where his fingerprints might be located. The patrol officer stood guard by the door as Mase and the lab guy combed every inch. They were just about finished.

"Thomas, any prints?"

"Nothing. They must have worn gloves."

"Well, let's get out of here. I think we're done." Said Mase.

As they walked towards the door, the officer standing guard noticed a cigarette butt by the door.

"Any of you guys smoke?"

"Yeah, but not here. Why?"

"It's probably nothing, but I see one cigarette butt just outside the door. And it looks fresh."

"I'll take it for DNA testing just in case." Said Thomas.

Mase agreed. It might be the one piece he was hoping for.

***

Vrain was waiting for the team to return, and while he waited, he started thinking about New Rochelle. Wilmot Woods in Quaker Ridge was where an old girlfriend of his used to live. She came from a wealthy family, and that was the area. What was it about Quaker Ridge? Didn't Mase mention it? He couldn't remember, but he'd ask him when he returned.

Where would a wealthy guy live in New Rochelle if he needed to keep low, be best protected and hidden? It would have to be some place that was well-disguised or hidden away from view. It couldn't be too hard to find in a place like New Rochelle. Of course, it remained to be seen whether the wacko who did all this actually lived in New Rochelle. Vrain's brain was now in overdrive.

***

Mase told Vrain about the possible DNA sample and Vrain told him that even using SMBJ, an experimental technique for getting the results faster, the results wouldn't be known for at least a couple of weeks. No, this case needed old school methods, which was right up Vrain's alley. Mase felt great about having his Captain by his side on this one. He was a pain in the ass sometimes, but a damned good cop and an even better detective.

Vrain was looking for something very specific in New Rochelle. He jumped back into total detective mode like he'd never left.

This case begged for the kind of logic that only worked if they approached it from behind. So, after he reviewed the details that Mase had given him, instead of taking it apart, he searched the how's, but not the why's. In his experience, every time he faced a person who was a complete whack job, he would not waste his time looking for motives or why that person hated his father, or mother, or why he felt neglected.

He prioritized what each of them would work on; he set aggressive follow-ups between them. He agreed with Mase that there wasn't much time. Mase took the gut feeling approach and Vrain took the building block approach. Both hoped that either or both would lead them to Lara and the psychotic killer who had everything figured out, or, thought he had everything figured out.

Chapter 49

In the kingdom of Zakar, nothing changes very much from one day to the next. Oil was pumped out of the desert; money was collected from around the world. The royal family stayed to themselves in their palace and went about their daily routines unconcerned about the events of the day. They were the Switzerland of the Middle East, never commenting or taking sides in area conflicts, never insulting other world leaders or building up huge amounts of weapons. They remained neutral.

But, on this day, the summer sun seemed more intense than usual. Not a whisper of a breeze to take the edge off, nothing. Everyone was inside, huddled around their smart phones and computers. They were waiting for two things. The King's health had been declining for the past few weeks, and he seemed quieter than usual and he looked exhausted just to be alive. His death was imminent.

Today was the day when his son, the Sheik, would take on the greatest video game player in the world for a championship match, for the title of the greatest player in the world. Some of Zakar's citizens whispered that the King was ashamed of his son's obsession with gaming and that it was such a humiliation to his family and his kingdom that it was too much to take for the King. Perhaps he was giving up on life and welcoming death because of it.

The thought that his country would then be led by his son made it even worse for the older monarch. How would his son be able to take charge of the country he had created into a well-respected oil-rich jewel in the desert? All he thought about were those stupid games; too much distraction for a young man. He had such potential, such brilliance.

The health of his father concerned the Sheik. He loved his father and did all the right things to make sure he was taken care of.

However, it wouldn't let his concern take his focus away because he needed every bit of it. His personal attendants took care of his every need and then some. Nothing was going to keep him from winning this game, nothing.

The Sheik had two younger brothers, Ramar and Tariq. Ramar was sixteen and Tariq twenty-two. Both brothers were permitted to attend the game but only Tariq attended. Ramar stayed with his very ill father. The game was only two hours away. On the one hand, the citizens of Zakar wanted to watch the game, but they were also worried about the King's health and found it hard to enjoy the event that was being watched all over the world.

***

Jonah Christian never lost focus, regardless of the situation. His attention to detail, every detail, comforted him even during the most difficult times. This game was not a distraction. In fact, it gave him no pleasure at all. It was simply another event in another day in a life that was solely built around computer programs.

This was a language he was born to speak. His face was not his face. He was a disfigured, mouthless monster that spoke only occasionally and preferred to communicate through his programming. His artificial mouth was only put on when his assistants were in attendance, and even though they never reacted to his facial deformity, Jonah knew they were horrified at the sight of it.

When Jonah placed the mouth down in order to carefully cleanse his face, the lips sometimes kept moving because he hadn't finished what he was saying. He could talk without them, but it wasn't easy, and he was slightly embarrassed about it himself. So, he made it a point to leave the mouth on when anyone was around him, which wasn't often.

With the amount of AI integrated into his gaming program coupled with his innate skills and strategic awareness of his opponents, there was no way he could lose the upcoming game. It was more than a foregone conclusion; it was a fact. No one knew that, of course, but him.

With an hour to go, Jonah double checked his program, played a few games while he waited, and limbered up his hands by stretching them and cracking his knuckles a few times. He felt as ready as he would ever be. He called Toy Francisco and asked him how Lara was doing.

"She's fine boss. She's coming out of her sedative now. It won't be long."

Jonah didn't respond. He hung up and refocused on his computer screen. Every possibility had been pre-calculated along with backup options only a mind like his could think of, right down to the heart rate he needed to perform at his best to the temperature of the area around his massive gaming computer. Everything was ready. Jonah was always ready, especially when it came to making money.

He watched the clock tick down on his screen. Now!!

Chapter 50

Mase got himself a hotel room for the night. Both he and Vrain knew his apartment was being watched. Vrain told him to get a room and expense it. Mase was surprised at the generosity of the cheap son of a bitch. Vrain would never admit that he had a special bias toward his best detective and that he reminded him of himself twenty years prior.

Mase ordered room service, figuring that he might as well go for it since it would never happen again, including one beer with the medium rare ribeye and mashed potatoes. Why not, he thought, didn't they always give the condemned man whatever he wanted?

He'd forgotten about the big video game championship match, the one that had the world's attention. He thought it might take place that evening. Mase could never figure out Sekiro, so he wondered which of the two heavyweights was going to out maneuver and out strategize the other.

The Brougham Hotel in Chelsea had top of the line video streaming for its guests. The anonymous unofficial champ had secured a pay-per-view deal with Las Vegas and at $49.95, he stood to make tons of cash, not to mention whatever he and the Sheik had worked out between them. Mase paid for the stream out of his own pocket, using a credit card.

He sat at the table in his room and savored the meal that was in front of him and the match that was about to start. If you were a gamer of any level, this was Ali-Frazier all over again. The wealthy Sheik with the high-level skill set against the man, or woman or child, who never lost. Besides, Mase wanted to watch their moves so he could learn from them and finally figure out how to win that bitch of a game. He kicked back on the recliner and turned off the lights in his room. The game was about to begin.

The anonymous champ was represented by a sad face emoji. Simple as it was, it presented a face that would be transferred to any opponent that would challenge him. It was child-like but definitely unnerving. The Sheik seemed to blow it off as the split screen close-up of him playing and the screen to his right.

The people of Zakar were also split, right down the middle. Some despised the Sheik for his shallow obsession, while the younger citizens cheered in the streets, for hours before, for victory by their young Royal. A huge screen was placed in the main square of the capital city for everyone to watch. The Sheik had purchased it himself. His confidence in his skills left no doubt in his supporters that he would end the match in victory for himself and his country.

A play-by-play announcer agitated the enthusiasm of the crowd in the square to a frenzy. They were chanting the Sheik's name and Allah's name all in the same phrases. It was all too much for the King. He told his aides to turn off the match. His revulsion at this frivolity was too much. As the room was darkened to allow the King his sleep, the King stiffened in his bed and passed away. The word was sent out to his citizens and although it was a sad moment, no one seemed to care.

They seemed to be more interested in The Match. As the Sheik stretched his hands and sat in his chair facing the screen, Tariq stood patiently behind him, in the shadows. Everyone in the room was told to leave except Tariq.

As The Match countdown clock neared zero, Tariq approached his brother slowly, emerging from the shadows, saying not a word, looking intense. The Match began as Tariq lunged at his brother, plunging a large knife into his neck, and then shooting him in the back of his head. He dropped both weapons on the floor, walked calmly out of the room, motioned to his men to take care of the body. The late King's order was fulfilled. Tariq was now the new King of Zakar.

***

The broadcast ended with a note from the streaming service that flashed in large red letters. *"Due to technical difficulties, our broadcast has been interrupted. We will attempt to reconnect our broadcast. Your credit card will not be charged for this broadcast unless we can bring it to our viewers. We apologize for any inconvenience."*

Mase wondered what had happened. He checked his phone to see if there were any reports on the match. Apparently, all communication with Zakar had ceased. There were speculative reports from CNN and other outlets, but nothing definitive. *Bummer*, he thought. *This was the heavyweight championship.*

He turned off the TV and lay down on the bed in the room. Many thoughts ran through his busy mind, mainly because of how close he had come to dying and that he felt guilty about Sherman Weiss' passing.

There were noises in the hallway, just outside his room that sounded nothing like people walking by, coming and going to their rooms. He even walked over to the door and put his ear against it, hoping to get a clearer sound. It was quiet.

As he pulled the covers over his worn out body and flipped onto his side, he heard more noise. At that moment, something crashed into his door. Someone was trying to enter his room. He grabbed for his gun, rushed over to the door, pulled the lock free and decided right then to open it. His gun was ready for whatever was out there.

He squatted down, ready to fire, when he noticed an older man, lying on the ground in a puddle of vomit. The smell of alcohol was all over him. Mase smiled and called security. Housekeepers came and cleaned the mess after the man was pulled away to sleep it off, somewhere. He'd never been so glad to find a drunk on his doorstep!

He lay in his bed wondering why he was sleeping in a hotel when his own place was less than five miles away. The idea was taking shape that instead of hiding from whoever took him prisoner, he should offer himself up. It would be the best way to uncover the mystery. But, as long as he was here in the room, he might as well just rest up.

***

It felt like reality as he walked around the huge black granite or marble interior of the castle. He knew it was his castle, and that Lara was in one room, but which one? He walked around the upper level and checked each room. The rooms were empty. He heard echoes from his boots stomping on the inlaid marble floor. Jewels and elegant figures in medieval costumes were painted into the marble.

He checked every room, nothing. She was Cornelia Summerlyn; he remembered now. He'd taken her from her father, but why? Why would he do something like that?

He walked down the expansive stairway that led to the great room. "Cornelia. Cornelia. Where are you Cornelia?" No answer came. He sat down on a large chair by the fireplace, sitting alone and staring at the flames. The flames were the same. They seemed to repeat themselves, same flames, same crackling sounds, same logs that never burned. He thought to himself that none of it was real, but yet there he was. But what was this place? He touched the chair to see if it was real and it was.

Chapter 51

The evening was uneventful for Mase. He went to work early. It was a grind it out and see what pops up kind of day for him and Vrain. They both knew they were getting closer, but the crucial next step proved to be elusive for both. When Mase walked in to Vrain's office, he saw the Captain sorting through papers scattered all over his desk and the surrounding floor.

"Has anyone put in a missing person's report on Deming?" Asked Vrain.

"I put one in this morning, myself. I figured a cop oughta be able to put one in."

"Good."

Vrain picked several documents out of the pile that got his attention. Then he swiped the rest on to the floor and sat down to study them.

"I asked cyber forensics what they thought about the programs and the subliminal messaging incorporated into the video games. One of those little geeks asked me if I had checked the power usage records of the homes in New Rochelle. He said that for sure, the number of servers needed to work with those programs was enormous, meaning that the power draw was significantly more than a normal home, and not by a little, much more! So, I've contacted Con Ed, but of course the manager is off today so they're getting alternative approval which might take a couple of hours."

"How about narrowing it down to extensive properties, mansions, like that?"

"If this guy uses that amount of power, he'd want to be hidden somewhere. Is that what you're driving at, like a wooded property with a lot of trees and shrubbery to camouflage a large operation?"

"My guess, Cap, this guy's too smart to use the power company. He's probably got fuel cells, solar arrays, banks of rechargeable batteries, that kind of stuff."

"What are you working on?" Asked Vrain.

"The way I figure it, that abandoned warehouse has got to be owned by a private party after they put that section of the naval yard into mothballs. I'm tracking land ownership in an around that area."

"How?"

"My options are limited for a quick turnaround. I can fill out a Request for Information, get consent from the owner, which is stupid because we don't know who the owner is, we can get a warrant, which is the way I think we should go."

"Nate Bernstein is the judge on duty right now. He's probably at home feeding his prized goldfish. I'll call him while you fill out the affidavit and tell him what happened and why you need those ownership records. He's a no bullshit kind of guy so don't try anything stupid, like lying. OK?"

"Me, lie?" Smirked Mase.

"You do whatever it takes, which is why I like you. But with Bernstein, he'll see right through it, believe me. I've tried, and it won't work."

***

The elegant brownstone in Brooklyn Heights that Judge Bernstein owned looked like it had been there forever. It was solid stonework from top to bottom. Mase knew he could never afford a place like that.

Nate Bernstein was a short, stocky man, small gray-flecked mustache, a Yankee's cap on his thinning gray hair, and a perpetual affable smile on his face. Mase had the feeling that the smile was the perfect front for deception, never revealing how insightful he was or how much he knew about the law. It's much easier to smile like that when you know as much as he knew.

"You're Mason?" Asked the Judge. "Dick Vrain called me about a warrant you want."

"Yes, sir. I have the affidavit here for you to look at."

Captain Vrain was right about the goldfish. They were everywhere. Mase had no idea there were so many sizes and colors. The judge put down the feeding and tank cleaning equipment to listen to Mase's story. He was particularly interested in Mase's personal involvement with the case, seeing the bandages that he still wore on his wrist and the general truthful tone of what he said.

After he read the affidavit, the Judge expedited the Warrant.

"You really feel as though this Miss Deming is in serious trouble, don't you?"

"Yes, sir. Whoever is doing all this is a cold-blooded murderer. I just hope we're not too late, that's all."

"Yes, I see."

"Thank you, sir."

"I'll make a call to the registrar of deeds to expedite the ownership search for you. They should have everything ready for you by the time you get there. Good luck, detective. I hope you're able to save the woman and catch the perpetrator."

"Thank you, sir. Oh, I like your fish. I might get a few goldfish for my place, one day..."

Mase raced away down the cobblestone streets. At least he had the means to get the information. Maybe it was a wild goose chase, and maybe it wasn't. But he needed something, anything. Things were moving too slowly. Something had to break quickly.

***

While Mase was getting the deed ownership documents, Vrain was making some headway. He'd checked all the satellite photos and the topographical maps of New Rochelle to narrow down his choices. Of course, his theory might be way off, but he had a good sixth sense about the direction he was going. This one felt right and he would continue going with it as long as he could.

He had narrowed down the properties that had the right configuration of extensive properties with a wooded area to hide the obvious, such as solar panels and storage structures, a large enough house to fit in banks of servers and possibly even large electrical storage areas.

There was no point in getting search warrants yet, since he hadn't narrowed his choices down to the few that looked promising. But, when he would finally get to those few homes, he would not only jump on the search warrant but the Con Ed data on electrical usage as well.

The data comparisons began. He knew it would be an all-nighter. Whether it would lead to anything promising was a whole other story. But, the search was like the good old days when he began as a detective and did the all-nighters all the time.

When Mase arrived with the deed ownership data, the look on his face was glum and Vrain knew he'd struck out.

"Did you get it?"

"Getting it wasn't the problem. The name on the deed is the problem."

Mase pulled the document out of the large manila envelope, unfolded it and laid it on the desk. "North Side Enterprises, LLC."

"North Side Enterprises, LLC. What the hell is that?"

Vrain lifted his right index finger and looked at his watch.

"Damn it, they just closed."

"What just closed?"

"The best way to identify the registered owners of an LLC is through the New York Department of State's Division of Corporations, State Records and Uniform Commercial Code, which I've used many times trying to find owners of corporations. They're open from 8:45 AM–4:30 PM. It's five O'clock right now. We'll have to wait until tomorrow."

"Where are you with your property search in New Rochelle? It has to be there." Asked Mase.

"I agree. Where am I at?" Replied the Captain.

Vrain looked at the two stacks of geographical information on his desk and looked at Mase. When he was on to something, he furrowed his brow and scratched the back of his head. But then he thought about something and his eyes opened wider than usual. And then he smiled.

"I could narrow my search if I found a property with a running stream of water, which I think exists out there. I swear I remember walking with my old girlfriend through some woods and seeing fast-moving streams."

"Streams that might cool a bank of servers?"

Vrain didn't answer. What he did was divide the stacks in half and gave Mase instructions on what to look for. Large wooded properties with large homes and running streams. There couldn't possibly be more than a few of those? But there were. Eleven properties matched Vrain's criteria.

"If I were a betting man, I would have predicted two, maybe three, but no way eleven. Jesus fucking..."

"Well, we've also got the SUV info. What if we put these eleven on the desk, checked the car info against it and see if there's a match. There's gotta be something."

#

The evening extended and the two men were exhausted trying to match information that didn't match.

"You know, it takes an act of congress around here to get power usage records from Con Ed, which I think is the key to this damn thing." Said Vrain.

"What about thermal imaging. We could send one of our helicopters out there and do thermal imagings of the entire area. There might be a good heat signature that would indicate something."

Vrain called for a copter and he and Mase went with them to New Rochelle. He didn't enjoy doing it because the brass were cheap and these little copter excursions were expensive and if something happened during the trip, his ass would be whipped.

It was a little windier than the pilot liked and he looked dubious that they could go. After a thirty-minute wait, the wind died down enough to make the trip.

The flight was uneventful and the Infra-Red thermal imaging camera in the helicopter's nose worked perfectly. They took enough pictures and made notes on the places that showed up as higher heat locations than the surrounding areas.

Chapter 52

In certain Arab countries, it is said that the sun shines at least three hundred and sixty-one days a year. And it is also said that their sons are the most important treasure to their kings. In Zakar, the sun shone so bright that it looked like polished silver in the sky.

Extra Palace guards were stationed in strategic locations, fighter jets buzzed the capital city, and helicopters flew in and out of the Royal Compound air space. A Royal Decree had been issued announcing the passing of the King and his eldest son, Sheik Habib. The middle son, Tariq, was appointed King and the youngest son, Ramar, was next in line for succession.

A news blackout was in effect in Zakar, but the world soon found out what had happened. The exact details wouldn't be released because of the sensitive nature of Middle East tensions, but it was obvious to their inner circle that Sheik Habib's obsession could not be tolerated any longer.

The one billion dollar bet was forfeited because of the preset rules agreed upon by the two competitors. Jonah Christian was now instantly and fabulously wealthy beyond his wildest dreams.

In the murky universe of cyber currency, money appears and disappears as if it never existed. It is washed, cleansed, rewashed and converted instantaneously into an unlimited number of anonymous accounts throughout the world. It has become the universal currency of greed.

But, for Jonah Christian, the attainment of wealth was secondary to winning the match. His thoughts were focused on the win, and it didn't happen. His mind had created an unbeatable system, and it was his brainchild. He wanted to show the world that he couldn't be beaten, even though he was cheating his way to invincibility. Artificial Intelligence would have gotten him the win and somewhere along the line he had convinced himself that it was his skill that would give him the victory.

The path to victory can go in many different directions. Jonah created the program that was unbeatable and undetectable. Since he created it, the victory would be real, as real as any video game could be. To this, if you desire to live in a dream world, your new reality becomes a fact.

Jonah had assimilated his winnings and washed away his disappointment with champagne. In his heart, he knew he could beat the Sheik without the help of Artificial Intelligence. In his mind, he couldn't accept the concept of loss. It simply wasn't permitted to exist. This is the new world order. Make yourself the master of your own existence and allow no one to enter it unless they follow every one of your rules.

He was satisfied. But now it was his other passion, Cornelia Summerlyn, in his world, living under his roof, subject to his rules, forever.

***

Vrain and Mase were making some headway, but not enough. They both heard the clock ticking, and it pushed them into rushing their investigation. Each small clue needed pruning and watering like a seedling in a hothouse.

Mase slammed his pencil down hard on Vrain's desk. He leaned back in his chair and rubbed the top of his head briskly. Maybe it would generate some new idea that would pop another idea which would give him the answer.

"She's in danger, and we're sitting here like two idiots."

"We're getting closer than you think." Said Vrain.

"Everything is wait for this, keep busy while we wait for that. Tomorrow we'll get this approved. Wait, wait, and wait. That's all we do and each time we do it, we're still sitting here wasting our time."

"OK, let's say whoever this is, he's got Lara Deming. Which I agree. He probably does. But it's obvious that he wants her for himself, with no competition. He's apparently eliminated what he thinks is the competition. With one exception."

"Who would that be?"

"Isn't it obvious? It's you, Vic."

Mase stood up and hit himself in his forehead.

"Of course! I'm in his video game and I've got Lara, I mean Cornelia Summerlyn. How stupid can one cop be?"

"But the game is the key, and it's not the key. I think it's more than that."

"OK Cap, now you've lost me."

"Think about it, Vic. He's got everything he wants, right? Now, think about this. I think she's safe and sound and probably in the lap of luxury and comfort, befitting a princess, right. So, my guess is that she's in no immediate danger, which buys us some time."

"You sound like that's a guarantee. We can't make that assumption, can we?"

"No, we can't sit on our asses. That's for sure. But we can do this the right way, Vic."

"Meaning, your way, right?"

"Exactly."

"The slow way."

"No, the right way."

Mase walked out of the office and went for a walk around the block, clearing out the jumbled thoughts that had converted themselves into cobwebs. This wasn't working. Everything Vrain was doing was like walking in concrete. Each step was slower than the one before and soon, soon, they'd be stuck in it.

***

An idea was forming in his mind as he rounded the corner back to the office. *If the killer wanted him dead, it would have been easy. Why didn't he just finish him, right there, in the warehouse? The only logical answer had to be that he wanted him alive. Alive! But why? What reason could there be?*

The large swinging glass door to the building reflected a dark sedan near the corner. There was a hooded man in it, looking down. It was a round dark face, but the evening muted any details. He avoided glancing at him, but pinned that note to his mind. He wanted some feedback from Vrain on his new idea.

When he entered the Captain's office, Vrain was leaning back in his chair with his eyes closed and his head facing the ceiling. He was motionless and silent, no movement, no sound, not a flicker of anything. First, he thought the Captain was dead, but as he approached him from the side, Vrain was startled and woke up in a flash.

"Why don't you go home to Virginia and get some sleep. You need it."

After a few breaths, the Captain's eyes regained their focus.

"I'm fine. How about you? Want some coffee?"

"Sure, I'll make it. The stuff in your pot looks like it's been there a while. Besides, we need a new look at what we were bouncing around. They're all good ideas...but..."

"They'll take too long, and I agree."

Mase was definitely surprised at his Captain's change of mind. Now was the time to go at it straight on. There might be risks, and whatever they decided had to be now and decisive or Lara might not make it.

The coffee maker beeped a few times and Mase brought the Captain's his coffee the way he liked it, black with nothing in it. He fixed his own with cream and sugar.

"I don't know how you drink that shit."

"I like to taste the damn coffee, not drown it with bullshit."

Mase tried to contain his excitement. His idea was taking shape in his mind and to him anyway, it made sense. They settled in and Vrain could see anticipation all over Mase's face.

"Go ahead. Spill it. What's on your mind?"

"Can you get a wire for me? I mean like in the next ten minutes."

"I don't like it already, but go on."

"We already know the general area, right?"

"So?"

"They're out there following me, right now. Let me go back to my apartment, wait for them to show, or maybe they're even in the apartment already, and let them take me. They don't want me dead, we already know that. Let them take me, and even if they don't take me to the place where Lara is, they'll take me there eventually."

"And if we have enough unmarked vehicles nearby, we could follow them. Is that what you're trying to say?"

"Pretty much."

"Can't do it. If anything goes wrong along the way, you're a dead man, probably, and so is Lara Deming. I can't afford it. Too much risk. No. No way."

"When did you start taking the safe way? I distinctly remember you taking risk after risk and most of the time they paid off. What happened Cap?"

Vrain didn't respond. He sat there with his hands together in front of his mouth, tapping his lips and thinking. He was shaking his head almost imperceptibly. He was waiting for whatever he was thinking to clear out of his brain before he answered Mase. The long breath he took through his nose seemed to last forever.

"If, and I'm saying if, if I approve this, then what? I mean, we have no idea what we're getting into, what you're getting into, do we? Whoever this is, he's a complete whack job. A whack job without a conscience and without a sane thought in his brain. He's way out there, Vic. So far out there that we couldn't even predict what he's going to do. I can't take the risk of losing two, rather than one, and, believe me, Vic, that's what it boils down to."

"No choice, Cap. That's what it comes down to. True, we don't know what this guy's really up to, but he's holding the cards and dealing. I've got to get myself in the game or we're out, and so is Lara. You know it and I know it."

Vrain reached for his phone and ordered a wire.

Chapter 53

In order to make it look routine, Mase was supposed to stall for a while before heading back to his apartment, give Vrain enough time to position his units in the best strategic locations around his apartment and in New Rochelle. Then, and only then, was Mase supposed to enter his apartment and start playing video games. By the time the killer found out that Mase was home, Vrain would be ready to track him using the wire and GPS device on one of the buttons of his jacket.

Unfortunately, once again Mase lost his patience and went into a few bars to stall. After a beer or two, he lost it, and drank three scotch and sodas in a row. Vrain had a bad feeling when the wire on Mase picked up nothing but bar noise and glasses clinking and wild laughing. The tracking device showed him stationary, no direction home.

Vrain had no choice. He let Mase do his thing, hoping against hope that he was just marking time and not really drinking. Eventually, he'd get home and they could watch for visitors.

It didn't take him long. Mase once again got into it with a surly bouncer at his neighborhood watering hole and got tossed out into the rain-swept street. The rain had started hours before and the sidewalk in front of the bar now reflected the face of the drunk. He opened his eyes and saw himself staring into his own eyes, rain pouring down, and people walking by in wide arcs to avoid the guy who now looked like an ordinary vagrant.

What no one knew was that he lost his jacket in the fight along with the wire and the tracking device. The bartender threw it under the bar, figuring Mase would return soon enough to retrieve it at which time the bartender could give him a good piece of his mind.

***

Vrain tracked the tracking device an hour later at the very bar Mase lost it in. When Vrain flashed his badge at the bartender, the story was retold and the jacket was handed over to the Captain, reluctantly.

They went to Mase's apartment, but he wasn't home. They scoured the area bars and nothing. He'd simply vanished. Vrain wondered if he'd been snatched already. His only choice was to go back to square one, his original plan, the one that took forever. He called off the four unmarked vehicles that were supposed to bracket New Rochelle without being noticed. He never contacted the New Rochelle Police Department which went against everything he stood for, and he was glad that he called them back. But not glad enough because now two innocent people were probably in grave danger and he had no clue where they were.

***

When Vrain arrived back at Headquarters, he dove into his investigation, making heated calls to everyone involved, lighting fires under lazy bureaucrats sitting on their asses, and acting like the usual pain in the ass he always was. He had to do something. Mase was right when he said they were taking too long and Lara Deming's life was in danger. But Vrain had one fact on his side. The jerk who was doing all this wanted Mase, and that bought him a little time.

Mase found himself in a $10 a night flophouse. Another drunk had found him in an alley on Rivington Street and helped him up and walked with him to a place used by any alcoholic with ten bucks. After the fake do-gooder took everything he had, he paid the ten dollars and took the detective to his bed where he left him to sleep it off.

***

Vrain was still in his office at 6 am. Mase woke up in his rent-a-bed residence and felt like a pile of steaming shit sitting in a sewer. It took him a while to remember what had happened, but when he did, he realized what his actions had done. He'd let down his Captain and all the others who were helping him and he'd let down Lara. He found a coffee place with a filthy counter and an even dirtier cook playing with the last remnant of a cigar that looked well-chewed. Mase looked up from his coffee and then at the cook. He had no money in his pocket to pay for the coffee, so he ignored the cook's demand for payment and kept walking. After two weak demands for the twenty-five cents, the cook gave up and continued playing with his cigar stub. Mase shuffled his way along in the general direction of his apartment.

The walk home was a long one, but walking it off seemed like the best way to handle himself. His stupidity was clearing in his mind and he hated himself for being that weak that he lost control. Once again, everything he cared about was trashed, and he couldn't do a damn thing about it.

He wobbled a bit as he walked, holding on to lamp posts and parked car bumpers along the way. A car crash took place right in front of him as he crossed Second Avenue. He couldn't have cared less about it, but he knew he should have tried to help. But everyone seemed fine in both cars and he knew getting home was what he had to do.

The long walk home eventually cleared his mind. It was two blocks ahead, which felt like walking to Jersey on one leg. He was beat, in more ways than one. His head was clear, but his body was wasted and filthy.

When he felt in his pockets for his keys, he realized that not only had the Good Samaritan taken all his money, but everything else, including his car keys, which had his apartment key attached. Mrs. Finnegan, the apartment manager, was his only hope. Unfortunately, when he arrived at his building, she wasn't at home. So now he was stuck. He looked like shit and smelled like a bum.

He went to his apartment and saw a sliver of light came through the bottom of the door. He slowly turned the doorknob to see if it was open. It was unlocked! At last, something good had happened. He was happy, until he opened the door and saw what looked like a dead body in the middle of his living room. He looked around to see if anyone else was there and bent down to see if it was a corpse.

As he felt for the carotid artery, he kept looking around, turned the body over to see who it was and sure enough he recognized the Good Samaritan who had stolen his money and given him a place to sleep it off. Now, what was he going to do?

As he stood up, something came down on the back of his head with enough force to send him on a one-way trip to the Big Bang. He thought he heard words, muffled, two different voices talking, but it made no sense to him. Waves of pain and dizziness took turns with his head.

He looked up from the floor and glimpsed two men and one of their big shoes kicking him on the side of his head and then, nothing...

The men lifted the wayward detective, placing themselves on either side of him and putting their arms around his waist. It was bright daylight outside. They walked with their 'drunk friend' as they mentioned to a couple of nosey neighbors to help him 'walk it off', laughing as they did it with the two bobble head neighbors pointing at Mase like they knew this was what he got for drinking so much.

As they walked out onto the sidewalk, they looked around, quickly ushered their catch into their large SUV, and sped away as quickly as they could. Not five minutes later, Captain Vrain and two patrol officers pulled up to the apartment building. They were still searching for Mase and figured he'd be home by then.

He was not there, of course, and Vrain flicked his wrist at the other two and told them to continue searching.

***

Lara Deming was fully awake now. Her head had cleared and she wondered why she was dressed in a full-length lace dress, probably Italian and very expensive, with a heavy diamond necklace and earrings. A long dressing mirror with gold braided edging stood up near the window. She walked over to it and was baffled by what she saw. It was her, but it wasn't her.

The person she saw in the mirror looked just like the Princess in the Fantasy Dream she'd been having. Cornelia Summerlyn. The entire Fantasy rushed back into her mind: The Black Knight, Creighton LaVelle, and her father, Lord Summerlyn.

She looked around the room, pulled the curtain away from the window and realized there was nothing on the other side of it. She tapped on the window with the knuckle of her left hand covered in rings of rubies and diamonds. It looked like a window, but it wasn't.

As she turned around, the large metal door to the room opened. An older, frail looking woman dressed as a servant came in with her head bowed and holding a tray with food.

"Good evening Princess. I've brought you your evening meal, as you requested."

"I didn't request a meal. What is this?"

The woman looked as though she didn't hear a word Lara said. Left the tray on the gilded table in the center of the room and exited as quickly as she had entered.

Chapter 54

Vrain flicked his thumb at the two patrolmen that had remained with him, and after a couple of shoulder slams into Mase's apartment door, they popped it open. Vrain stepped in first and spread both arms out wide.

"Don't touch anything. You hear me?" Said the cautious captain. "Just wait. Tolan, use your elbow to turn on the light switch by the door."

When the light came on, Vrain saw the body of the Samaritan. He tilted his hat back on his head and rubbed the back of his neck. He toed the body to make sure he was as dead as he looked. And he was.

"Call the lab boys and the M.E., right now."

The dead guy was maybe thirty, about five feet ten, dressed like a bum. He'd been taken from behind and by the look of his Adam's apple, his air was cut off by a very strong person. The look of surprise on his face was the first sign that whoever did it was a pro. That was all he knew at that moment.

Vrain carefully walked around the apartment with his gun drawn just in case the pro was still around, but he doubted it. And he was right. The apartment was as empty. He knew Mase would never do something like this, let alone do it in his own place, run away and leave the body.

As with the rest of this case, every dot to connect remained unconnected.

"Time for some legwork, boys. You know what to do. I'll stay here and wait for the lab boys and M.E."

Vrain looked at his watch more than once. Then he went to work, walking carefully through each room, noticing every detail. He took out his little notebook that he rarely used and wrote small notes.

He was stuck there and he knew damn well he should be out there looking for two people that he was responsible for. The way the scene looked, without question, the suspect would be Vic Mason, especially since he'd probably been on a bender and lost it, at least that's what the Chief would say, covering himself and his department's reputation no matter who had to take the fall.

It didn't look good at all. There were no casings that he could see. Probably no prints, since whoever did it were very good. He was glad that his men were doing the legwork so he could be alone with his thoughts. And, no matter what he thought, it still led back to why.

#

Two hours and a pack of cigarettes later, the lab boys had finished, the ME gift-wrapped the body and the scene was taped off and ready for Vrain to really check it out. He had the contents of the dead man's pockets on Vic's kitchen table. A set of keys, thirty-seven dollars and fifty-three cents in cash, Vic's wallet and two New York Lottery tickets. He looked at the keys and walked to the apartment door. The key opened the lock. No question, they were Vic's keys.

The ride back to headquarters was filled with questions for the men who did the legwork. Apparently, two men were seen walking out with Vic. He looked drunk when a neighbor saw them leave. Both men held him upright and told the neighbor they were helping him walk it off, which, knowing Vic, the neighbor wouldn't give it another thought. The descriptions of the men were vague enough to be worthless, but just the fact it fit the Captain's initial theory was enough.

The theory was: The dead guy was in Mase's apartment, taking whatever looked like he could sell. Two men were in the apartment, probably waiting for Mase, and snuffed the burglar. Mase came back to the apartment and, probably still wasted, got toasted by the two big guys. No way he would have been taken by those two guys if he'd been the good Vic.

The bad news was, they got his boy. The good news was, he was still vertical. Now it was time to finish the work they'd started and hopefully find his boy in one piece and the girl.

He sat at his desk for a few minutes, sifting through the paperwork, moving piles and thinking, reshuffling piles of paper, reshuffling again. There had to be a better way. Wait a minute! Wait just a minute...what if...?

***

The large digital map of New Rochelle glared on the large monitor in the conference room of headquarters. Vrain brought all his piles of papers and laid them on the table. But they weren't stacks of papers anymore. He was simulating the map in front of him on the large monitor.

The IT department had pinpointed various electrical power transformers in New Rochelle. He remembered a case, years before, when an illegal sports betting operation had been ID'd when the power went out and everyone scrambled out of the building looking for another location to watch the games. They'd been caught on camera and they were able to flip the operation and catch the operators.

His brain was clicking, which it always did when things were at their worst and everything seemed hopeless!

***

When Mase woke up, all he could feel was a headset around his head, and he thought his arms and legs were tied tightly together. And he was losing the sensation of feeling anything in them now.

The room was warm and the air had an odor of roses and lavender. The headset came on and the video began. A soothing voice came on with split second images repeatedly passing by too quickly to recognize. Then, after a pause, he was back in Anthonia, walking around his castle, looking in rooms and wondering where Cornelia Summerlyn was.

He found her. She was on the luxurious bed, covered in damask and silk weavings, bouquets of flowers covered her bed; roses, lavender, poppies. She didn't appear to be worried, but she looked unhappy. Sadness drooped her facial expression. The scene changed instantly and what sounded like opera came through to his ears. Creighton LaVelle was in grave danger as the swamp of fire was rising up. As he cut himself climbing one of the large thorn trees, a gigantic winged dragon swooped down and plucked him from the tree.

The winged dragon was immense, probably sixty feet of wingspan and a large mouth that spewed fire and heat as he moved his wings in a mechanical, almost silent flight. He turned his head and long neck to see if his passenger, Creighton LaVelle and his two white horses were OK.

The Swamp of Fire stretched out in front of them as far as he could see. The Dragon flew effortlessly, higher and higher into the sky, occasionally looking down into the smoking, boiling quagmire below. Creighton LaVelle and his two horses stood atop the dragon, looking around in amazement and wonder. The opera music kept playing as if urging them onward. It appeared nothing could stop them.

The horizon changed colors, and far into the distance the swamp appeared to be changing into an ocean or a large lake. The dragon picked up the pace of his flying and was edging down slightly. A large cloud appeared in front of them, as if out of nowhere. It was immense and red.

Nestled in the cloud was a tall and stately stone castle of gigantic proportions. It towered into the sky and seemed to float weightlessly and without moving. It looked like an unreal vision, but it was what Lord Summerlyn had told him. It was the Kingdom of Anthonia, there, right in front of him.

The Dragon seemed to smile now and spoke to Creighton.

"I will place you at the gate below. You can see it there, at the base of the castle. Once I open the gate, there will be three staircases that circle the castle that you must climb, each one having a doorway and a key. The keys are hidden, but you will find them, you must find them or the Princess will die at the hands of The Black Knight."

Creighton had the location of each key written on the instructions given to him by Lord Summerlyn. When Lord Summerlyn had been a leader of the Royal Knights in his youth, he'd stormed this palace once before and killed The Black Knights' father, King Philip of Anthonia. The kidnapping of Cornelia Summerlyn was revenge for the death of his father, and the Black Knight was not to be denied.

The Dragon stretched out one of his large wings and Creighton LaVelle with his two horses walked swiftly down the wing and toward the gate. He bid the Dragon farewell and watched the winged giant as he flew higher and higher, breathing fire out in front of him and disappeared without a trace. Creighton LaVelle knew what he had to do and also knew that the Black Knight would do everything in his power to stop him.

Chapter 55

The State funeral for the dead King was filled with the usual pomp and circumstance. The King was beloved by his people and although he'd been ill for the past year, he still fulfilled his kingly duties as prescribed by the law of the land. The new King of Zakar, Tariq, assumed his role flawlessly.

There were questions asked, but no more than is usually asked when intrigue at the top handles its own problems. When Sheik Habib lost his mind, he took his own life after he thought he was going to lose his match.

There are courts in Zakar, but not for the royalty of the country. They Royals were truly above the law. In their own words, The King is The Law.

There was little doubt that King Tariq was now in full charge of his government, the oil industry of Zakar, and the future succession of rulers after him. But, there was one bit of business that still needed to be resolved. The small matter of the one billion dollar bet. According to the press release, the government of Zakar would seek damages from various parties involved in the match's marketing and the anonymous player who won it, although there were doubts. The full weight of the Kingdom's legal team, backed by seemingly endless capital, would spare no expense in recovering the lost funds.

According to the official government Press Release; "It isn't the amount of the money that was wagered illegally, it is the 'pride in our country as a sovereign nation that is our primary motivation in the recovery of the funds."

But, the actual story was much stronger than the phony press release. A secret group of agents was formed within the small but effective Zakar Special Forces team to find the anonymous player, extract the lost funds from him, murder him and leave no trace.

***

A meeting of low level State Department officials in Washington, and the Zakarian ambassador was intended as the official US response to the death of the King and the suicide of his son. It was formal, short and documented with official State Department media releases and photos. Everyone in the photos looked and acted solemn and slightly concerned.

Secretly, the ambassador met with one of the Under Secretary of States in a closed meeting attended only by their top aides. In the meeting, because of recent events in other countries, the Under Secretary expressed deep concern that there would be bloodshed because of the recent unexpected events.

Assurances were given that no such violence would take place because all government activities were now functioning normally and well within the rule of law in the country. Everyone shook hands, everyone smiled, and no one believed a word of it. The ambassador knew he was being shadowed by the US Government, so every step he took was intended to show his strict adherence to US Law and International standards of diplomacy. His plush residence in New York City was six city blocks away from the United Nations building.

He was well known for the lavish parties he hosted and the connections he managed with diplomats from many other countries. He knew for a fact that there were listening devices throughout his apartment building and in his own apartment. The language he used was coded and the men he worked with, the secret Special Forces team. Their plan was in place and the actors were all set. No more than two more weeks of internal investigation into the anonymous player's identity would be needed and they would execute the plan.

***

If you have enough money, you can buy whatever you want. With Zakar, they had access to some of the world's top computer programmers and analysts. Their job was to find that player. The investigation took place in three different locations; Moscow, Tehran, and London. Each location was given separate tasks of backtracking everything that originated from the player, no matter how obscure or innocent. None of the locations knew what the other ones were doing, in case the player got wind of it.

What none of them knew was that they didn't have two weeks. Events were about to take place that no amount of money or technical expertise could have bought or expected.

***

Vrain was used to living under pressure, especially with the idiots upstairs always panicking and worrying about their jobs. "Your ass is on the line on this one", or "You might as well retire now before you're fired on that one", or many other finger pointing episodes that were far too numerous to remember. It came with the job and he often wondered why he hadn't remained a detective and not taken this job.

College tuition for two teenagers and a mortgage that he never should have been sucked into, that's why.

He glanced quickly up at the monitor in the large conference room and noticed one particular stack of papers on the large wooden table. It was the listing of large-sized estates near wooded areas in New Rochelle. There were only three of them! All he had to do was get three separate unmarked vehicles and place them close but out of sight of the people in those homes! He was guessing of course, educated guessing at that, but guessing nevertheless. One of those had to be the place!

He called for three unmarked vehicles to get ready and called in his three best men, ones with enough experience to handle any unforeseen problems and who would not panic or make it obvious what they were doing. Three men walked into the conference room. Joe Summers, thin, lanky, pencil mustache, large hooked nose. Trevor Bottoms, the longest tenured detective on the squad, was calm, tall, broad shouldered, and funny; always cracking jokes no matter how bad things were. And Alston Meers, college educated, piercing blue eyes, stocky, worked out at the gym all the time and had a body builder physique. He was a guy you wanted around when things went rough.

None of them knew what was going on as they entered the conference room.

"Have a seat gentlemen," Said Vrain.

"What's this all about Cap? I was just about to take my after dinner siesta when ..."

"No jokes today, Trevor. Someone's taken Mase. We're not exactly certain why, or who, or where, but I've got some ideas and I want you guys to handle it. Are you good with that?"

The three officers nodded slowly but with intense interest. To a man, they all liked Vic Mason, even with his problems, and had all worked closely with him and he'd always had their backs. They had no problem returning the favors. The captain smiled when the men's facial expressions looked not only interested, but fully engaged.

"If I sound a little unsure of where I am with this thing, it's because I am. But, as you all know, sometimes these cases look like blind alleys and dead ends, but they really aren't. They're just complex problems with simple answers."

"What's with the map of New Rochelle up on the screen?" Asked Bottoms.

"There's someone in New Rochelle that to all the world looks wealthy, is wealthy, but is acting strange. From what I can determine, one of these estates is where Mase is, where a Behavioral Therapist name Lara Deming is, and where a serial killer disguised as a computer genius lives with way too much money at his disposal."

Vrain quickly laid out the clues that had piled up and how none of it seemed to make much sense, but that it all pointed to New Rochelle, a nice, well-mannered, and fairly nice place to live community. Vrain also pointed to the one stack of papers that gave him his idea. Each of the men would be assigned one of three mansions in three different locations. Each fit the profile of what Vrain was looking for but each one had to be handled carefully. Lives were at stake, and they had no idea who the killer was or what else he was planning.

Vrain handed each one a location.

"Now, please understand, I could be totally wrong on this, but my gut tells me I'm headed in the right direction. The locations I've chosen may or may not be the place we're looking for, but I believe one of them is. Questions, so far?"

No one was ready to speak up, but a look on Bottom's face caught Vrain's attention.

"Trevor? Speak up."

"Well, Cap, why don't each of us knock on their doors, tell them we're looking for an escaped prisoner in the area and that we were wondering if they'd seen anything suspicious? That would at least give us a chance to look inside and maybe we could see something, anything that would be a lead for us, since we're still in the dark."

"I like that idea, but I want to hold on it until we get a better handle on what we find when we get there. I'm going with you, in my car, and park myself somewhere in the middle of your locations. We may just do that, Trevor, but let's wait and see what we've got. Let's go, boys!"

Chapter 56

The small, frail woman attending Lara in her room would not or could not speak and kept her head lowered as she did her work in straightening up the room, bringing in and taking away food and dishes and whatever else was needed to make sure the Princess was perfectly taken care of. No amount of coaxing by Lara could induce a word out of the woman.

Lara noted that the woman's hands looked like they'd not seen much hard work. She noted a large diamond ring on the woman's hand.

The exact number of days that Lara had been imprisoned in that room was lost in her mind somewhere between her capture and her kidnapping both in the game and in reality. She wasn't exactly sure where she was or if she was there. All of the scenes blended seamlessly and without borders. Was this small woman real, or was she part of the game? Lara had realized that this was all a game, at some point, but not why it was a game or how it was a game. All she knew was that it was horrible.

The therapist in her began piecing together the intricate way in which her new life was woven together. The idea was to make her doubt her own sanity, which Lara had secretly done many times after the death of her husband.

There was a voice, however. It would come through the speakers that were placed at the four corners of the ceiling, a smooth baritone voice, sounding confident, self-assured and forceful. She dreaded hearing that voice because it always indicated the fantasy part of this drama. She vaguely remembered hearing it before this situation took over her life.

Lara also noticed that when the voice came on, the attendant would flinch a bit upon hearing it. It was just for a split second, but she definitely flinched, and then she would go about her business.

More than likely, there were other devices in the room to watch her every move and monitor any little deviation in the desired behavior. She knew she was being kept alive as long as she went along with her captor and that eventually they would meet.

She planned to take a deep dive into her role as Cornelia Summerlyn and push the characterization to its limit. No point in dragging this thing out, but she knew her acting ability would eventually be what saved her. Her Barnard College days in the Theater and Drama Department were brought back to life. She'd played Ophelia and Desdemona and her skills were noted by her favorite Professor, Dr. Bernstein, in the program. She remembered him telling her, *Lara, your acting skills are significant, but only if you delve into your Character's true psychological motivation will they come alive. Then and only then will you become your Character.*

Funny that she would remember that right then. But her audience now was probably much more discerning than the hormone drenched university students that came to her previous performances. It was time to take Dr. Bernstein's advice, and delve into the character of Cornelia Summerlyn, and along the way, into her captor's psyche.

She reasoned that someone must known she was missing and that a search was under way for her by now. In order for her to buy time, she had to be as believable in her role as possible. Everything she would now say and do would be to delay the inevitable, whatever that was, and to reverse the mind control now taking place by her captor.

She'd decided that every time the voice would come through the speakers, she would try to engage the person on the other end of it, and see if she could get indicators, any indicators, of what this person was thinking. Lara figured out that the VR Headset was the key to his mind control efforts, but, as bad as that was, it never caused her any physical pain.

There was no point in trying to combat her opponent on his own turf, which he obviously was a master of, but switch it over to her own turf, psychological analysis and deep understanding of the other person's problem. Then and only then could she win the contest.

Whoever this person was, he or she was brilliant, incisive, and not prone to making mistakes. Every move she would make had to be well-planned and aimed at the eventual goal, freedom!

***

Two levels below ground, Mase was being held in a room that looked like a medieval prison. Mase looked around and tested everything for strength and resistance to escape. It was solid everywhere. He was free to walk around and sit on a stone bench or lay down on a basic bed with a straw mattress.

A speaker that was built into the ceiling was the only communication tool used. From time to time, instructions were given. There was a hole in the ground for toilet use and that was it. The barred window high above was fake. It glowed different colors depending on the time of day. It was a solid wall with lights. It was too high for him to even look through, so he discounted its future use.

Food was occasionally pushed through the bottom of the heavy stone door, through an opening wide enough for a tray. It was closed and locked immediately after the food came through. Alcohol in various forms always came through as well, beer, wine, whiskey was always available.

Sound would come through the speaker. Sometimes, loud music, other times opera or punk rock or rap. The volume would vary, enough to irritate even the most avid music enthusiast. Mase knew exactly what was happening. But, it was going to get worse, and he knew it. The alcohol was put there as a temptation and he was craving it as bad as he ever did. He'd stacked up the unused bottles in the corner near the bed. A deep, mellifluous voice came over the loud speaker.

"Good evening Mr. Mason. I hope you are finding your accommodations satisfactory. We don't always have such distinguished guests as you."

Mase waited as long as he could.

"Cat got your tongue, Mr. Mason?"

"Why don't you get to the point?"

"The point? I'm afraid I don't understand." Said Jonah Christian.

Mase didn't respond.

"I'm feeling a little, shall we say, resistance, on your part. And honestly, I completely understand. Sometimes, when we find ourselves in a strange and different place that we don't appreciate, we often feel threatened. But I assure you, Mr. Mason, there's no need for you to feel threatened. In fact, you are most welcome here and let me assure you that your good friend, Lara, is also welcome here."

Mase stood up and screamed at the speaker.

"If you as much as touch Lara, I will destroy you and everything here. Do you understand me?"

"Well, I see I've gained your undivided attention, Mr. Mason. That is excellent. Now, let us move to the principal subject of this conversation. The Princess Cornelia Summerlyn is your captive. Since you are The Black Knight and you have certain powers that must be overcome by me, Creighton LaVelle, I need your full cooperation. Do you understand me, Mr. Mason?"

"That you're insane? I absolutely understand."

A crackling, high-pitched tone came through the speaker. The intensity and pain that entered Mase's head was unbearable, even when he put his hands over his ears. He dropped to the floor and pleaded for it to stop.

The sound stopped and the voice came on again.

"Mr. Mason. My sanity is not the issue here, is it?"

Mase lay flat on the floor, barely recovering from the horrific sound that made his head feel like someone was stabbing his head with steel needles. He reluctantly answered.

"Yes. Yes. You're right..."

"Very well. I see we agree. Good. I'm going to give you a thirty-minute rest period, after which my assistant, Mr. Stanley Burnett, will bring to you a headset that you will place on your head. The rest, as they say, will be between you and fate. But remember one thing Mr. Mason. Your life, Mr. Mason, depends on your cooperation. Without your full cooperation in the last level of this game, your life will end and Miss Deming's fate, shall we say, will be in my hands. Now, enjoy your rest, Mr. Mason. I want your complete involvement in this drama. This is not life imitating art. This is life!"

The voice was cut off and soothing music came through the speakers. Mase got the message, stared at the bottles next to his bed, and grabbed one. He looked at it, held it up to the light, and smelled the top of it. The smell was intoxicating. Mase threw it and it crashed into the wall next to his bed. He lay down on the bed, covered his eyes with his arm, and thought long and hard about what he needed to do to get out of this mess.

Chapter 57

Vrain was growing impatient at Headquarters. Just as he was about to leave his men, he received a call from his wife saying that their son had to be taken to the hospital. From the symptoms he showed, it looked like his appendix, but they weren't sure, yet. She had called 911 because the teen was writhing in pain and she couldn't take any chances.

He told the three units to wait for his return, because he had to check on his son before they left. The decision wasn't a decision. His family came first no matter what. He didn't think Mase or Miss Deming was in immediate danger, but his son was. He turned on his siren as he sped to Mt. Sinai hospital's ER.

He left his vehicle near the ER entrance and raced into the ER waiting area where he met his wife, Sara. They'd been happily married for twenty-two years. She was petite, had curly blond hair and no nonsense steel-blue eyes that never lost their intensity and focus. She wasn't a person who wanted sympathy or empathy; she wanted results. The respect Richard Vrain had for her was nothing short of immense. She was his rock and their family's center of gravity!

He tried his best to act composed as he approached her. She was sitting in one of those indestructible plastic waiting room chairs.

"How's he doing?" Asked Vrain.

"Emergency surgery. It didn't burst, thank God, but it was about to."

"How much pain is he in?"

"Too much." She put her hand up to her mouth.

Vrain saw her eyes tearing up, which they never did even in their worst moments, so he knew this was bad. He had no idea how he was going to tell her he couldn't stay very long because Mase was in danger as well. He waited, but it was killing him.

He moved closer to Sara and put his arm around her as gently as he could. She wasn't one for sentimentality and would tighten up when he would try to give her a hug, but that was just her personality, not her true feelings. She was just one of those people. She had a heart of gold inside a refrigerator of a soul.

When she rested her head on his shoulder for a few seconds, he knew how bad it was. He couldn't remember the last time she had done that, if ever. It felt good, even though he knew it was temporary until she recovered from her momentary need of comforting.

"Can I talk to a nurse or someone?"

Sara pointed at the reception area where a large receptionist, almost too large for her desk, was texting or playing or wasting time on her cell phone. It was obvious that she didn't want to be there, but, as long as she was she might as well entertain herself. She had a black nose ring, three studs around her lips that had small chains connected to her little diamond earrings.

Vrain tried to be courteous.. She knew he was standing there, but she continued on with her phone distraction.

She jerked her body back and forth and occasionally pursed her large lips as if she was involved in a desperate game of survival, cell phone survival; digital meanderings of meaningless movement. She lost whatever she was playing and rolled her small round head back on her neck and closed her eyes in defeat. When she opened her eyes, she saw an obviously angry Richard Vrain.

"My son, Connor, is in emergency surgery. I'd like to know what's happening. I just arrived."

His angry gaze was met with an equally angry 'so what' look from the large receptionist.

"Name?"

"Connor Vrain."

"No, your name. I have to be sure you're a relative. You know, patient privacy and all that."

Vrain pulled his badge from inside his jacket and flipped it open. She looked at it, reached for it to look at it closer, but he pulled it back. He held it up so she could read it at which point he wondered if she could read.

"It's too far for me to read. I left my glasses home today."

Sara watched the drama play out from her chair and immediately knew that the receptionist didn't stand a chance. She shook her head slowly and smiled. She nodded when her husband opened the door to the ER examination rooms and walked in. The receptionist actually stood up and tried to stop the pissed off the NYPD Captain. He brushed her aside. She almost fell down but caught herself and landed perfectly in her swivel chair, pushing the seat down as far as it would go and hitting the bottom with a hard stop.

Vrain found a doctor in the back, a young Middle Eastern or Indian looking young man who helped him immediately and with no problem. The receptionist twisted her face into a tight purse and went right back to her cell phone like a good girl.

Sara watched it all with bemused interest. It took her mind off Connor for just a few seconds. She could see her husband and the doctor discussing Connor's condition and what was happening. She couldn't read the faces from so far away, but the amount of head-nodding was encouraging enough to put her in a less worried mode.

As the doctor touched the top of Dick's shoulder, the police captain stopped and listened to the last words of the doctor, and he nodded slowly. He walked back towards the waiting area, passing the good girl with the cell phone addiction, and slowly opened the door. Sara still couldn't read his face, which was unusual, because she'd learned every expression he had, except this one. He sat down deliberately, and paused a few seconds before speaking, a pause Sara did not like in the least.

"He's still in surgery, but they're finishing up now."

"Did the doctor indicate how he was doing?"

"As good as expected, was what he said. Nothing more, but the way he said it was encouraging. The appendix was bursting when they opened him up and removed it. The problem is that they never know how a patient will handle it. But, he said he's young and strong and with the proper care, should be OK."

"That's not enough for me; maybe it is for you, but..."

"Look, Sara. The doc seemed positive enough for me. Whatever will happen, he's in the right place with the right people to take care of him. Eighteen to twenty-four hours was the way the doc inside put it. We'll know nothing until then."

"You have to leave, don't you?"

Vrain looked down at his hand holding Sara's hand in her lap. He didn't say anything, but Sara knew. Her anger was building, but it was more disappointment than anything. She pulled her hand away from his.

"Then go already. Go!"

Her voice went up an octave and many decibels. An older couple in the waiting room was startled by the outburst. A thin, frail-looking man with thin tousled hair and arthritic hands put his arm around his wife as if to protect her from the raised voice and who knew what else from the Vrain's.

Captain Vrain looked at the scared couple and formed his lips into a forced smile, in case a smile would help the situation, which it did not.

"Connor will be fine. He's young and he's tough. The tough part comes from you, right?"

The weak attempt at fake compliments wasn't working. Sara clenched her jaw and wouldn't look at her husband.

"Look, Sara, if I could stay here I would. You know that. But, I've got two other people who are in just as much trouble as Connor only they've got no one to help them except me."

Sara turned her twisted up face and aimed it right at her husband.

"Are you the only cop in this god damned city?"

The old man squeezed his wife even harder in case the wild woman on the other side of the waiting area was about to lose it."

"I'm the one responsible. No one else knows the situation like I do. Look Sara..." Sara tried to look away, but Dick Vrain wouldn't let her. She knew he was going to win because he always did. That was who he was, and she loved him for it. If it was right, Dick was going to do it and sometimes it pissed her off, but most of the time she was glad she had a husband like that. She looked at him deep in his eyes with a few tears forming in hers.

"It's OK, Dick. I'll be alright and I know you have to go, even though I want you to stay here with me. In case, you know, something happens. That's all."

"Nothing is going to happen. They've got everything under control. But I need you to handle this until I can get back. You're the only one I can trust. You're my rock. You've always been my rock. I need you, Sara."

When Sara heard the words, 'I need you, Sara', she snapped out of her anger and nodded at her husband firmly and with conviction. They both knew what needed to happen and they were both resigned to it. Their team was still intact as Dick gave Sara a hug and a kiss on her lips. A brief smile from his wife told him it was OK. The older couple seemed relieved, but the old man across from them still held on to his wife.

As he departed, Sara held on to his hand for a split second, not wanting to let go.

"Be careful, babe. I have a feeling it's going to be dangerous."

Richard Vrain left and thought about her warning. He knew she was right.

Chapter 58

Mase had to play it right down the middle. If he played it too hard, he'd never find Lara. If he played it too soft, whoever this guy was would know he was up to something. What couldn't happen was to give into the subliminal suggestions totally. He wouldn't stand a chance if he gave in to it, so he lay on the stone bench in his cell, looking out of it and half-stoned.

A bottle of whiskey lay in shattered pieces against the cold concrete wall. He stared at it over and over again. What it would have brought him was peace and escape from this madman's hell. He needed it more right then more than anything. The battle of wills was on. How fantastic it would be to slide into comfort and silence and sleep away everything that was happening to him.

There were small puddles of the whiskey right there at the base of the wall; he wanted that little sting of it on his tongue and then to take just a little more. But, if he did that, he'd be done, more done than he'd ever been. He'd let his family down, his brothers in blue, his mentor and himself; each time enjoying the taste and the smooth, seamless deadly numbness in his mind. And off he'd go, again.

And then he'd wake up feeling hung over and sick to his stomach and then it would start all over again, into the night, spinning in circles through bad dreams and skull splitting pain. The cycle never ended. Should he do it, should he start all over again? Of course he shouldn't. Of course, he should. He had to. This, all of this, was useless, absolutely useless.

The voice came on the loud speaker again, at a higher volume and with more purpose.

"Not yet, Mr. Mason. Later."

Mase stared at the speaker and tried to speak but he couldn't. No words came out. He remembered. "Yes, OK."

"Excellent! And now, Mr. Mason, the finale of The Quest for The Golden Shield of Anthonia. Are you ready, Mr. Mason?"

"I have no choice. Let's get on with it."

"Yes, well, that's not necessarily true. One always has choices, doesn't one?"

"My assistants will take you to your castle where you will fight Creighton LaVelle for the hand of Cornelia Summerlyn. The competition will begin once you enter the castle. Is that understood?"

"Well, whatever. I'll win, you know."

"Excellent, Mr. Mason. Your fighting spirit will enhance the intensity of the challenge to make the battle worth fighting. After all, the hand of the beautiful princess is at stake, is it not? It's Level 8, Mr. Mason. The last level where one of our lives will continue and one will end."

"If that's the way you want it. Let's get on with it. Anything to shut you up."

"My men are on their way. You will be provided with a new headset. I designed it especially for this last engagement. I hope you particularly enjoy the three-dimensional depth of the images you will live through. I designed them with you in mind, Mr. Black Knight."

His laughter bellowed through the loudspeaker as Toy Francisco and Stanley Burnett entered his cell, lifted him up and escorted him to a room that looked exactly like the cell, but with one dimensional images flashing around on the walls.

He was forced to put on the headset and instantly the space he was in became a three dimensional medieval castle again, black marble walls, gyrating dragons on pedestals, portraits of old royalty on the walls that winked and waved at him. The flashes of light that entered his eyes were not lightning strikes; they were subliminal messages that were intended to control his mind.

Somehow, he squeezed his eyes closed with such force that the pain kept him aware of everything that was actually happening to him. He knew he had to suffer that pain if he was going to act quickly when he needed to. *Pain was his antidote!*

He was just getting used to his surroundings, when in walked the Princess, Cornelia Summerlyn. His hand touched her arm and she felt real. But, feeling real didn't mean real. He kept telling himself that as the sequence of game play continued.

The Princess looked sad and helpless as he tried to convince her that being his bride was the best thing for her and that Creighton LaVelle was not right for her. The more he talked, the more she sobbed, holding her face in her hands, her body shaking with grief.

Then the sound of cannon shot echoed in the chamber!

***

The Black Knight was ready for battle. Numbers appeared at the top of the action scene, just above the head of the combatants, and they flashed every time a sword fighting scene took place between The Black Knight and LaVelle. Each had their own numbers that kept increasing above their heads. The Knight was leading by 5000 points and appeared to be ending the battle.

The Princess fell down to her knees and grabbed the ankles of The Black Knight, temporarily distracting him and giving LaVelle the opportunity he needed. The sword play was scored by the number of aggressive strikes made by the swords. The Knight tripped and LaVelle was all over him.

The clinking of the swords continued, with The Knight on the ground fighting desperately to stop the sword from penetrating his body, but it appeared LaVelle had the advantage. The Knight was fighting for his life and the points were mounting for LaVelle. The score was now tied as The Knight jumped up to his feet and lunged desperately toward LaVelle.

It was now a fight to the finish. The Knight was wearing his armor and was holding the Golden Shield and LaVelle had his tunic with his family shield. It looked now like a fencing match, each fighter lunging and parrying with their swords, each not retreating. Something had to give. The numbers were exactly equal above their heads.

A loud bell was heard and the fighting ceased! A deep baritone voice announced the tie breaker was now in place ready to go.

"The Princess Cornelia will decide the winner. She will stand in between the two warriors and point to the winner. A challenge will not be considered and the winner will be chosen. Princess Summerlyn, which combatant is the winner?"

A flourish of trumpets preceded the decision as the Princess stepped forward. She pointed to Creighton LaVelle. The winner!

#

As the game ended, LaVelle and The Princess walked out of the castle and mounted their white steeds. The music played softly as a mist shrouded the castle and the castle slowly dissolved into its cloud. The horses floated down to the ground and pranced along a golden path, shining in the bright sunlight.

Creighton LaVelle was the winner and he was bringing Cornelia back to her father, Lord Summerlyn. Over their heads, the word 'Winner' flashed repeatedly, as they smiled at the sun on their way home.

***

Lara Deming felt exhausted. She was now in an unfamiliar room without the costume she'd worn previously. Everything was different, from the furniture, which was now plain and simple in design to the curtains, which looked like woven plastic. A breeze was felt in the room coming from a vent in the ceiling. It smelled artificial and clean, but not from the air outside.

She sat in a plastic chair that faced the door. The door opened, a lone figure entered her room and looked at her. He was about six feet tall, well-built, wearing an expensive looking black turtle-neck sweater, tailored gray gabardine slacks, black leather shoes that shined in the light, and a gold men's necklace with a large ruby that seemed to sparkle as he walked towards her.

Lara didn't move. She stared apprehensively at the man as he approached her. His face seemed to lack emotion of any kind, except for his eyes. They were dark brown, almost black and had a terrible gaze that struck fear in her, but she didn't move.

This had to be the person behind this huge charade, this game, this evil drama that was trying to prove some point.

He stopped about six feet from her and lowered his head as if he was trying to hide something.

"Good evening Lara."

She couldn't see his mouth, but the words didn't sound right. They sounded slightly mechanical and programmed, as if he wasn't actually speaking. She furrowed her brow and lost her fear of the man. Whoever he was, he looked shy and scared, not evil. All she could see was his eyes and the top of his head. His hair was black and wavy and perfectly combed.

He took a few steps back and turned around.

"I've been waiting for you for a long time." Said the stranger with his back still turned towards her.

"The moment I saw your photo, I knew I had found the person I've always dreamed I would find; the one woman who would become a part of me and my life. It was instantaneous and a miracle. But that was so long ago now."

"Who are you?" Asked Lara. "Why are you doing this?"

"All your questions will be answered in due time. My first goal is to prove my worth to you. You will see, Lara that you could never find a man like me, ever. If a man and a woman are to be as one, they must respect each other and cherish them and never waver in their love for each other."

Chapter 59

When Vrain reached New Rochelle, his three units were posted at the designated positions, and he placed his car near their midpoint. Nothing new had been determined as to power usage or solar panels or anything else that indicated which of the three estates would probably be the one. Maybe Bottom's had the right idea.

Without the proper warrants, they couldn't just demand entry into these homes. But, what if each Patrol Officer simply knocked on each door, told the residents that they were in the area looking for a possible serial killer and had they seen anything unusual recently. And, if they looked cooperative could they allow them to look around their home. Bottoms knew all the tricks, even though he was the Precinct jokester, he knew his way around difficult investigations.

"OK, boys, here's how we're going to handle it; on my signal, and my signal only, each one of you will approach the home, knock on the door and show the resident your ID. Tell them you're looking for a serial killer who's been seen in the area and you wanted to know if they'd seen anything unusual."

Detective Bottoms starting laughing as Vrain explained what Bottoms had suggested back at headquarters. He didn't mind Vrain taking his advice, in fact, he couldn't wait to get back and needle him about it for weeks, if not months on end. Vrain and the other units heard the laughter.

"OK, Bottoms, it was your idea, which, after seventeen years, good on you, you finally had one. Boys, it's Bottoms' idea, I take no credit for it."

Bottoms finally calmed down as Vrain finished his orders.

"Bottoms will try it first, then Meers, and then Summers. When each has finished, you'll report back to me and the group. And make sure you listen carefully to the last part of this. Only approach the homes and ask the question. Don't take any chances and don't do anything stupid. No matter what you see from the open door, don't go in. Just report back to us and I'll make the decisions. Oh, and turn off your lapel cams. As it is, we shouldn't be here in New Rochelle, but at this point I don't give a fuck about territories. Everyone clear?"

They all agreed and Bottoms started out. Vrain waited patiently for the reports, as the night had completely engulfed their vehicles in darkness. He knew they were all sitting ducks if one of these homes was the right one. He knew it was still a long shot, but time was running out and he had to do something.

***

In a small office space at the C.I.A. an administrative assistant type was getting coded reports from the field regarding unusually high volumes of chatter coming from their NYC operatives. Something was happening. They couldn't identify it exactly, but they were pretty sure a hit squad operating under the direction of the Zakarian Government was about to contact a hacker type who'd stolen a lot of money from their government, and was about to take him out.

The notice, unusual as it was, came through to NYPD as a warning to be on the lookout for any unusual activity, anything, any unmarked cars, any computer assisted online searches that might indicate anything suspicious, anything.

While he was waiting for Bottoms to report back, Vrain heard the warning and tucked it in the back of his mind. The part he didn't like was that they were using unmarked vehicles and he wondered if the New Rochelle Police Department would scour their city for generic looking vehicles that were acting suspicious, which Vrain and the boys were.

The best he could hope for was that it was confined to the NYPD for now and not New Rochelle. He tapped his steering wheel to a song in his head. Summers asked him to stop the tapping because it was driving him crazy. Vrain stopped, for a few minutes, and then started again, without even realizing he was doing it again.

Bottoms came on the speaker and gave his report.

"Nothing, Cap. Not a thing. Some kind of cocktail party was going on and everyone was enjoying themselves with a little band playing high society dance music. The owner came to the door and said they had seen nothing lately and wished me a good evening. How's that for nothing?"

"OK, Meers, you're next. Remember, just observe the reactions, see as much as you can when they open the door and do nothing else. Report back quickly. We don't have all night."

"OK, Cap, I'm going now. Shouldn't take very long."

"Be careful Alston."

Vrain was running out of patience. He kept thinking about Mase and how much trouble he was in, and they just seemed to be spinning their wheels. Maybe Meers would find something.

***

"While Meers checks out the Van Storen home, I want everyone to keep quiet, me included. Understood?"

No one answered. Vrain asked one more time.

"Understood?" No answer concerned the jumpy Captain. "Hey!" Still no answer. Then Trevor Bottom's voice whispered.

"You told us to shut up. Which one is it Cap, answer you or shut up?"

A little snickering from Summers ended quickly as dead silence took over. The wait seemed like an eternity, but finally Meers reported back.

"Cap, nothing. The Van Storen daughter was shacked up with her boyfriend while mom and dad were out partying in Manhattan. The girl came down in her nightie, all sweaty, and when she opened the door, she smiled at me. Then I asked her about whether they'd seen anything recently that looked odd, like someone sneaking around or any serial killer stuff, she just giggled at me and chewed on a long strand of her blond hair."

"Get to the point, already, please, we don't have all night." Said Vrain.

"The point is that she was ready to chuck her boyfriend for me and I hadn't been laid for a while, so I thought…"

"Never mind, Alston. Get yourself a date some other time. OK, Joe, you ready?"

"Ready Cap. The Boyd Mansion looks pretty dark, like there's no one around. I'll check it out. See what's going on. There's a long circular driveway to the house, so it's going to take me a while. Have a little patience and I'll let you guys know what I found."

"Just go already, jeezus Christ."

The only thing Vrain could do was lean back in his seat and look into the darkness. He heard sounds and distant cars honking their horns, a few night birds yakking it up in the trees, but every minute was interminable. He kept thinking about how his ass was in deep trouble for doing this, but he'd have to deal with it later.

Then his son's smiling face kept appearing in his busy mind. The fact that he wasn't in the hospital with Sara bugged him. He hated himself, but that wasn't anything new. He thought about all the years they'd been together, all the close calls and missed soccer games because he was too busy.

His phone was on mute when he saw the call come through from Sara. He couldn't even think about it being a problem. That would be just too much. But Sara knew if he didn't answer, it was because he couldn't, so she texted him that Connor was out of surgery and resting comfortably, and not to worry. A smile crossed his face. He checked the time on his phone and wondered what was taking Summers so long. It seemed like too long.

When he tried to remember when Joe had left, he couldn't remember. Maybe ten minutes, maybe less, maybe who knows? If you watch a clock, it slows down. But he still felt it was too long.

"Any of you guys know how long Joe's been out?"

"At least fifteen minutes, maybe a little longer. Seems like he should be back by now."

"Yeah, I know. But he said it might take him a while. Can one of you drive quietly over to the Boyd home and see if you can find out what's happening? Check that. We're all going over to the Boyd home, since it's our only option right now. But, let's find Joe's unit first and park near it. We'll stay separated, but just in case we need to move we'll all be there."

Vrain, Meers, and Bottoms each drove to the Boyd home slowly, without their lights on, the crunching gravel the only sound that came over the radio. Bottoms got there first and parked about fifty feet from Joe's car. When Vrain and Meers did the same, Vrain emerged from his car and looked around. It was so dark in that area that he couldn't see anything. Still no Joe. Vrain looked at his watch one more time.

A hand reached out of the bushes behind Vrain and tapped him on his shoulder. Vrain spun around and was ready to fire his weapon when he realized it was Joe. Vrain notified Meers and Bottoms that Joe was OK.

"Nothing Cap. Some old lady maid came to the door and said the Boyd's were out of town, in Italy, and that nothing unusual had been seen. I looked over her shoulder and everything looked pretty quiet. Only one thing, Cap."

"Yeah, what?"

"Well, I'm no expert on servants or anything like that, but if you ask me, she looked too old to be a servant. And, her hands looked like they hadn't seen a hard day of work, ever. Manicured, and all that."

"All right. Let's get out of here while we can. This seems like nothing all the way around."

They all drove off. Vrain went to the hospital to be with his family, and the other two went to Precinct Headquarters. Vrain told them he'd meet them there as soon as he found out how his son was doing.

Chapter 60

Creighton LaVelle had been declared the winner by the Princess Cornelia Summerlyn. They were now on the golden path that led to the Summerlyn Estate. They stopped briefly by a small stream and rested under a large willow tree that tinkled like crystal wind chimes as the wind passed through its branches. He held her in his arms as they sat romantically under the tree and listened to the water bubbling past them.

"Cornelia, this is our moment of everlasting love. You will…"

"Stop this. Stop this now." Cornelia ripped off her headset and smashed it on the ground.

The fantasy game ended and all the lights came on in Cornelia's room. Creighton watched it on his monitor and couldn't understand how this had happened. He'd done everything correctly, the mind control, the headset, the programming, all of it exactly as it should have been. How did she stop it in her mind? He had to know.

Two levels below ground, Mase woke up out of his nightmare and realized that Lara and he were now in grave danger. He had to think strategically and quickly because he was dealing with someone who lived in two, possibly more, worlds.

Pain and Deception were the answers. The Pain would distract him from being controlled and the deception would get him closer to the maniac he and Lara were dealing with. He spoke to the loud speaker in the ceiling.

"Creighton, listen to me. This is the Black Knight. I can help you win back the Princess. Let me talk with her for just a few minutes and I will convince her you are the love of her life and that she will find no one like you."

"And how will you convince her if she's already convinced herself I'm not?"

"It's quite simple. She knows me and I know her. I've never lied to her, ever, in all the time we've known each other. I promise you I know exactly what to say to her to convince her. Just give me that one chance. You'll see."

"I will think about your proposal and in due time I will let you know. In the meantime, enjoy my hospitality and relax as much as you can. I foresee, shall I say, certain problems that you will deal with, and a little R & R will work wonders for your constitution."

Mase walked around his cell for a while, visualizing all the options and probabilities of different strategies. Then, he knew he had to think how this wack-job would react to them, using his previous reactions as his base of understanding. Then, he had to work out options that went against everything this guy would expect and surprise him into a mistake. One mistake was all he needed and he would get them out of there.

***

Back at Precinct Headquarters, Vrain had made it back to find a surprise on his desk. A small manila envelope was waiting for him. He hesitated for a moment, not knowing exactly what it contained. The words 'Con Edison Data' were printed in the corner.

When he opened it, six months' worth of power usage for all New Rochelle residents was right in front of him. It was one piece he'd been waiting for. As he scanned the thousands of names on the paper, he focused momentarily on the three large estates they'd just visited.

The column that gave the six-month average usage gave highlighted accounts that went over their normal usage for the previous year. When he cross-checked the three estates, although the Boyd Estate didn't exceed its average, he noticed the one piece of information that he was looking for.

Its power usage, its average power usage was over four times the amount of the other two and far and away higher than every other home in New Rochelle. He used a highlighting pen and drew an opaque yellow stripe. He slammed his fist on top of the paper and looked up at his team.

"Boys, come here. I think we've found our man. Look at this."

They gathered around the Chief and saw the highlighted information. They looked at each other and high-fived.

"Not so fast. I've got to get a search warrant for the Boyd home on pretty thin evidence. I know the DA won't buy it. So we've got to try something else. I'm going to call Captain Reeves in New Rochelle. I hope a little brotherly honesty will help him understand the pickle we're in and try to figure out a quicker way. We can't wait for the DA. It's an election year and he's walking a slippery tightrope. He won't take any chances so we might as well roll the dice and see what happens. You guys in?"

The vote was a unanimous yes!

***

Not only was Reeves in a bad mood that night, but he thought Vrain was losing his mind asking for help on this bullshit power usage indicators that couldn't mean anything important when he knew some of these rich bitches in New Rochelle used electricity like running water for pools, air conditioners, charging their stupid electric vehicles, and don't bother me Vrain with any of your bullshit putting Vrain back to square one.

The last comment Reeves made got him thinking. He said, jokingly, why don't you just cut the main power to the house and see what happens? That idea had merit, because if the power was cut, even if they had alternate power sources, they'd be functioning at a much lower level, which might, just possibly, make them do something they don't normally do. Anyway, driving out there, fighting the rush hour traffic, Vrain had time to think and figure out how he was going to get Mase and Deming out of there. He was positive it was the Boyd Mansion.

***

Jonah Christian set a grand feast to celebrate his overwhelming victory over The Black Knight. Victoria, the elderly attendant, had put the dishes together during the day and was ready for the guests. Creighton, Cornelia, and The Black Knight, walked in to the main dining hall, accompanied by Toy Francisco and Stanley Burnett.

Jonah had everything prepared. The lights were set at the best level to enhance not only his appearance, but Cornelia's as well. They were angled to highlight their best features, enough to make them as attractive as possible, and put the Black Knight in poor lighting, accentuating his evil intentions.

Creighton glowed in the spotlight he'd created, lessening the artificiality of his mouth. He made sure he was first into the room to double check every detail and when he was certain everything was perfect; he walked towards Victoria.

Victoria stood meekly at the doorway to the kitchen, awaiting her final orders. Before he signaled for the guests to be brought in, he adjusted the lighting and the piped in orchestral background music, set low at first with the controls next to his place setting, giving the finishing touches to his masterpiece.

He nodded at his men and Victoria to commence the feast. Cornelia had been mildly sedated once again and The Black Knight, dressed in their designated costumes were escorted in, Burnett bringing in Mase and Francisco escorting Cornelia, her hand on his outstretched arm.

All Mase could think about was Pain and Deception, Pain and Deception, as he was placed opposite Jonah at the far end of the table. Burnett stood close guard to him. Cornelia was placed to Jonah's immediate right, not over six feet away.

The pain part was working. Unbeknownst to Jonah, Mase had placed a shard of broken glass from the broken whiskey bottles in his shoe. Every step or slight movement caused shooting pain to start at his heel and traveling all the way up his leg. It hurt like hell, but he needed it to fight the mind control he was about to be subject to. He could feel the blood seeping into his shoe and his foot sloshing around in pain. The pain was excruciating!

Seeing Lara again made all of his efforts worthwhile. At first, she ignored Mase and looked to be in a strange mood, not caring, indifferent to everything that was going on. One quick dart of her eyes toward him gave him some hope. He wasn't sure if she was under this guy's mind control games or she'd simply given up.

Mase's mind kept busy by noticing every detail of the people in the room and the weapons he saw bulging from the two men's waists. These were the same guys who'd taken him from his apartment. Neither of them showed any expression on their faces. They simply stood on guard as if they were automatons ready to kill.

He tried not to squirm from the shooting pain that wouldn't stop, and control his own face that would give away his intentions. Each painful pulse in his foot reminded him how dangerous this situation was. She still looked as beautiful as ever, even though he'd almost forgotten.

"You look a bit uncomfortable, sir." Said LaVelle to The Black Knight.

"Not at all, sir. I'm simply enjoying this, this, feast you're about to present. It's magnificent and I'm quite hungry after such an enjoyable battle. That's all."

"Good, good. I'm delighted that you've taken your defeat with such grace. It shows your noble upbringing. And Cornelia..."

"Elated to be here, Creighton? I've waited a long time for this celebration of our future marriage. Everything here is amazing!" She said the words with no emotion in her voice.

Creighton LaVelle stood up with a large wine goblet in his hand. The music stopped and the lights dimmed, as he cleared his throat to propose a toast:

"May I propose a toast? To the most beautiful woman on the face of the earth: May our future battles be victories and may our children favor your beauty."

Creighton LaVelle drank all of the deep red wine in his goblet and nodded to Cornelia and The Black Knight to do the same. Mase stood up and smiled broadly at Creighton and added a less than heartfelt "And to the victor belong the spoils" toast. Cornelia remained seated and sipped a small amount, maybe none, it was hard to tell. But they both pulled it off. Mase sat down carefully, in agony from the pain. As he sat down, and pulled in his chair, he noticed a small amount of blood had leaked from his boot onto the floor. He quickly covered the blood with his other shoe.

The feast was about to begin.

Chapter 61

If you could see them, it was only for less than a split second. Even their shadows faded into nothingness as they sifted silently through the bushes along the edges of the Boyd estate's extensive acreage. It was as if they were hauntings of a past coming back for their evil doings. Their steps were soft and muted; their soundless movements were a silent symphony of non-dimensional ephemera.

These were men who adapted themselves to their surroundings, camouflaged, existential beings in search of their only intention, death. They didn't talk to each other because it wasn't necessary. Their stealth looked rehearsed but natural and flawless in its design. They exhibited patience, tranquility, and focus.

It wasn't time, yet. But, soon they would be going about their business; they were now in the pre-positioning stage. Each man moving effortlessly toward their assigned location on the estate, each pre-set place and action determined well ahead of time to avoid any mistakes. Mistakes were not considered, because if something went wrong, one of the other shadows would eliminate the mistake and immediately take over.

***

Vrain had contacted an electrician that had been used on previous cases. He was trustworthy, dedicated, and most of all a man who wouldn't talk to anyone after their work was completed. His name was Curt Sammons, middle-aged, short, squat, hands of steel, and more than just a journeyman, he was an expert in anything electrical.

Curt brought his little van to the Precinct before Vrain left for New Rochelle. He was ready for anything. The thrill of danger, that adrenalin rush, the pressure of limited time to accomplish your work, was what Curt fed on. It wasn't danger to him; it was life, living with purpose. Vrain always told him he should have been a cop, but he was too short, didn't enjoy taking orders, and an overall pain in the ass. But, he liked Vrain and they worked well together.

Vrain gave Curt the basics of what they had to do, but, the van had to stay. There was no way they would take it. After Curt got the update, he knew exactly what he had to take with him, threw it in the back of Vrain's car and they were off.

"I brought my US Energy Atlas with me. It's all I need, as far as locations of power sources and where we'll make the break."

"You sure it's accurate?"

"It's less than a year old and should show us all we need. Tell me the address and I'll start working on it as we drive."

When the coordinates were located, Curt pinpointed a location less than a mile from the property. It was the only way they could stay clear of any security cameras, guards, guard dogs or whatever measures were in place to stop intruders. Vrain always enjoyed working with Curt Sammons because his techniques were flawless and he worked fast. Of course, the thought that they were trespassing without a warrant, or working around the local police, was still in his mind, but Vrain filed those in the dead letter file for now. This was nothing new to him, mainly because certain situations call for logic and daring, not fear. He had the feeling that whoever this maniac was, his mind was as sharp as they came and Vrain had to take drastic actions and not wait to get permissions from every bureaucratic pencil pusher. No, this one was his.

When they finally arrived at Sammon's chosen location, Vrain positioned his men equidistant in a rectangle around the spot. Before they started, he asked each of his men to search power poles, buildings in the area, and homes that might have security cameras. They found only one and Meers threw an old blanket over it from behind. It turned out to be a lucky toss, which Vrain enjoyed immensely.

Sammons got to work immediately. The spot he'd chosen ran through an empty lot, underground, and indicated by certain markers used by Con Edison. He didn't have to look around at being spotted, because he knew and had confidence in Vrain to cover his back. The best way to handle this job was to put two clamp resistors three feet apart and after they were put in place, cut the line. The resistors would send false short circuit messages intermittently to Con Ed, giving minor interruption signals for a while. But, eventually, they would figure it out and find the source.

This job required perfect timing. Once the slice would be made, the window of opportunity was thirty minutes, no more, and then they had to get out fast. Vrain told Curt to wait there, behind a large oak tree near the north wall of the empty lot, leave his cell phone on mute and when he sees a call from Vrain, it means 'cut' the wire.

They all knew the plan was fraught with potential screw ups, but it was the best they had. No point in overthinking this, not with so much on the line. The plan was simple: Make sure all the power was cut to the mansion at the exact time they were positioned to storm in and take charge of whatever was taking place. If the network they were using was reliant on the power, everything would shut down. Vrain's big gamble was that even if they had backup power, it wouldn't be sufficient to maintain the amount of energy they needed to keep a massive system functioning. And that was all that he needed. Even if he could partially immobilize whatever this guy was doing, that would give Mase enough time to work out whatever he was planning, and then they would roll in.

***

Inside the mansion, the elaborate dinner feast that Jonah Christian had served was ending. Two new VR Headsets were brought in by Toy Francisco on a silver tray. They almost looked alive, as small yellow and blue lights flashed brightly on the edges of the goggles.

"Mr. Francisco, please give Mr. Mason his ticket to a new universe. And make sure it is adjusted properly. I will do the same for Miss Deming."

It was the first time Jonah Christian was within reach of the love of his life. It's hard to imagine what he was feeling, or even how he could have transformed Lara Deming, in his mind, to take her rightful place on such an exalted pedestal. His hands were trembling as he approached Lara. It took every acting skill she had from her college days to act as if she was about to enter the realm of love and affection she'd only dreamed of.

When his hands touched the smooth and lustrous blond locks flowing down to her shoulders, his hands almost couldn't hold the VR set. It was as if her hair sent a passion volt of electrical energy through his body that was impossible to control. He worshiped her and he'd never even touched her. He positioned himself behind Lara and gently placed the VR set on her head, making sure he didn't harm her.

She couldn't see him as he spoke to her, his artificial mouth smoothly mouthing the words in her ear.

"Are you feeling OK, my dear? Is the headset comfortable? We'll be ready to go shortly."

Mase knew the time was rapidly coming when he would face one of the most difficult experiences of his life. And the only way to survive it would be to not give in to it. He sensed that his VR set and Lara's were synced up and that they would experience similar pulses of mind controlling subliminal messages.

Jonah had a keyboard placed in front of him at the table and typed in a few words. A large monitor screen appeared on the far wall, replacing what appeared to be a member of some royal family riding a horse and wearing armor. When images appeared on it, they were split screen images of exactly what was appearing to both Mase and Lara.

First, Lara! Alternating photos of her late husband and of Creighton LaVelle began slowly. Then a photo of Lara and her late husband kissing each other on what looked like a cruise ship. They were selfies from their honeymoon. As the various photos flashed on her headset, Creighton's image replaced her husband's image. It was so smooth and seamless that it was impossible for the human eye to detect the change.

He was attempting to replace her memory of her husband's image with his own. It was pure mind control and Artificial Intelligence. There was now a child, a young girl that was Cornelia and Creighton's child. Virtual time had passed. Passionate piano sonatas accompanied the image swapping, perfectly timed, and pulsing like two heartbeats beating as one. Cornelia Summerlyn and Creighton LaVelle were one heartbeat together, one presence, two people becoming one person.

Chapter 62

Mase watched everything. At first, he was confused and angry and, of course, jealous. He felt like a voyeur looking through a keyhole, only a full screen keyhole at live action, passions unleashed and full-on obsession. Whatever he was watching pissed him off and there was nothing he could about it, except sit there and take it. But, no matter what he saw or felt, the one thing he knew was that pain was shooting through his body, first from his foot and then from his eyes.

Watching this scene of intense passion made his heart beat wildly fast. The thought came to him that the faster it beat the more blood was pushed through his body and the more he would bleed, eventually losing too much. He couldn't sustain this because all could think about now was the pain. It was beyond excruciating. Then he realized that he'd done that to himself on purpose. Yes, he did it to himself, to stay focused, not to give in to the mind control that was being pushed into his brain.

He kept telling himself to smile and not give in, just smile and look like you were enjoying the passion play in front of you. The pain triggered stone cold logic to enter his mind.

"Mr. LaVelle. I'm tired of this headset and this make-believe bullshit. Allow me to kiss Cornelia one last time, that's all I ask. Then you'll see who she really wants."

Jonah Christian, or Jonah Boyd, or Creighton LaVelle or whoever he was, was startled by the speech. This had never happened before. At first, he didn't believe it, but as Mase rattled on, the smile caught the computer genius by surprise. His subliminal mind control was unbeatable. No one stood a chance against the science and the technology behind it. It was all his, and he knew everything about it. He stopped the scene by putting the program on pause and by inducing a temporary hypnotic pause in the program Lara watched.

"Very good, Mr. Mason. You are to be commended. Your tenacity and self-possession are excellent. Unfortunately, they're no match for what I have in store for you next. But I'm always up for a good 1v1 and since we're all here together, I say let's play. What say you, Mr. Mason?"

Mase liked what he heard. Everything had stopped because of the pain he'd inflicted on himself. Now, total deception was called for. There wasn't a lot of time left because of the amount of blood he was losing and he was feeling weaker, woozy, and shaky. He had to act fast.

"I've got a much better idea."

"Speak Mr. Mason. I can't wait to hear what you have to say."

Jonah laughed heartily, followed by the smiles on his two assistants. They knew what was in store, but, playing the game was what their boss enjoyed most.

"Creighton, if I may be permitted to call you that, Creighton, there's only one game that means anything here; the love of Cornelia Summerlyn."

"Go on..."

"It's quite simple, really. We take off our headsets, stand directly in front of Cornelia, and ask her who she finds more attractive, you or me."

The blood coming from his foot had formed a small pool around his shoe. He tried not to move his foot, but it was almost impossible. Instead, he squirmed a little in his chair, his foot moving under the table.

"Isn't it obvious who she's more attracted to? Didn't you see it in the headset? We're a couple who lives for each other, we have a child; we can't be separated by life. If we can't live together in happiness, then we'll die together in sorrow. Your idiotic proposal is a waste of time, and frankly you're boring me."

"Well, Creighton, sometimes a little boredom is good for us. If your life was constantly filled with entertainment and wealth and riches like you have, that would really be boring. And, it seems to me that if you're so sure of Cornelia's affection for you, then you certainly shouldn't fear a little 1v1 competition that you couldn't possibly lose. I mean, you said you were always up for a challenge, which, in this case you couldn't possibly lose, if you get my drift?"

Jonah looked at his two assistants who stood next to him stone-faced and immobile.

***

Not very far away, two silent shadows slid in and out of the woods that surrounded the Boyd Mansion. One shadow wore an eyepiece and a small microphone. This environment was as easy to move in as a young boy in a meadow. His years of training and physical aptitude were created for just this.

Vrain and his men, on the other hand, weren't as comfortable as the stealth shadows.

"Stay low and hold in place until you hear my signal. And then... shhhhhh, quiet now."

Vrain had indicated to his team exactly where he wanted them to remain.

"Curt, can you hear me?"

"Yes, you're coming through perfectly. I'm just putting the finishing touches on the resistors and we'll be ready. I'll let you know when I'm ready. Shouldn't be more than a few minutes."

"Good, we're not quite ready ourselves. Remember, do nothing until I tell you to."

"Sure. Curt out."

Joe Summers had no idea that his car was placed less than fifty feet from one of the two shadows in the woods. Vrain asked each if they were in their assigned locations. He wanted the mansion strategically surrounded just in case there were secret doors or tunnels that they couldn't see.

Vrain had heard the weather report for the area before they arrived, and he didn't like it at all. Heavy rain and fog were due in within the hour and it meant his time frame might be shortened, which he hated, because he liked doing things his own way. Fuck the weatherman! Unfortunately, a low heavy fog was already moving in, the temperature was dropping fast and he could feel the humidity increasing. Rain was inevitable.

The lead shadow had night vision. His weather tight insulated clothing shed the fog and tiny rain droplets now falling like a ducks' feathers. He watched carefully and with a professional killer's patience. He could see each of Vrain's cars and had the plan in place to handle any eventuality.

The fog was thickening rapidly in the woods. Joe Summers would be the lead in this.

"I'm ready Vrain." Said Curt Sammons.

"Ten-four, hang tight."

Their sight was almost completely fogged out, and Summers' window was covered in mist and rain. He couldn't see anything. He looked behind him and all of the other windows were useless as well. He had no choice. At least the front window had to be wiped clean, and the only way was to lower his passenger side window enough to let him slide his arm out to wipe the moisture off.

An almost silent pop was heard by Summers, which turned out to be the last thing he would ever hear. His arm was still sticking out through the window, a stream of blood coming down the left side of his head. All that was left of Joe was a surprised look on his face. The thin pencil mustache that the other guys always gave him grief about didn't move, as misty rain covered his face, dripping down with his blood.

"Come in Joe. Joe, come in."

Because Summers wouldn't answer, he told everyone to stay in place and do nothing until he found out.

"Meers, drive by Joe's car and see what you can find out. Maybe the rain is interfering with his radio, maybe he fell asleep, who the fuck knows. Just drive by his car and tell me what you can see. Don't get out of your car under any circumstances. Go slow and be as quiet as you can be. You hear me? Oh, and if possible don't turn on your lights. Got it?"

"Knowing Joe, he probably dozed off, dreaming about one of his bimbos? Sure, I'll go check it out for you."

Meers did exactly as Vrain had asked and when he got to Joe's car, he knew his buddy was dead; his arm sticking out through his window and a head wound still leaking blood.

"He's dead cap. Joe's dead."

"Get back to your spot, now, don't wait."

Meers was out of jokes. None of this was funny anymore. In an instant, Vrain knew his plan was broken and needed an immediate fix, and he didn't have any time to waste. They were in a trap and so was Mase.

"Curt, you still with us?"

"Yes. Still waiting."

"Joe's dead, Curt. We've got to improvise. Not sure yet how, but the way we were going to do this is all wrong. Someone's out there and they know we're here. I've got an idea, but, we have to regroup and talk it through before we proceed. Boys, let's meet by Curt and figure this out. And, whatever we do, this one's for Joe, and Mase, of course."

Chapter 63

"You're not very clever Mr. Mason, are you? The Princess has already decided who she favors and it certainly is not you. Can't you see that? It should be perfectly clear to a detective."

"Not clear at all. You are speaking for Cornelia. Don't you think she has a mind of her own and doesn't need someone to speak for her? That doesn't show much respect for the woman of your dreams, now does it, Creighton?"

"Your simple mind games are so trivial as to be embarrassingly laughable. The Princess is a woman above all other women. She exists in a perfect world of purity and innocence. I wouldn't waste my time or embarrass her with your stupid little tricks that a child could see through. Come on Mr. Mason, really."

It took every ounce of strength left in him to hold it together. LaVelle wasn't budging, but Mase had to push ahead. He had to get close enough to him to do the next best thing, show Lara who this man was, what he was and shock her completely out of her haze, that is, if she was in a haze.

"You call this a trick. I call it a proof beyond all proofs. It doesn't matter what you say because I know inside you, there is doubt. The doubt is this: are you really good enough for this perfection in the person of Cornelia Summerlyn? How much more effort are you going to put into fooling yourself that this is all real. Come on Creighton, or whoever you are, you know if she saw you for who you really are, there's not a chance in the world that she would choose you over me. No way in hell. You know it and I know it and you're afraid to find out if she finds out who you are and what you actually look like. If you can't be honest with me, at least be honest with yourself. Don't insult yourself."

"Better, Mr. Mason. Quite a bit better, actually. You want honesty? Here's some honesty for you. You are a wasted alcoholic.

You can't stand the reality of your own life, let alone someone who's made a success of themselves far beyond anything you'll ever know. So, Mr. Mason, be honest with yourself and realize that no woman like Cornelia Summerlyn would ever, could ever, love someone like you. You're a bottomless pit and she won't jump in there with you. How's that for honesty."

"Not much of a choice then, I mean, choosing between a delusional psychopath and a useless alcoholic."

A bolt of pain shot through Mase. He flinched enough to catch the psychopath's attention. The grimace on Mase's face brought a smile to Jonah Christian. Pain was enjoyable to him; it validated his opinion of the world and how much control he had of anyone he came in contact with.

"I see Mr. Mason, by the look on your face, that you are enjoying yourself. But, unfortunately, your time is running out."

"My time ran out a long time ago. That's not a problem for me. But you, Creighton, you think your time is infinite. You think you control everything, including your own immortality. But, your fantasy will end, believe me, and not the way you want it to. We may be your prisoners, but you're the one in prison, Creighton, or whoever you are. You're a prisoner of your made up world."

"Don't we all live in our own little worlds, Mr. Mason?"

"Yeah, but some of us can change it if we want. We don't have to live there if we don't want to. You're stuck in yours and you'll never get out. It's a life sentence without the possibility of parole. Face it, Creighton, and you'll be free. Don't you want to be free? It's the only way out of this hell you've created. Don't you want to be free? Answer me, Creighton."

Creighton paused his speech program and stepped into a side area and went behind a closed door. He soon reappeared, looking more composed, pressing his hair back on his head and touching his artificial face carefully. His eyes had a new look to them. It was doubt above all else. However, the artificial smile on his face gave the impression of confidence.

"Very well, Mr. Mason. I agree with you. Let Cornelia decide who she wants to spend the rest of her life with; you or me. Mr. Francisco, please remove Mr. Mason's headset and bring him over to stand next to me. Then, Mr. Burnett, please remove Cornelia's headset so that she can clearly see us, side by side. Lower all the lights, and put the spotlight on us, so there will be no distractions. I want her vision to be clear and unobstructed. Turn off all the music."

***

Curt Sammons was ready for whatever Vrain wanted. Vrain, despite some doubts about when to do it, was ready. His gut was telling him to do it, but his mind was stalling.

"Here's what I want you to do, Curt. When we go back to the mansion, I'll send you a birthday text. You'll know it when you see it. Next, I want you to turn the power back on again, and then wait ten seconds and turn it off again. Can you do that?"

"Why?" Asked Alston Meers.

"Because, it will indicate to everyone, including whoever killed Joe, that this is not a power outage, it's a short, but if we do it enough times, it'll piss them off and hopefully they'll show themselves. It's a long shot, but it's all we've got at the moment."

"Kinda thin Cap?"

"Very. Here's where I want you to position your vehicles. All of you will get the birthday text, and when you get it, turn on your bright lights. Joe's killer is out there and if enough lights are put on the wooded area, we'll see them."

"Do you want me to keep flashing the power outage? I don't want to overheat the bypass I've created."

"Do it for as long as you can. Frankly, I don't give a damn what gets overheated. We're past that now."

Curt nodded along with Meers and Bottoms. Vrain had that look on his face. Doubt with a twist of anger. The scene was set and as the men returned to their positions, Vrain checked his cell phone. He had only 15% battery left. He hoped to God it would be enough.

The two shadows from the Middle East were getting closer to their entry point, a small window on the back end of the east side of the house that led to a small storage area. From there, they'd figure it out. Vrain thought they were still in the woods, but, as they had done already, the shadows were ahead of all of his plans. It was getting close to entry time and they were poised to enter at the lead shadow's nod of the head.

They could see lights inside the house, some coming through the upstairs windows, one from the small entry window they were about to enter. It was enough light to make out the initial steps of their plan and so far, none of what they saw presented any difficulties. There were alarms and security cameras in many locations, but for this team of two, they were child's play to disconnect.

The smaller shadow scaled the stone wall to the left of the cameras, and from behind it, he attached a small electronic device that fed preprogrammed images that took the actual view and transformed it using Artificial Intelligence to make the field of focus seem normal, nothing to worry anyone. They could tell by the looks of the security system, that it was sophisticated and far above the run-of-the-mill household security system. But, they were up to the challenge with their own counter security devices. They could easily buy enough time to do what they had to do.

***

The shadows watched Vrain and his men re-enter the area, but they were already in far enough that these fumbling police officers wouldn't even notice. As Vrain and his men set themselves in place,

Vrain glanced at his phone once again. 12% battery. That was a problem. They had little time left.

Curt Sammons was getting nervous, not so much about what they were doing, but because a boy and his dog were entering the lot where Sammons was working. It looked like they were going for the dog's evening walk, but kids have a way of sticking their noses into places they shouldn't. The dog must have caught Sammon's scent. He was friendly and so was Curt.

"You good boy. Good boy." Said Curt, rubbing the top of the mutt's head.

"Trouble, Trouble, where are you, boy. Here, boy."

The boy saw Curt and ran to get his dog.

"Your dog, boy?"

"His name is Trouble. Always gettin' into it, so we named him that. Say what's goin' on here?"

"Power Company asked me to fix a bad circuit. That's all. You go home now, boy, it's late."

"OK, mister. Come on, boy? Come on Trouble. Let's get out of here before mom gets angry at us."

Curt watched the boy run through the lot with his dog sniffing junk in the lot and eventually catching up to his master. Curt was glad he didn't have to do anything else.

Chapter 64

Lara Deming pulled off her headset, her eyes adjusting to the darkened room as she rubbed them hard. At first, everything seemed blurry, but as she got them refocused, she saw Vic and the strange man whose voice didn't sound real. They were staring at her, side by side, a spotlight from the darkened ceiling focused on their faces, Mase towering over the shorter Creighton LaVelle.

"Make sure you get a clear look. Remember Cornelia, I'm the one who really loves you and I'm the one who saved you from this beast. Remember, our fates are intertwined forever, our hearts beating as one. Make your choice." Spoke Creighton LaVelle.

Lara was clearing the cobwebs out of her brain as he talked. Mase could see an awakening starting in Lara. She wasn't completely there yet, but he could see her putting things together. He had to make his move and soon and, that's when he did. He had to move faster than he'd ever moved in his life. In one quick shift of his body, he reached around Creighton's face and pulled off the artificial mouth, cheeks, and skin, to reveal a living facial skeleton.

His right arm was now around Creighton's neck as his two aids made a move to save him, but Mase had moved too fast.

"Make one move boys and your boss is dead!"

Francisco and Burnett stopped in their tracks as Creighton waved them back. He was having trouble breathing, bleeding badly all around his head from his skin being ripped away and they were facing Lara now.

"Lara, don't look away. Look at this man. Is this what you want?"

The horror show in front of her brought on a new focus. The sight of a man without a face was horrendous. She couldn't face the sight. It was too much to take, when suddenly the lights went out in the room, and then muted gun shots came from many directions, bouncing off of metal and plaster, shattering glass and then, the lights came on again.

The smell of gun powder was coming from the doorway. Mase saw Stanley Burnett dead in a corner and Toy Francisco disappeared. The lights came on again. He still had Creighton LaVelle in a choke hold. The lights went out again. He went over to Lara in the dark and held her hand while he whispered to her.

"Lara, this is Vic. We have to get out of here and now. Can you walk out of here once it's time?"

Lara was still too stunned to reply, but Vic assured her she would be OK if she just held on to him as they were leaving, but not yet. She put her head gently on Mase's shoulder and he knew she would be OK. The lights flashed on again and when he looked around, LaVelle, or whoever he was, was gone. Burnett was still dead.

Vic held Lara's hand as they cautiously left the room through the large wooden door. Mase heard gunshot pops that were silencer shots coming from not too far away.

"Boss, you OK?"

Francisco's question couldn't be answered by a man without a mouth. LaVelle was too smart to answer and give away his location. Shuffling feet could be heard everywhere. LaVelle knew his home better than anyone, and he had enough weapons and traps throughout the mansion to stop an army. Mase could tell that whoever was shooting, was a professional assassin.

Then a loud flash bang explosion was heard which sounded like the entry door was blown off its hinges, as a loud thud sounded, the door crashing down and glass shattering in all directions. Mase heard a voice that he recognized immediately.

"Police! Drop your weapons now. This is the Police."

"Captain, stay low, there's active shooter in here and they're hidden. Stay low."

"Vic, is that you?"

They couldn't see each other and Vic wasn't happy about giving away his position, but he didn't want his boys walking into a trap.

"Yes, don't move. I've got the best spot to finish them. I've got Lara with me and she's OK. Shine all your lights on the outside of the house. The shooters will try to leave through a window."

The lights kept going on and off, repeatedly, and then, they remained off and Vrain was confused. Something must have happened to Curt, or the entire circuit blew. But, it gave Mase his chance. He held Lara's hand firmly and even though his foot screamed with pain, he dragged her with him blindly through the house.

Mase had Burnett's automatic weapon. The chances were increasing that he would meet up with the shooters or LaVelle and that could go either way. Just as he and Lara were approaching the end of a long hallway, they noticed two small figures cowering in the corner, shaking and crying. When they got closer, Lara called her name.

"Victoria. Is that you?"

The older woman looked up furtively, not sure of what she would see, but as she recognized Lara, a brief look of relief crossed her tired face. A cowering smaller figure was next to her huddled under her arm.

"Come with us Victoria. You have to come with us. It's your only chance."

Lara pulled away from Mase's hand and bent down to help Victoria and the child next to her stand up. Mase gave them whispered orders and they complied.

"Stay close behind me, and no matter what, don't say a word, not a word. I'll get us out of here, and Victoria, you point us in the best direction to get out of here."

When Mase looked closely at the little girl, he recognized her immediately. It was Kathy Barlow! He knew right then that she must have been kidnapped by LaVelle. It wasn't Kristina's fault after all!

Creighton was now Jonah Christian, recovering from Mase's choke hold and replacing his face with a spare. He was back in his element and knew from the start that he was facing at least three opponents plus the Police. He nimbly traveled through all three levels, readjusting his security settings and then laying his traps.

The two shadows were now at Jonah's mercy. In all of their training, they had never come across a mind as complex and dangerous as his. He had recovered from Lara's rejection and was about to turn the attackers into the attacked.

Vrain had backed out of the house but stood close to the entry door. His instincts were working overtime, survival, save the people he knew that needed help, keep low, assess the immediate situation at hand and act, act quickly and with violent intent.

"Curt?" Whispered Vrain.

"Yeah?"

"Turn the power on and leave it on and get the hell out of there. We'll pick you up when we're done here."

"Will do."

Then all the lights came back on, outside and inside. The shadows were caught in Jonah's web. Toy Francisco took out the lead shadow, leaving him dead in a spare bedroom. It was like child's play for him.

As the second shadow tried every stealth maneuver he knew, each move was met with a locked door or bullets from Francisco's automatic weapon. Somehow, he survived. But, now, it was Jonah's time. From a large control panel in his computer complex, he had the man trapped and by clicking a security button on his screen, a large amount of sleeping gas was emitted from the vent in the ceiling.

Mase knew he was in for it now. With all the lights on, they were sitting ducks. But with Victoria guiding them, they could keep moving. What no one noticed, because it was well hidden, was that a small fire had started in the two backup generators because of being overheated by Curt's power manipulation.

Victoria knew the only safe spot on the property because she'd found it accidentally one day when she just wanted a place away from all of her step son's madness. It was in a hidden cove of the wine cellar. She also knew there were no security cameras at that spot. The best way to that spot was to go outside through a service area used for food deliveries. It had enough overhanging awnings to keep them hidden as they went through an opening in the basement wall that had never been repaired or closed.

The fire that had started now engulfed the two generators and set off the fire alarm. The screeching of the alarm now added music to the chaos that was about to take place. Jonah gave Toy Francisco exact instructions of getting the cops taken out. From a small wooden landing pad on the roof, he would have a clear shot. But, the fire was spreading along the far wall near the generators.

Vrain had moved his men farther away from the house. He knew they needed protection from whatever was about to come at them. They waited and saw a large man on the roof with what looked like an automatic rifle. But now they could get behind the cover of the trees.

Flames were now coming towards Francisco from the roof line. He paused for a second and turned around, looking directly into the flames now engulfing the roof. The path back into the house was blocked. The only way to save himself was to climb down from his sniper position, which was now burning under his feet.

Vrain saw the sniper and knew he had him. Meers was the best shot of the three, so Vrain threw his chin at Toy Francisco and Meers took him out with one shot just above his left eye. The sniper fell forward and down to the ground as if he was taking part in a high dive competition, landing directly on his head. He never felt a thing. Vrain flashed the thumb up and now, it was time to rush in.

He could see the flames spreading inside the house quickly. Now, one of the best sounds he ever heard could be faintly heard coming to them from a distance. But, they were getting closer and he knew he had to take action, immediately.

Jonah Christian was temporarily trapped in his computer center. Smoke was now pouring in. He had to leave fast, but he was breathing toxic smoke, still bleeding around the edges of his replacement face, weakened by his fatigue. This would be his last ditch effort to save himself and everything he'd worked towards. Defeat could not be permitted.

Mase could see the smoke and the flames coming through the stone-lined wine cellar and knew they had to get out quickly. Victoria, elderly and frail, was running low on energy and a reason to live and Kathy was crying and shaking uncontrollably. When Lara and Mase attempted to lift them up from the stone floor, Victoria pulled her arms back, not allowing them to pull her out of there.

There was little time to argue with her, so Mase told Lara to take her, anyway. They lifted them up forcibly and were ready to leave. Flames were now everywhere in the building and they could hear the fire truck sirens arriving on the scene. Victoria was dragging her feet and resisting their efforts to save her and Kathy clung to Lara. As they climbed an old stone stairway out of the wine cellar and turned a corner to get out of the building, an ominous figure appeared.

Jonah Christian in singed clothing, blood seeping from around his artificial face, barely able to talk, stood in front of them with his weapon pointed directly at the four of them. His face was too distorted to read, but his eyes had vengeance in them. Mase read it perfectly and knew what he had to do. The madman pointed at Kathy with his weapon.

"Cornelia, what about our child?"

Instantly, Mase grabbed Victoria and held her in front of him and Lara. He was banking on the fact that whoever this maniac was, he wouldn't kill this older, frail woman who was apparently someone he cared about. But, all he needed was a few seconds. Jonah, without the slightest hesitation, shot Victoria in her chest, the bullet exiting and striking Lara in her shoulder. Kathy was still clinging to her when Mase rolled on the ground and grabbed Jonah's legs, pulling him down with him and easily disarming him.

But, Jonah was not about to give in. As the flames were now above their heads, Mase took drastic action. Victoria was dead, Lara seriously wounded but holding on to the screaming Kathy and his foot now bleeding even worse than before. He overpowered Jonah, grabbed his automatic and shot him in his head, killing the Jonah Christian instantly.

Mase stood up, looked down at Jonah Christian and pointed his weapon at the man who had caused all the murders and chaos.

"This one's for Chuckie." Mase shot a bullet in Jonah's chest. "This one's for Sherman Weiss." He shot him once again in his forehead. "And this one's for everyone else you murdered, you sick son of a bitch."

Mase picked up Lara in his arms and walked out of the burning building with her and Kathy walking beside him. The old mansion was now completely engulfed in flames, its fire alarms screeching and the firefighters walking around with their fire hoses trying to put out the flames. There wasn't much left of the once magnificent mansion.

Two paramedics took Lara from Mase, put her on a stretcher and when they saw his bleeding foot, ordered a stretcher for him as well. Kathy held Mase's hand while he was put on the stretcher. Vrain was right there with Meers and Bottoms. As they led him towards the ambulance, Mase glanced up at them while they joked about his attempts to impress a woman.

"Cap?"

"Yeah Vic?"

"Call Kristina Barlow and tell her Kathy's OK. She needs to know."

Kathy was checked out by the paramedics and she was Ok. Vrain took the little girl in his arms. Lara and Mase were loaded into the same ambulance. After IV's were attached to their arms and the doors were closed, Mase reached over to Lara and she held his hand as the Ambulance sped off into the night.

Sometimes, when all the odds are stacked completely against us, we somehow beat them. Never give up. Never give in. The human spirit is within each of us and will be there for us when we least expect it!

Epilogue

"Even in dark times, we cannot relinquish the things that make us human." [1]

Khan from *Metro 2033*

The Boyd Mansion lay in ruins, visited occasionally by citizens of New Rochelle, retired couples mainly, who gawked at the old stonework and ornate wood left in burned remnants on the ground.

"Shame, isn't it. They just don't make them like that anymore." Most of them shaking their heads and taking selfies in front.

Where are we, as humans, when all we can leave behind after we're gone are charred ruins and broken lives? Is what we accomplish enough to sustain memories of us by the people we've known?

A man is just a man and nothing more. But, a man's place in this world sets him apart and keeps his memory alive. What matters is, did you accomplish something that helped others in their lives? Did you contribute something useful to the world?

For Jonah Christian, unfortunately, the answer was no. But, what is it for each of us, trudging throughout our little lives, struggling here, succeeding there? What did each of us do in our small battles with life? Perhaps many of us will never know. But, if we've made someone's day better by smiling at them or helping them in some small way, perhaps we will know when someone smiles back at us and thanks us for our help.

Such was the smile on Kristina Barlow's face when she was reunited with her Kathy. Their lives were changed forever, for the better; better than drugs, better than games!

---

1. https://www.gamesradar.com/best-video-game-quotes-all-time/

Don't miss out!

Visit the website below and you can sign up to receive emails whenever Andy Slade publishes a new book. There's no charge and no obligation.

https://books2read.com/r/B-A-SZBX-WGXZC

BOOKS 2 READ

Connecting independent readers to independent writers.

Did you love *Games*? Then you should read *Betrayal Is Beautiful*[2] by Andy Slade!

In a world of shadows and secrets, John Chayne's return home becomes a dangerous dance with betrayal and bloodshed!

When John Chayne, a handsome, tall, and mysterious MIA from the Iraq War, is spotted by an ex-member of his old platoon, he is forced to leave the farming family he's lived with for two years. He doesn't want to cause any more problems than he has to so heads off to his home pueblo in the Four Corners area of New Mexico.

To those who knew him, his arrival at the Pueblo was unexpected. But not to Paul Begaye, an old schoolmate from John's high school days. A drug cartel has completely taken over the pueblo and Paul is their head man. Paul had always been strange, violent,

---

2. https://books2read.com/u/bxr5Qo

3. https://books2read.com/u/bxr5Qo

and absolutely brilliant. But now, he's taken his evil ways to a whole new level.

Paul's primary goal is to take over the cartel for himself. He's got the money, the weapons, and the brilliance to pull it off. But the cartel won't go away easily, and Paul soon realizes that he needs solid battlefield experience and attempts to hire John Chayne to complete the battle against the cartel.

Will John Chayne give in to the evil?